Muzzle Match

The Case of the Midnight Vandals

Michael R. Hastings

Table of Contents

Chapter 1
A Disturbed Peace

The tranquil suburb of Greendale, once a haven of late-night serenades by crickets under the starlit sky, now resounded with a discordant clangor that fractured the night. It emanated from the downtown area, a realm of quaint shops and rustic charm now marred by a string of unsettling disturbances. At the heart of this night's turmoil was the local jewelry store, its front door shattered, an invitation to darker possibilities.

Whiskers, a German Shepherd of notable repute and a retired police dog, lay on the porch of a modest, vine-covered bungalow that belonged to Jerry Maitland, his former handler and a retired detective. Despite the veil of retirement, the night's stark silence, punctured only by that abrupt clamor, had pulled Whiskers from his slumber. His ears twitched at the discordance—a shattering glass followed by the distant, wailing siren of an alarm system kicked into abrupt protest.

His nose, still as adept as in his prime, twitched, picking up the stress-scented adrenaline that painted the cool, night air. The scent was familiar, too familiar—an echo of his past life. With a low growl vibrating in his throat, Whiskers stepped off the porch, his senses leading him towards the chaos, his body moving with a precision that belied his age.

The neighborhood, a picture of suburban tranquility by day, had taken on a sinister shade under the moon's gaze. As Whiskers trotted down the leaf-strewn sidewalks, the muted sounds of his paws were drowned out by the accelerating beat of his heart. It wasn't just duty that called him tonight; it was a resolute desire to protect, a remnant of his years on the force.

Jerry, awakened by the same noise and now by Whiskers' absence, followed swiftly. His steps were quick but burdened with a heaviness—a mix of anticipation and the familiar weight of responsibility. As he caught up, Whiskers was already nearing the jewelry store, his silhouette a dark, moving patch against the backdrop of flashing patrol lights that had just begun to converge on the scene.

The store looked ravaged, its door hanging off the hinges, the windows smashed, and inside, the faint glimmer of scattered jewelry catching the intermittent flickers of red and blue lights from the arriving police cruisers. Whiskers moved cautiously, his every step deliberate, sniffing around the broken glass and metal, mapping out the scent trails left by the intruders.

Jerry approached Captain Sandra Clarke, who was commanding the response tonight. Their greeting was terse, a nod of mutual respect between professionals who knew their roles all too well.

"Looks like they made a significant haul," Jerry observed, peering into the chaotic interior of the store through the fractured glass of the front window.

"Third time this month, Jerry," Sandra replied, frustration lining her voice. "We're looking at a professional job. They knew exactly what they were after."

Meanwhile, Whiskers continued his survey of the scene, his nose skirting the ground, his tail stiff, an indicator of his focus. His paws, though aged, moved with purpose, tracing the phantom steps of those who dared disrupt the peace of Greendale.

He paused, his ears perking up at a faint sound—a whisper of movement at the alleyway beside the store. Without hesitation, Whiskers bolted towards the sound, with Jerry and a couple of uniformed officers following close behind. As they rounded the corner, the shadow of a figure dashed from their sight, the clatter of a knocked-over trash can marking the path of the fleeting suspect.

The chase was brief, Whiskers' agility surprising the younger officers. The suspect, a young man barely out of his teens, was cornered by the old dog, his escape thwarted by the very creature he'd likely dismissed due to age.

As the officers handcuffed the trembling suspect, Jerry knelt beside Whiskers, his hand brushing the dog's side in quiet appreciation. "Good boy," he murmured, "still got the instincts of a protector."

Whiskers responded with a soft nuzzle against Jerry's palm, his eyes still on the captured youth, a silent affirmation of his unyielded vigilance. The scene, bathed now in the glaring lights of law enforcement, marked the beginning of a renewed battle against the creeping shadows of crime in Greendale—a battle Whiskers and Jerry were once again ready to face together.

As Whiskers stood guard over the subdued suspect, his ears remained perked, tuned to the lingering undercurrents of the night. Jerry conversed quietly with Captain Sandra Clarke, their figures cast in the alternating wash of red and blue lights that pulsed silently in the background.

"This one's young, Sandra," Jerry said, eyeing the suspect, who sat on the cold pavement, hands cuffed behind him, watched over by one of the officers. "Think he's part of the bigger problem or just a one-off?"

Sandra shook her head, her eyes thoughtful. "Not sure yet. But the M.O. is similar to the last two incidents. High-speed, in-and-out job, minimal mess aside from the break-in itself. They're getting bolder, or more desperate."

"Or both," Jerry added, folding his arms as he turned back to glance at Whiskers, who was sniffing around a discarded backpack near the alley. "What's the plan for the kid?"

"We'll take him in, obviously. Interrogate him first thing. If he's part of a larger group, maybe he'll give up his buddies." Sandra's voice carried a mix of hope and skepticism, a balance born of years in law enforcement.

Meanwhile, Whiskers nudged the backpack with his nose, signaling Jerry to come over. Jerry excused himself from Sandra and approached, kneeling to inspect the bag under Whiskers' watchful gaze. Inside, he found an assortment of tools—lock picks, a compact crowbar, and even a small, high-torque drill. "Looks like our friends were prepared for more than just a quick smash and grab."

Whiskers whined softly, his gaze shifting back towards the store. Jerry followed his line of sight and noticed a small, electronic device peeking out from under a nearby trash bin. He carefully picked it up, examining it under the light of his flashlight. "Looks like a GPS tracker. Amateur hour or smart cookie?"

"Could be either," Sandra, now beside him, remarked after taking a look at the device. "But it's sloppy to leave it behind. Might be stolen goods, or could be used to track their movements. Either way, we'll check it out."

Back at the patrol car, the young suspect, a boy with shaggy brown hair and a face too soft for crime, kept his head down, avoiding eye contact. Jerry decided to engage him directly.

"What's your name, son?" Jerry asked, his tone softer, trying to pierce the boy's resigned exterior.

"Kyle," came the whispered reply, barely audible over the distant sound of another siren.

"Kyle, I'm Jerry. That's Whiskers over there," he gestured towards the German Shepherd, now sitting alert beside them. "He's retired, like me, but it looks like we both can't seem to stay out of trouble. Can you tell me why you were at the store tonight?"

Kyle hesitated, his eyes flickering between Jerry and Whiskers, then back to the ground. "I... I was just supposed to grab something. That's all they told me."

"They?" Jerry pressed gently. "Who are they, Kyle? Friends of yours?"

"Just some guys I know," Kyle muttered, his voice a mixture of fear and defiance. "I don't know much about them. They just tell me where to go."

Whiskers moved closer, his presence seemingly comforting rather than intimidating. Kyle's hand reached out, his fingers brushing the dog's fur. Jerry noted the gesture, the first sign of openness since the start of their conversation.

"Kyle, those 'guys you know' left you out to dry tonight. You're here, and where are they?" Jerry's words were pointed but not unkind. "Help us understand what's going on, and maybe we can help you too."

The boy looked up, his eyes meeting Jerry's for the first time that night. "I... I don't want to go to jail," he stammered, a flicker of panic crossing his features.

"We'll do what we can to help, but you need to be honest with us," Jerry reassured him, his voice steady and calm. "Let's start with the names of these friends."

Kyle nodded slowly, the resistance in his posture easing as he began to speak, his words spilling out in the quiet night, overshadowed only by Whiskers' soft panting and the distant call of an owl. As he talked, Jerry listened intently, piecing together the fragile threads of a story that was larger than a simple burglary, a narrative woven into the darker edges of Greendale's sleepy facade.

Under the harsh glare of the street lamps, with the night air growing colder around them, Jerry and Whiskers stood by as the police officers escorted Kyle to a waiting cruiser. The young man's words hung in the quiet, his story unfolding like the layers of an onion, each one revealing a new depth of complexity to the seemingly straightforward crime spree that had unsettled the town of Greendale.

Whiskers, his senses ever alert, remained close to Jerry, his gaze intermittently scanning the shadows that danced along the periphery of the street lights. There was a tension in the air, a palpable sense of urgency that seemed to pulse from the ground itself, as if the town awaited the resolution of a deeper mystery that had only begun to surface.

Jerry watched the cruiser pull away, his thoughts turning over the information Kyle had provided. It was not just a band of reckless youths; this was a coordinated group with ties deeper and more dangerous than he had initially suspected. The details were sparse, the names and places mentioned by Kyle only breadcrumbs leading into a labyrinth of criminal intent that Jerry knew he had to navigate carefully.

Turning back to the scene, he noticed Whiskers sniffing along the edge of the broken window, his nose twitching as he traced the lingering scents that the intruders had left behind. Whiskers' demeanor suggested a trail, one that Jerry knew could lead to critical insights. Perhaps it was the old detective instincts kicking in, or the silent communication that had always flowed between him and Whiskers, but he felt a surge of anticipation — the hunt was on, and every clue was a vital piece of the puzzle.

The street was quieting down now, the initial chaos of police activity dying down as the officers finished their preliminary investigations and prepared to leave the scene. Jerry approached one of the younger detectives, a woman named Marla who was methodically logging evidence into her tablet.

"Find anything else that might help us?" Jerry inquired, his voice low, almost blending into the night sounds.

Marla looked up, her eyes reflecting the fatigue of long hours. "Just this," she held up a baggie containing a small, digital device that wasn't part of the store's inventory. "Found it tucked behind the counter. Doesn't seem like it belongs to the store."

Jerry took the offered baggie, turning the device over in his hand. It was a small, black USB drive, unremarkable yet clearly out of place in the context of a jewelry store burglary. "Thanks, Marla. I'll see what I can make of this."

With the last of the patrol cars pulling away, Jerry felt the solitude of the crime scene wrap around him like a cloak. Whiskers, sensing his partner's shift in focus, stood beside him, their shadows merging on the pavement. It was time to move deeper into the investigation, to follow the leads that Kyle's confession had unearthed and the digital breadcrumbs now in Jerry's possession.

They walked back to Jerry's house, the USB drive a silent promise of secrets waiting to be unlocked. Inside, Jerry's old computer hummed to life, the screen flickering as he inserted the drive. Files loaded, rows of dates and times, documents that hinted at transactions and meetings. The content was cryptic, coded in ways that suggested these were not mere vandals but part of an organized network.

As Jerry delved into the files, piecing together the data with what they had learned from Kyle, Whiskers lay down beside the desk, his presence a comforting constant in the solitude of the night's work. Each document opened, each file decrypted added layers to their understanding of the gang's operations. It wasn't just about theft; there was something bigger at play, a scheme that perhaps went beyond the town's borders.

The clock ticked past midnight, the screen's glow the only light in the room. Jerry leaned back in his chair, eyes tired yet mind racing. Whiskers lifted his head, his ears twitching at the silence that enveloped the house. In that quiet, with only the sound of Jerry's deep, measured breathing and the occasional click of the mouse, the pieces began to fall into place. This was more than a series of crimes; it was a challenge to the very peace of Greendale, a puzzle that Jerry and Whiskers were determined to solve.

As dawn approached, the room bathed in the soft glow of early morning light, Jerry continued to scrutinize the information sprawled across his computer screen. Whiskers, sensing the shift in his partner's intensity, had risen, his focus now as sharp as it had been in his younger years. The quiet of the house was broken only by the occasional murmuring of Jerry as he pieced together the complex web of transactions and messages from the USB drive.

"Looks like we're dealing with more than petty theft, boy," Jerry murmured, clicking through another encrypted file. "These guys are organized, branching out into more than just vandalism or simple burglaries."

Whiskers barked softly, his eyes locked on Jerry as if understanding the gravity of the situation. The early morning silence was soon interrupted by a knock at the door. Jerry glanced at the clock—just past 6 AM—and rose to answer it. Standing at the door was Captain Sandra Clarke, her expression grim.

"Morning, Jerry. I didn't wake you, did I?" Sandra stepped inside, her gaze falling on the open files on the computer screen.

"No, been up for a while," Jerry replied, leading her to his makeshift office. "What brings you here so early?"

"We got a match on the prints from the scene—turns out your young friend Kyle isn't working alone. There's a whole network, just like you suspected. We picked up two more of his associates overnight," Sandra explained, her eyes scanning the digital map on Jerry's screen that displayed various points across Greendale.

"That fits with this," Jerry pointed to the screen, showing a series of emails detailing times and locations that matched the crime scenes. "They've been coordinating hits all over town, possibly even outside Greendale."

"Any idea what they're after? It can't just be random theft. There's too much planning involved," Sandra inquired, pulling up a chair beside Jerry.

"It looks like they're funneling the stolen goods. It's not just for resale—it's funding something bigger. But what exactly, I'm still trying to piece together," Jerry clicked through another encrypted file, his brow furrowed.

Sandra nodded, taking notes. "We need to lean on Kyle harder. He's not just a foot soldier; he knows what the end game is."

Jerry sighed, glancing at Whiskers who sat attentively by his side. "I agree. But we also need to be careful. If we push too hard without understanding the full scope, we might spook whoever's running this operation."

"Agreed. I'll arrange for an interview with Kyle. See if we can get him to cooperate fully. In the meantime, keep digging into this," Sandra stood, her tone resolute. "Whatever you find, Jerry, it could be the key to blowing this whole thing wide open."

As Sandra left, Jerry turned back to the screen, his fingers paused over the keyboard. Whiskers moved closer, his presence a silent support as Jerry delved deeper into the digital maze.

"Let's see where you lead us," Jerry whispered to the screen, opening another document. The names and numbers it contained could potentially link the local crimes to larger, more sinister operations. It was a puzzle that required patience, a quality both he and Whiskers had in abundance.

Hours passed, the morning light shifting across the room, casting long shadows against the walls filled with books and memories of past cases. The room was quiet, save for the occasional click of the mouse and Jerry's deep, thoughtful sighs. Each piece of data added a layer of complexity to their understanding of the criminal network operating under the quiet facade of Greendale.

As the morning waned into early afternoon, Jerry finally leaned back in his chair, his eyes tired but sharp with the adrenaline of the chase. Whiskers, sensing a break in the intensity, lay down at Jerry's feet, his head resting on his paws.

"We're onto something, Whiskers. Something big," Jerry spoke, more to himself than to the dog. The room felt charged with the weight of their discoveries, the air thick with the promise of untangling a criminal web that could shake the very foundations of their peaceful town.

Chapter 2
The Night Prowlers

In the comfortable confines of Captain Sandra Clarke's office, the morning sun streamed through the blinds, casting stripes of light and shadow across the room. Jerry sat across from Sandra at her desk, cluttered with the detritus of active investigations—papers, files, and the omnipresent digital screens flickering with crime stats and dispatch calls.

"So, Jerry, what have we got?" Sandra initiated, her voice tinged with both urgency and fatigue, evidence of sleepless nights compounded by the stress of their investigation.

"It's a network, Sandra. These aren't random acts. It's all connected," Jerry started, leaning forward, his eyes intent on the captain's, trying to convey the gravity of his findings. "The evidence from that USB is clear. They're funding something big. Possibly out of town. But everything starts here, in Greendale."

Sandra nodded, processing the information. "And Kyle? Does he fit as a key player, or is he just another pawn in their game?"

"He's in deeper than he admits," Jerry replied, his tone certain. "He's scared, and that's good. Scared means he knows enough to be useful. We need to push him harder, see if he can lead us to the head of this snake."

"Agreed," Sandra affirmed, tapping a pen against her notepad. "I've arranged for another sit-down with him today. I'm hoping he's more cooperative, given the pressure."

"Use what he gave us last night. Show him we know he's not just a bystander. It might make him open up more if he thinks we can protect him from the bigger fish," Jerry suggested, his detective instincts in full play.

"Right," Sandra said, jotting down a note. "Now, about these locations from the USB. Any idea why they target these specific places? There's a pattern, but I can't make sense of it."

"They're strategic, each hit funds the next. The goods from one heist fund the next operation. It's systematic, organized. They're building resources for something that requires significant capital. We need to map out their activities, project their next moves," Jerry analyzed, his hands moving as if to draw the connections in the air between them.

Sandra leaned back, her gaze fixed on Jerry. "And the other names Kyle mentioned—have we looked into them?"

"Yes, every name he's given us checks out. They're all linked to minor incidents around town over the past year. Petty crimes, mostly. But now they're escalating," Jerry replied.

"Alright. I'll get the team on it. We'll pull everything we have on them, see how they connect to the larger picture," Sandra decided, her voice firm with resolve.

"What about external help? This might be bigger than our local PD can handle," Jerry ventured, knowing the limitations of their small-town force.

Sandra paused, considering. "I've been reluctant to bring in outside agencies. But you're right, this could be beyond us. I'll make some calls, see who we can bring in without causing too much disruption."

"Good," Jerry nodded, satisfied. "In the meantime, I'll keep digging into the financial angle. There's a trail of money leading out of Greendale. I need to see where it ends."

Sandra stood up, signaling the meeting's end. "Keep me posted, Jerry. Every bit helps. And be careful. We don't know how they'll react once they realize we're onto them."

Jerry stood, feeling the weight of the investigation on his shoulders. "Will do, Sandra. And I'll keep Whiskers close. He's got a nose for trouble."

The two shared a brief smile, a moment of lightness in the midst of their daunting task. As Jerry left Sandra's office, stepping back into the corridor, the reality of their situation settled around him like a heavy cloak. Each step took him deeper into the unfolding mystery that threatened the peace of Greendale, each move he made shadowed by the unseen eyes of those who would prefer their secrets to remain hidden.

As the sun climbed higher, casting its warm glow across the bustling streets of Greendale, Jerry set up in his makeshift office at home. Papers and digital maps were strewn across the table, each marked with notes and pins indicating the locations involved in the recent spate of crimes. The town, with its quaint shops and peaceful parks, seemed an unlikely backdrop for the sinister undertow of organized crime that Jerry was uncovering.

Whiskers, ever-present, lay at his feet, occasionally lifting his head whenever Jerry paced around the room, his mind racing as he tried to connect the dots. The quiet buzz of the computer and the occasional rustle of paper filled the room as Jerry plotted out the possible next moves of the criminal network.

The sound of his phone ringing broke the concentration, and Jerry quickly answered. It was Marla, the young detective who had been assisting him with the data analysis.

"Jerry, we've run the names through the database like you asked. Three of them have priors related to theft and fraud. Looks like small-time crooks getting big ideas," Marla reported.

"Thanks, Marla. Keep digging. See if they have any common connections to businesses or other individuals in town. It might help us predict their next target," Jerry responded, his voice steady despite the brewing frustration of the slow progress.

"Will do, Jerry. Oh, and Captain Clarke said she'll have more for you after the meeting with Kyle this afternoon," Marla added before ending the call.

Jerry hung up and turned his attention back to the maps. Each location had been chosen with a purpose, none random. This was a chess game, each move calculated, but the kingpin remained in the shadows, orchestrating without revealing themselves.

With a deep sigh, Jerry leaned over the table, his fingers tracing the paths between the points on the map. The network was intricate, woven into the very fabric of Greendale's day-to-day life. It was clear that the stolen goods were only part of a larger, more complex scheme. Financial records from the USB hinted at transactions that extended beyond the local scope, suggesting external backers or perhaps a more extensive criminal syndicate using the town as a staging ground.

The afternoon sun began to wane, casting long shadows across the room, mirroring the growing darkness of the case before him. Jerry's thoughts were interrupted by Whiskers' sudden movement, the dog's ears perked up as he stared intently at the window. Jerry walked over, following Whiskers' gaze, but saw nothing beyond the ordinary: children playing in the nearby park, neighbors going about their day.

Despite the normalcy outside, the tension lingered, a stark contrast to the peaceful view from the window. Jerry turned back to his work, the pieces of the puzzle slowly forming a clearer picture, yet the most crucial piece remained elusive. The identity of the orchestrator of these crimes was carefully shielded, hidden behind layers of transactions and false names.

As the day shifted into evening, Jerry continued to work, his resolve hardening with each passing hour. The town of Greendale, with all its charm and tranquility, was relying on him to root out the threat that lurked in its shadows. This realization weighed heavily on him, yet it also drove him forward, fueled by the need to protect his community.

Whiskers stirred, breaking Jerry's focus momentarily. The dog seemed to sense his partner's determination and the importance of their task. Together, in the quiet solidarity of the office, they prepared for the long night ahead, ready to uncover the truths that would bring light to the darkness that had fallen over Greendale.

Jerry found himself back at the police station later that evening, seated across from Captain Sandra Clarke in the dimly lit interrogation room. The walls, bare and colored a stark, unwelcoming grey, seemed to absorb the tension that filled the space. Kyle sat between them, his hands cuffed loosely in front of him, his eyes darting nervously from Sandra to Jerry and back again.

"Kyle, we know there's more to this than you've told us," Sandra began, her voice steady but carrying an edge of impatience. "The names you've given us, the places you've been—they're all part of a larger plan, aren't they?"

Kyle swallowed hard, his gaze falling to the table. "I... I told you everything I know. I just did what they told me to do."

Jerry leaned forward, his demeanor calm yet assertive. "You did well giving us those names, Kyle. But we believe you're holding back on us. Who's coordinating the operations? We can offer more protection if you help us get to the core of this."

Kyle's eyes flicked up, meeting Jerry's. There was a flicker of consideration, perhaps even trust, before he responded. "It's... it's not just about the thefts. There's something bigger going on, but I'm not..." He hesitated, looking over at Sandra before continuing, "I'm not sure of all the details."

"Who are you protecting, Kyle?" Sandra pressed, her tone softening slightly. "You're in deep enough that walking away isn't an option anymore, but helping us might be your best way out."

Kyle bit his lip, considering his options. After a moment, he sighed and spoke, "There's a guy, calls himself Marco. He's the one who plans where we hit next. I've never met him, just phone calls. He's careful, always changing numbers."

Jerry exchanged a quick glance with Sandra before asking, "Do you have any of these numbers, any way we could trace them back to this Marco?"

"I might have something on my phone," Kyle admitted reluctantly. "But I left it at my place. I can show you."

"That's a start," Jerry said, nodding to Sandra, who made a quick note.

"Okay, Kyle. We'll arrange for an officer to accompany you to your place to retrieve the phone. Cooperate with us, and we'll make sure you're protected," Sandra reassured him, her voice firm yet reassuring.

As the meeting concluded, Jerry and Sandra stepped outside the room, their conversation continuing in hushed tones as they walked down the corridor.

"He's scared, but he's talking. That's a good sign," Jerry murmured, his hands tucked into his pockets as he walked alongside Sandra.

"Yes, but we need to move fast. If this Marco suspects Kyle is talking, he might pull the plug on the whole operation, or worse," Sandra replied, her expression fraught with concern.

"We should also consider bringing in some tech specialists to trace back any communications from Kyle's phone once we have it. If this Marco is as smart as Kyle says, he won't be easy to track," Jerry suggested, his mind already racing through the possibilities.

"I'll get on it," Sandra said as they reached her office. "And Jerry, be careful. We don't know how far this network reaches, or how dangerous these people really are."

Jerry nodded, the weight of her words settling over him like a cloak. As he left the station, the night air felt colder, sharper. He walked back to his car, the echo of his footsteps a stark reminder of the solitude of their battle. Whiskers, waiting patiently in the backseat, wagged his tail as Jerry climbed in, a silent acknowledgment of their partnership in the looming shadow of the unknown.

Jerry drove through the quiet streets of Greendale, the dim glow of the streetlights casting long shadows on the road. Whiskers, ever vigilant, sat up in the backseat, his gaze fixed out the window, ears perked at every passing sound. The car pulled up to a modest house on the edge of town, where Kyle had been living alone since his involvement with the criminal network.

The night was still and silent as Jerry and Kyle, accompanied by two uniformed officers, approached the front door. Kyle fumbled with his keys, his hands shaking slightly under the watchful eyes of the officers.

"Right here," Kyle said as he pushed the door open, stepping into the small, dimly lit living room. He moved straight to a small desk cluttered with papers and various electronic devices.

Jerry followed closely behind, observing every move. "You said the phone is here?"

"Yeah, just give me a second," Kyle muttered, rummaging through a drawer before pulling out a smartphone. "Here it is."

One of the officers stepped forward, extending his hand. "I'll take that. We'll need to examine it back at the station."

Kyle handed over the phone reluctantly, his gaze lingering on the device as if saying goodbye to a part of his life.

Jerry watched the exchange, then turned to Kyle. "Is there anything else here that might help us? Any other devices, papers, anything at all?"

Kyle hesitated, then nodded slowly. "There's a laptop, in my room. I used it to communicate with Marco a few times. He was cautious, always using secure channels, but maybe you'll find something."

"Let's take a look," Jerry said, following Kyle to a small bedroom cluttered with clothes and books. Kyle retrieved the laptop from under a pile of laundry and handed it to the other officer.

As they walked back to the living room, Jerry kept the conversation going, trying to glean more information. "Kyle, how did you get involved with Marco and this group?"

"It started small," Kyle began, his voice low. "Just doing favors, running errands. Then it escalated. I was in too deep before I realized what was really going on."

"And the others? The ones you mentioned before?" Jerry probed.

"They're just like me, I guess. Caught up. Marco has a way of making you feel like you're part of something bigger, like you're important," Kyle explained, a note of regret in his voice.

Jerry nodded, understanding the allure all too well. "And what about the targets? Was there a pattern, something that dictated the choice of locations?"

"It was all about opportunity and payoff. Marco had it all planned out. He'd tell us when and where, and we'd just follow orders," Kyle said, sinking into a chair, his shoulders slumped.

"Alright, we've got what we need for now," Jerry said, signaling to the officers to prepare to leave. "You did the right thing tonight, Kyle. We're going to do our best to sort this out."

Kyle looked up, a mixture of hope and fear in his eyes. "Thanks, Jerry. I just want this to be over."

Jerry gave him a reassuring nod as they stepped out of the house and back into the cool night. As they drove away, Jerry looked back at the house through the rearview mirror, his thoughts on the complexities of human nature and the thin lines between right and wrong.

Whiskers, sensing his partner's contemplative mood, rested his head on the seat, his presence a comforting reminder of the unspoken bond between them. The case was deepening, spreading its roots through the heart of Greendale, and as they returned to the station, the early morning hours whispered promises of more revelations to come.

Chapter 3
The Consultant

Back at the police station, the atmosphere was charged with the urgency of the ongoing investigation. The early morning hours crept by as Jerry, Captain Sandra Clarke, and a team of officers huddled around a large table littered with maps, photographs, and digital devices seized from Kyle's home. The room was alive with the low hum of conversation and the occasional beep of incoming data from the tech team working in the next room.

"We've managed to extract some data from Kyle's laptop and phone," one of the tech officers reported, handing over a USB drive to Sandra. "There are encrypted files we're still working on, but we found communications with several numbers that are not in service anymore. Looks like they were burner phones."

Sandra plugged the USB into her laptop, her eyes scanning the contents. "Good work. Keep on those encrypted files. There might be something there that could lead us to this Marco."

Jerry leaned over to view the screen, pointing at a series of emails. "These communications—any idea what they were discussing? Dates, times, locations?"

"Some of it is code, but we're piecing it together," the officer replied. "We should have a clearer picture soon."

"Time is something we might not have much of," Jerry muttered, rubbing his chin thoughtfully. "If Marco senses that Kyle's turned, he might accelerate whatever they're planning."

Sandra nodded in agreement. "We need to anticipate their next move. Jerry, take a couple of officers and go over everything we have from Kyle's devices. Look for any mention of future plans or dates. We need to stay ahead."

Jerry acknowledged with a nod and gathered the materials, setting up a workspace in the corner of the room. Two officers joined him, both eager to contribute to cracking the case.

As they sifted through the digital documents, Jerry's phone rang. He answered it quickly, his expression growing serious as he listened. "Alright, I understand. Keep me posted." He hung up and turned to the officers. "That was Marla. She's following up on the background of those names Kyle gave us. Turns out one of them has a record of weapons charges. Could be nothing, or it could be part of what they're planning."

"Should we bring this person in?" one of the officers asked, ready to act on Jerry's command.

"Not yet," Jerry decided. "We don't want to spook them until we know how they fit into the larger picture. Keep digging here."

As the morning shifted into day, the room buzzed with the kind of focused energy that comes from a team working seamlessly towards a common goal. Each officer, each analyst brought their expertise to bear, pulling on the threads of the tangled web of criminal activity that had ensnared their town.

Sandra walked over to Jerry's table, her face etched with concern. "Any luck with those encrypted files yet?"

"Not yet, Sandra. But there's a pattern in the dates and locations linked to what looks like trial runs for something bigger. These aren't random hits; they're planned with precision," Jerry explained, showing her the map with the marked locations.

"That fits with the profile we're building on Marco. He's meticulous, cautious. Which means he's dangerous," Sandra concluded, her gaze lingering on the map. "Keep at it, Jerry. Every piece of information helps."

As the day wore on, the pile of evidence grew, but so did the urgency to piece together the puzzle before Marco could strike. Whiskers, who had been resting by Jerry's side, stood up, stretching, as if sensing the growing tension in the room.

Jerry patted him gently, then turned back to his work. The stakes were high, and the clock was ticking, but he was not one to back down from a challenge. With each document, each decoded message, they were getting closer to preventing whatever storm was about to hit Greendale.

As the relentless tick of the clock marked the passage of the morning, the pieces of the puzzle in the Greendale police station's makeshift war room began to coalesce. Sandra and Jerry, along with a few selected officers, had spread across the long table a mosaic of digital prints and phone records, each possibly hiding secrets of the criminal network slowly being unearthed.

"Look at this pattern," Jerry pointed out, tapping a complex chart with dates and locations spread across. "These aren't random choices. Each location picked for a hit had a high payoff potential and minimal security. Marco's careful—he's building up to something big, and he's using the profits from these smaller jobs."

Sandra leaned in, her eyes narrowing as she traced the pattern with her finger. "And the timeline? These jobs are ramping up in frequency. That could mean they're nearing the end of whatever phase this is."

"That's my read too," Jerry affirmed. He shuffled through some papers, pulling out a series of emails decrypted that morning. "And there's communication here that suggests they're planning something soon. Something that needs more resources, possibly more dangerous than the thefts."

"What sort of resources? Are we talking explosives, weapons?" Sandra's tone was laden with concern.

"It's unclear, but one of the emails referenced 'heavy equipment.' That could mean anything from firearms to something much larger. Marla's still running down leads on the weapons charges associated with one of the names Kyle gave us," Jerry replied, handing her a printout of the email.

Sandra scanned the document, her lips pressed tightly together. "I'll push for a deeper dive into this. We can't afford to be caught off guard."

"Agreed," Jerry said, as he returned to the documents. Just then, his phone buzzed—a text message from Marla, signaling a breakthrough. "Marla might have something. She's asking us to come to the tech room."

They quickly made their way to the tech room, where Marla was waiting, her eyes bright with the adrenaline of discovery. She greeted them with a quick nod and gestured to her screen.

"I've been monitoring the phone numbers Kyle provided, and one of them reactivated briefly last night. We traced the signal to a warehouse on the outskirts of town," Marla reported.

"A warehouse? That could be their staging area, especially if they're amassing 'heavy equipment' as you suggested, Jerry," Sandra said, turning to Jerry with a renewed sense of urgency.

"Can we get a warrant to check it out?" Jerry asked, already thinking a few steps ahead.

"I'm on it," Sandra replied. "Marla, good work. Keep monitoring any activity related to that number. Any blip could lead us to Marco or whoever is running this show."

"Will do, Captain," Marla affirmed, her gaze returning to her screens, the lines of code scrolling past reflecting in her focused eyes.

Sandra and Jerry stepped out of the room, their minds racing with the potential implications of this new lead. "If we're right about this, we could catch them in the act, maybe even get ahead of whatever they're planning," Sandra voiced her thoughts aloud.

"That's the hope," Jerry agreed. "But let's prepare for all possibilities. If they sense we're onto them, they might accelerate their plans or go to ground."

"Understood. I'll have SWAT on standby, and I'm pushing that warrant through now. We need to be ready to move at a moment's notice," Sandra said as they walked back to the war room, each step heavy with the weight of their responsibility.

The rest of the afternoon blurred into a flurry of preparations. Each officer had their role, each piece of information was a vital thread in the fabric they were weaving to catch a shadow. As the sun began its descent, casting long shadows through the windows of the station, Jerry felt a momentary calm. It was the stillness that often came before a storm, and in that stillness, he and Sandra shared a quiet resolve to protect their town, no matter what the dawn might bring.

Night had fallen over Greendale, and the police station buzzed with a subdued tension as Jerry and Sandra reviewed the final preparations for the raid on the warehouse. The warrant had come through, and a map of the area lay spread out on a table between them, illuminated by the soft glow of desk lamps.

"Everything's set for the early morning. SWAT's briefed, and surveillance is in place around the warehouse perimeter," Sandra detailed, pointing at the map with a stylus, marking the entry and exit points the team would use.

Jerry, his eyes tracing the planned routes, nodded slowly. "What's our main objective once we're in? Are we looking for evidence, or are we trying to catch them red-handed?"

"Both," Sandra responded firmly. "If we find evidence of weapons or whatever 'heavy equipment' they've been accumulating, we secure it. But ideally, we catch them in the act. I want whoever's behind this in custody."

"Agreed. Do we have any intel on how many might be inside?" Jerry asked, his mind already running through various scenarios.

"Unclear," Sandra admitted, her face reflecting the gravity of the situation. "Surveillance hasn't picked up much movement. Could be they're keeping a low profile until whatever they're planning kicks off."

Jerry rubbed his jaw, thinking. "We need to be prepared for anything. These aren't amateurs. They've been two steps ahead until now."

"Exactly why we're not taking any chances. We'll have tactical teams at each entry point, and we'll cut the power to the warehouse to give us the advantage," Sandra outlined the strategy.

The room fell silent for a moment, the weight of the upcoming operation pressing down on them. Then, Jerry broke the silence with a practical query, "Communication lines?"

"All secure. And I'll be on comms personally, overseeing the operation from the command truck," Sandra added, ensuring the lines of command were clear.

Jerry nodded, satisfied with the setup. "I'll be on the ground with the first team. Whiskers will stay back this time." He glanced at his canine partner, who seemed to sense the seriousness of the conversation and lay quietly by Jerry's chair.

"That's wise. He's done his part already," Sandra acknowledged, giving Whiskers a brief but affectionate glance.

As they finalized the details, the door to the war room opened, and Marla stepped in, her face urgent. "Captain, Jerry, you need to see this. We picked up increased activity on one of the burner phones an hour ago. It looks like they might be moving something tonight."

Sandra's eyes widened slightly, and she exchanged a quick look with Jerry. "They're starting early, or maybe they caught wind we're onto them. We need to move now."

Jerry's response was swift and decisive. "Let's go. We can't afford to give them any more lead time."

The team mobilized quickly. Within minutes, the war room was empty, the map still lying on the table as the only remnant of the hurried preparations. Outside, police vehicles rolled out of the station, sirens silent, lights off, as they moved toward the warehouse under the cover of darkness.

As they approached the designated staging area, the quiet anticipation in the vehicle was palpable. Jerry checked his gear one last time, his focus absolute. This was the culmination of weeks of investigation, the moment of truth not just for him but for the entire town of Greendale.

The darkness of the night seemed to envelop them as they neared their destination, the warehouse looming ahead like a giant waiting in the shadows.

The convoy of unmarked police vehicles came to a stealthy halt a short distance from the warehouse, hidden from view by the darkness of the early morning hours. The air was crisp, carrying a chill that seeped through the seams of their tactical gear as Jerry and the tactical team prepared to disembark.

Jerry met Sandra's eyes across the vehicle interior, a silent exchange of readiness. "We go on your mark, Sandra," he whispered, his voice barely audible over the soft hum of the idling engines.

"Check your radios, one last time," Sandra commanded softly, ensuring every line of communication was clear and open. "We need eyes on all sides. No one moves in until we have confirmation of the situation inside."

Jerry nodded, his hand instinctively reaching down to check his own radio before stepping out into the night. The team assembled quickly and quietly behind the cover of the vehicles, the only sounds the soft rustling of their movements and the distant call of an early bird.

"Team one, you're with me. Team two, flank to the right. Team three, take the back entrance. Remember, no one engages until we have visual confirmation," Sandra instructed, her voice a calm command in their earpieces.

Jerry led team one towards the front entrance, his steps measured, his senses heightened. As they neared the building, the faint sound of movement from inside confirmed their suspicions.

"Position confirmed, we have movement inside," Jerry reported, his voice low. "Looks like we're on time."

"Teams in position," came the confirmations through the radio, one after the other.

"On my mark," Sandra directed, waiting for the precise moment. "Three, two, one—mark."

The teams moved as one, breaching the entrances simultaneously. The sound of breaking locks and crashing doors shattered the predawn silence. Jerry was first through the front door, his weapon raised, his eyes scanning the dimly lit interior.

The warehouse was vast, filled with rows of crates and boxes, some of them open and displaying various types of machinery and electronic devices. Shadows moved quickly in the chaos, figures attempting to escape or hide among the containers.

"Police! Stay where you are!" Jerry bellowed, his voice echoing off the high ceilings. The response was immediate; some dropped to the ground, complying, while others hesitated, caught in the act of fleeing.

"We have multiple suspects in custody," reported an officer from team two, his voice coming through the radio.

"Secure the area. Make sure we have all exits covered," Sandra commanded, her tone authoritative and composed as she coordinated the operation from the command truck.

Jerry moved deeper into the warehouse, his team covering him as they secured each section. His flashlight beam caught the glint of metal—a cache of firearms hidden beneath a tarp.

"We've got weapons here," Jerry called out, signaling to his team to secure the find. "Looks like our intel was good."

"Copy that," Sandra responded. "Good work. Proceed with securing all evidence. Forensics will be right behind you."

As the initial chaos settled into methodical searching and securing of the scene, Jerry took a moment to survey the area. The operation had been swift and effective, the element of surprise working in their favor.

"We need to catalog everything. Don't miss any documents or electronics. It could lead us to Marco," Jerry instructed his team, already thinking ahead to the next steps in their investigation.

The warehouse, now lit by the lights of the forensics team setting up their equipment, revealed the scale of the operation they had disrupted. Boxes of stolen goods, documents, computers—all forming the pieces of a puzzle that Jerry was determined to solve.

As the dawn began to break, casting a soft light into the dusty windows of the warehouse, the night's operation drew to a close. Jerry stood by as the last of the suspects were escorted out, his mind already running through the implications of their findings.

The morning light brought a sense of accomplishment, but Jerry knew the investigation was far from over. The network they had uncovered was extensive, and somewhere, possibly watching from the shadows, was Marco, the key to unraveling the full extent of the criminal activities that had gripped Greendale.

Chapter 4
First Clues

As the dawn stretched its early light across Greendale, Jerry stood outside the now-quiet warehouse, watching as the last of the forensic team packed up their gear. The successful raid had dismantled a significant part of the criminal network, yet the mastermind, Marco, remained a shadow just out of reach.

Sandra approached Jerry, her face showing traces of both relief and concern. "We got a good haul, Jerry. Weapons, tech, documents—it's more extensive than we anticipated. This should give us enough to keep digging."

Jerry nodded, his gaze lingering on the warehouse door. "It's a solid start, but it's not over. We didn't find anything directly tying back to Marco. No direct communications or paperwork."

"You think he's that cautious, or could we be dealing with someone else calling the shots?" Sandra pondered, her brow furrowed.

"It's possible," Jerry admitted. "But every lead points to him. He's careful, uses layers of people to shield himself. We need to peel back those layers."

"Speaking of layers, some of the documents we seized have references to other towns, other operations maybe. It looks like Greendale was just part of a larger network," Sandra revealed, handing Jerry a folder filled with copied documents.

Jerry flipped through the folder, his eyes scanning the contents. "This could be why it's been so hard to track Marco down. If he's operating on a regional scale, he could be anywhere by now."

"We're expanding the investigation, reaching out to other departments. If he's got operations in other towns, they might have seen similar patterns," Sandra explained. "We'll need to coordinate closely with them, see if they've got any leads that match ours."

"Good. I'll go through these documents, see if any names or places pop up that we've seen before," Jerry said, already walking back towards his car, the folder under his arm.

"Jerry, take a team. I want eyes on those other towns by tonight. Any delay could give Marco a chance to regroup," Sandra instructed, her tone assertive.

"Understood. I'll set it up," Jerry responded, pausing to look back at the warehouse. The morning light now fully illuminated the building, casting long shadows and highlighting the desolation of what had once been a hub of illegal activity.

Inside his car, Jerry made several calls, organizing a small team of officers to start checking the leads in the nearby towns. Each conversation was precise, each instruction clear—there was no room for error, not with Marco still at large.

As the car hummed to life, Jerry glanced at Whiskers, who had been a silent observer through the morning's discussions. "Looks like we're on the road again, pal."

Whiskers responded with a soft woof, seemingly in agreement, as they pulled away from the curb.

The drive was quiet, the early morning sun casting a golden glow over the landscape. Jerry's thoughts were occupied with the case, piecing together what they knew, planning his next moves. The road stretched out before them, leading towards the first of the towns mentioned in the documents.

"Whiskers, this isn't just about catching a criminal anymore," Jerry spoke aloud, as if trying to organize his thoughts. "It's about understanding how deep this goes, how many lives it's touched. Marco's just the key to unlocking it all."

The car rolled on, mile after mile, the landscape changing as they moved away from Greendale. Jerry knew that with each passing mile, they were stepping deeper into a web that had been years in the weaving. But he also knew that with each unraveling thread, they were closer to restoring peace to his town and perhaps many others.

The journey led Jerry and his team to a small town not unlike Greendale, where the quaint streets and bustling local shops belied the undercurrent of tension that had brought them there. Upon arrival, they convened at the local police station, a small, brick building nestled between a diner and a bookstore.

Jerry introduced himself to the town's sheriff, a stern woman with sharp eyes named Helen Morse. She welcomed them with a reserved nod, leading them into a cramped conference room where they could discuss the situation without the prying ears of the small-town community.

"We've had our share of troubles, Detective Maitland," Sheriff Morse began after the initial introductions. "A few break-ins, some suspicious activities at night—it's been unusual for our quiet corner of the world."

"Thank you for meeting with us on such short notice, Sheriff Morse. We believe these incidents may be connected to a larger network we're currently investigating," Jerry explained, laying out the documents they had brought with them. The papers rustled softly in the quiet of the room, each page a testament to the complexity of the criminal web they were unraveling.

Sheriff Morse leaned over the documents, her brow furrowed as she absorbed the information. "This Marco character you're pursuing—looks like he's been careful not to leave a clear trail."

"That's been our challenge," Jerry acknowledged, his voice low. "But we're hoping that by piecing together these smaller patterns, we can find him, or at least prevent him from doing further damage."

The meeting continued with a detailed examination of the recent crimes in the area, cross-referencing them with the patterns and methods outlined in Jerry's files. The local incidents, once isolated puzzles, began to fit into the larger picture, revealing a strategy that relied on the quiet desperation of small towns as cover for larger operations.

As the discussion wrapped up, Jerry and his team were granted access to local records and surveillance footage that might hold clues to their investigation. Sheriff Morse promised her full cooperation, her team ready to assist in any capacity needed.

With a new base of operations established in the small town, Jerry and his team spent the next hours poring over local crime reports and CCTV footage, searching for anything that might resemble the modus operandi of the network they were chasing. Each clip of shadowy figures moving through the night, each report of stolen items, added another layer of understanding to their quest.

The work was meticulous and draining, the room often silent except for the soft tapping of computer keys and the occasional murmur of discussion. As the sun began to set, casting long shadows into the office, the day's efforts had yielded modest results—several potential leads but nothing conclusive.

Exhausted but undeterred, Jerry stepped outside for a breath of fresh air. The streets of the small town were settling into the evening calm, lights flickering on in homes and storefronts, the normalcy of life continuing unaware of the darkness that lurked in its shadows.

As he stood there, Jerry felt the weight of their task. Each small town, each quiet street, might be unknowingly hosting elements of a dangerous network. But he also felt a renewed sense of purpose. The day had been long, and the leads were tenuous, but they were no longer grasping in the dark. They were building a case, piece by piece, and with each small victory, they drew closer to restoring peace.

The night air was cool and crisp, refreshing against the weariness that clung to his thoughts. Inside, his team continued their work, the glow of their screens a beacon of their dedication. Jerry turned back towards the door, ready to join them, the quiet resolve that had brought him here now strengthened by the promise of the breakthroughs that lay just beyond the horizon.

As the evening deepened into night, Jerry remained stationed at the makeshift desk, his eyes flickering across the glow of the computer screen, reviewing the data compiled from the day's investigations. The small police station was mostly quiet now, save for the low hum of the aging air conditioning unit and the occasional sound of an officer moving about in the adjoining rooms.

The information laid out before Jerry painted a grim tapestry of criminal activity that extended beyond Greendale's borders into neighboring towns, much like the one he currently occupied. It became increasingly clear that what had initially appeared to be isolated incidents of burglary and theft were in fact interconnected, each act a carefully placed domino in a larger scheme.

Maps dotted with colored pins covered one wall of the room, each pin representing an incident or sighting related to the case. Strings connected some of these pins, forming a visual network of crime that sprawled across the region. Jerry leaned back in his chair, his mind racing as he tried to predict the next move of this elusive criminal network. The patterns were there, subtle and complex, but decipherable to an experienced eye.

Outside, the moon cast a pale light over the town, the streets quiet and empty. The peace of the night was at odds with the storm of activity inside Jerry's mind. He stood up, stretching his legs, feeling the weight of hours spent in tense concentration. Moving to the window, he gazed out at the quiet town, his thoughts momentarily drifting to the people who lived in blissful ignorance of the dangers lurking in the shadows.

Returning to his desk, Jerry sifted through the latest batch of surveillance photos and financial records. His eyes were drawn to a series of transactions that seemed out of place for the small businesses they were attributed to. Notes scribbled in the margins of the financial ledgers hinted at a pressure to launder money through seemingly innocent local enterprises.

The puzzle was slowly coming together, each piece revealing the scale and audacity of Marco's operations. The realization of how deep these roots went was sobering. The network was not just stealing goods but was entwined in the economic fabric of each town it touched, corrupting it silently from within.

As Jerry compiled his findings into a report, his dedication to the task was singular. This was not just about solving a case anymore; it was about ripping out a malignancy that threatened to consume entire communities. He knew that the information he was gathering would be crucial in the coming days when the push to dismantle Marco's network would intensify.

The clock ticked past midnight, and the room was suffused with the soft buzz of the fluorescent lights overhead. Jerry finally leaned back, his report complete. He felt a mix of exhaustion and adrenaline, the latter fueled by the knowledge that each discovery brought them closer to the core of the criminal enterprise.

He glanced at his phone, considering a quick update to Sandra, but decided against it. It was late, and tomorrow's briefing would come soon enough. Instead, Jerry turned off the computer, the room dimming as the screen went dark. He gathered the maps and files, organizing them neatly for the next day's strategy session.

The night outside was still as he finally locked up the station, the silent streets a stark contrast to the storm of activity that had occupied his last several hours. As Jerry walked to his car, the cool night air felt refreshing against his tired face. The quiet of the small town at night was a brief respite from the chaos of his investigation. Yet, even as he drove back to his temporary accommodations, his mind continued to work, planning, theorizing—ever vigilant in the fight to restore peace and order.

Morning light filtered softly through the blinds of the small-town police station, casting strips of illumination that danced across the walls as the day began. Inside, the mood was far less tranquil, marked by the hum of activity as Jerry and the local team prepared for another day of strategic planning.

"Jerry, take a look at this," Sheriff Morse called from across the room, holding up a sheet of paper that seemed to have been freshly printed. Jerry approached, his expression focused.

"What have you got?" he asked, taking the paper from her.

"It's a list of registered vehicles that match the descriptions you provided from your surveillance. Three of them have been spotted in our area over the last two weeks," she explained.

"That could be our link to the next target," Jerry mused, examining the list. "Can we track down the current locations of these vehicles?"

"We're on it. I've got officers pulling traffic cam footage as we speak," Sheriff Morse replied. "If these vehicles are moving, we'll find out where they're headed."

"Good work," Jerry nodded appreciatively. "This might give us the break we need to anticipate their next move."

As they spoke, an officer approached, phone in hand. "Sheriff, we've got a hit on one of those vehicles. It was seen heading towards the industrial district an hour ago."

"Let's set up a team to head out there," Jerry suggested immediately. "If we move quickly, we might catch them in the act."

Sheriff Morse nodded, turning to the officer. "Get units ready to deploy in five minutes. Jerry, you'll want to lead this?"

"I wouldn't miss it," Jerry confirmed, his voice carrying a mix of resolve and urgency.

The preparation was swift, the police station a flurry of motion as officers gathered their gear and briefed on their roles. Jerry donned his bulletproof vest, checking his equipment methodically, his mind already racing through possible scenarios they might encounter.

"Stay sharp, everyone," Jerry addressed the team as they assembled outside. "We don't know what we're walking into. Keep communications open, and watch each other's backs."

The drive to the industrial district was tense, each officer mentally preparing for what might come. The area was less populated, a sprawl of warehouses and factories, many of which had seen better days. Jerry's eyes scanned every alley and access road as they neared the location where the vehicle had been spotted.

Upon arrival, Jerry led the team through a coordinated sweep of the area. They moved silently, communicating with hand signals, their steps echoing softly against the concrete. The suspect vehicle was soon located behind an old warehouse, abandoned and partially obscured by overgrown vegetation.

"Here's our vehicle," Jerry whispered into his radio, signaling the rest of the team. "No sign of movement yet. We're going in."

The entry was precise, the team breaching the warehouse doors with practiced efficiency. Inside, the vast space was dimly lit by shafts of light piercing through the boarded-up windows. Rows of crates and machinery formed a labyrinthine environment, perfect for hiding.

Jerry led the way, his senses heightened, every shadow and sound under scrutiny. As they moved deeper, the faint sound of voices confirmed they were not alone. With a signal to his team, they prepared to confront whoever was inside.

"Police! Show yourselves!" Jerry called out, his voice echoing through the warehouse. The response was immediate—movement, then figures emerging cautiously from their hiding places, hands raised.

"We're clear here," one of the officers reported, securing the scene. No further threat was found, but the discovery of the vehicle and several items of interest within the warehouse added another piece to the puzzle.

As the operation wrapped up, Jerry stood among his team, reviewing the morning's work. They had intercepted a possible staging area for the network's operations, and every bit of evidence collected would help in building a stronger case against Marco and his associates.

The morning's success was a testament to their diligence and quick action, but Jerry knew the investigation was far from over. As they prepared to leave the warehouse, his mind was already on the next steps, the next leads to follow. Each breakthrough brought them closer to the truth, and he was determined to pursue it to the end.

Chapter 5
Patterns Emerge

In the dimly lit briefing room back at the Greendale police station, Jerry reviewed the evidence collected from the industrial district raid with his team. Maps and photographs were strewn across the table, each annotated with notes and observations. Captain Sandra Clarke sat across from him, her focus on the array of documents that detailed their findings.

"So, what do we have?" Sandra inquired, looking up from a photograph of the items found in the warehouse.

Jerry sifted through the papers before him, pulling out a detailed list. "We found several crates filled with electronics, likely meant for resale, and documents that suggest they were planning another shipment out of town soon."

"Have we linked any of this directly to Marco yet?" Sandra asked, her eyes narrowing slightly.

"Not directly," Jerry admitted, shaking his head. "But the pattern fits. The way the goods were packed and the routes planned for transport—it's consistent with the operations we've already tied to him through other evidence."

"It's frustrating not to have him in hand yet," Sandra remarked, leaning back in her chair with a sigh. "What about the vehicle we tracked to the warehouse?"

"It was stolen, registered two towns over. No prints inside—cleaned out. But the type of vehicle and its use in transporting stolen goods fits Marco's M.O.," Jerry explained, displaying photos of the vehicle on a digital tablet.

"Okay, let's talk next steps. What's our strategy moving forward?" Sandra shifted the conversation towards action, her hands clasped together on the table.

Jerry leaned forward, his demeanor serious. "We keep pressing. I want to dig deeper into the transport routes we uncovered. If we can intercept the next shipment, we might not catch Marco, but we'll cut off his resources significantly."

"And the towns involved?" Sandra asked, scanning a map dotted with multiple locations.

"We need to coordinate with their local departments more closely. If we're seeing patterns here that match activities in those towns, they might be dealing with the same network without realizing it," Jerry proposed, his finger tracing the routes on the map.

"That's a good plan. I'll set up a meeting with the chiefs from those departments first thing tomorrow. We need all the cooperation we can get," Sandra decided, reaching for her phone to schedule the meetings.

"Also, I think we should re-examine all communications again," Jerry added. "Something might have slipped through. A different angle on the data might reveal something we missed."

"Agreed," Sandra said, nodding. "I'll have our tech team pull everything we've collected so far—emails, texts, call logs. We'll go through it all again."

As the meeting concluded, Jerry and Sandra stood, gathering the maps and documents. They were pieces of a larger puzzle that was slowly coming into focus, and each piece brought them closer to understanding the full scope of the criminal enterprise they were up against.

"Thanks, Jerry. Let's keep the pressure on. We're making progress, even if it doesn't feel fast enough," Sandra said, offering a tired but genuine smile.

"Every bit counts, Sandra. We'll get there," Jerry responded, his tone resolute. He collected his notes, ready to dive back into the investigation with renewed vigor. As he left the briefing room, the weight of their task was heavy but not insurmountable. The path ahead was clear, and every step took them closer to bringing the network down. As the station's doors closed behind him, the late afternoon sun cast long shadows across the floor, echoing the long reach of the law he was determined to uphold.

Later that afternoon, Jerry sat in the quiet of his office surrounded by the myriad elements of the ongoing investigation: maps marked with circles and lines, lists of suspects, timelines of crimes. The room was a visual representation of the complex web they were untangling. Sandra entered, carrying a fresh stack of reports and a cup of coffee which she handed to Jerry with a knowing smile.

"Here's the latest from the tech team. They've managed to pull some new data from the communications we seized," Sandra said as she set down the reports on Jerry's cluttered desk.

Jerry accepted the coffee gratefully and began flipping through the reports. "Anything jump out at you?"

"A few things. There's a series of encrypted messages that were sent from a device we haven't tracked yet. The team thinks it could be directly linked to Marco, given the encryption level and the context," Sandra explained, pulling up a chair next to Jerry.

Jerry's eyes narrowed as he read. "Have they managed to crack the encryption?"

"Not yet, but they're getting close. They believe it might contain details about upcoming transactions or possibly even direct communications to other members of the network," Sandra replied, watching Jerry's reaction closely.

"That could be the break we need. Good work on pushing the tech team. We need all the information we can get," Jerry said, his mind already racing through the possibilities. "What's the status on the inter-departmental cooperation?"

Sandra leaned back, her face reflecting the strain of the day. "It's going well. I've spoken to four other departments today. They've all reported similar activities and are willing to share their data. We're setting up a secure channel for information exchange."

"Perfect. That could widen our net significantly," Jerry noted, making a few quick notes in his notebook. "Have we got anything more on the potential routes for these so-called shipments?"

"Yes, actually," Sandra began, pulling a map from the stack she brought in. She spread it out on the desk, pointing to several highlighted routes. "These are the most likely routes for transport, based on the patterns we've established. Our best bet is to set up surveillance at key points along these routes."

Jerry studied the map closely. "Let's prioritize the routes with the least amount of public visibility. It'll reduce the chances of them spotting our surveillance."

"Agreed," Sandra said, marking the routes with a red pen. "I'll coordinate with the respective local units to get eyes on these points as soon as possible."

As the sun began to set, casting long shadows into the room, the weight of their responsibilities seemed to deepen. Yet, there was a tangible sense of progress that kept their spirits buoyed.

"I'll stay on top of the tech team about the encrypted messages. As soon as they break through, it could open up several new avenues for us," Sandra said as she stood, gathering the empty coffee cups.

"Thanks, Sandra. Let's keep the pressure up. We're too close now to let the trail go cold," Jerry replied, his voice firm with resolve.

Sandra nodded, a look of determination settling over her features. "We'll get him, Jerry. We'll get them all."

With that, she left the room, her footsteps echoing slightly in the quiet corridor outside. Jerry turned back to the window, watching as the last light of the day faded into the evening. The darkness outside was deep and vast, but inside, the light of their efforts cast long beams across the tangle of crime they were determined to unravel.

The following morning, Jerry found himself in a crowded conference room, surrounded by law enforcement officers from various jurisdictions. Maps and digital displays lit up the room, each one detailing parts of the operation spanning multiple towns. The interdepartmental meeting had been organized swiftly, underlining the urgency of their collective efforts against Marco's criminal network.

"As you all are aware," Jerry began, standing at the front with a laser pointer in hand, "we've identified several routes that are potentially being used for transporting illegal goods. These routes are less visible, mostly back roads and small highways."

One of the officers, a tall man with a graying mustache, raised his hand. "Have we considered setting up checkpoints? It could be a direct way to intercept these transports."

"We've thought about that," Jerry replied, "but the risk is high. If they spot the checkpoints, they could go to ground, and we'd lose any chance of tracking them further. Instead, we're recommending mobile surveillance units that can track movement without being too conspicuous."

Another officer, a young woman with sharp eyes, chimed in. "Are we coordinating with local traffic cameras? Can we integrate those feeds into our surveillance efforts?"

"Yes, we are," Sandra answered from her seat next to Jerry. "We've arranged access to traffic camera feeds along these routes. The tech team is setting up software to flag unusual activity or recognized vehicles associated with our cases."

Jerry clicked to a new slide showing a network of interconnected dots. "This map here outlines the network we believe is responsible for not only moving stolen goods but also laundering money through various businesses in our regions."

A murmur ran through the room as the officers absorbed the complexity of the operation.

"Money laundering?" another officer asked, leaning forward. "Do we have evidence linking these businesses directly to the crimes, or are they just potential fronts?"

"We're still gathering evidence on that front," Jerry admitted. "But preliminary investigations suggest that several of these businesses are involved, even if the owners aren't directly aware of what's going on."

An older officer from the back spoke up, "What about manpower? Some of our departments are stretched thin as it is. Coordinating an operation of this scale might require more resources than we currently have."

Sandra took the lead on this concern. "We understand the limitations. That's why we're also reaching out to state and federal agencies for additional support. The scale of this operation exceeds local jurisdiction capabilities, and we need all the help we can get."

Jerry nodded in agreement. "Exactly. This isn't just a local problem; it's regional, possibly even national. We need to treat it as such and pool our resources effectively."

As the meeting drew to a close, plans were made for follow-up communications and data sharing. Each department committed to specific tasks, with Jerry and Sandra overseeing the coordination of the larger strategy.

"Thank you all for your cooperation," Jerry concluded. "We'll be in touch with updates and further instructions within the next 24 hours."

The officers began to disperse, talking among themselves, their expressions a mix of determination and concern. Jerry and Sandra lingered behind, gathering their notes and discussing the next steps quietly.

"We've got a good team here," Sandra remarked, glancing around the now-emptying room. "I think we can really make a dent in this operation."

Jerry looked out the window, where the early morning sun was just beginning to brighten the sky. "I hope so, Sandra. With this kind of network, Marco's reach is extensive. But so is ours now. We'll get him."

The conference room emptied slowly, leaving Jerry and Sandra to their planning and the growing daylight that seemed to underscore the hope of their mission. As they exited the room, their resolve was clear; the battle was uphill, but neither was willing to back down.

By late afternoon, Jerry and Sandra had sequestered themselves in a small, quiet office to refine the tactical aspects of their operation. The walls of the room were lined with digital screens displaying real-time feeds from surveillance cameras and maps highlighted with the routes and locations identified as critical. The hum of computers and the occasional crackle from the radios provided a steady backdrop to their focused work.

Outside, the day was drawing to a close, the light fading into the deep blue of twilight. Inside, the glow from the multiple screens cast a surreal light on Jerry and Sandra as they reviewed the latest reports from their field agents. Each report brought them closer to understanding the full scope of the criminal network they were up against.

Jerry was particularly focused on a series of intercepted communications that had been partially decrypted by their tech team earlier in the day. These messages hinted at a larger shipment of contraband scheduled to move through one of their monitored routes in the next 48 hours. The specifics were still vague, but the timing mentioned in the messages gave them a narrow window to intercept.

Sandra was updating a digital map with the latest surveillance points when Jerry looked up from his screen. "The next 48 hours could define the success of this entire operation," he remarked, his voice low but clear.

"We've got our best teams on it," Sandra replied, without looking away from the map. "I'll be overseeing the coordination personally from the command center. We won't miss this opportunity."

Jerry nodded, his gaze returning to his screen where rows of data continued to scroll. He was piecing together the logistics, making sure that every team knew their role and was ready to act at a moment's notice. Coordination was key, and with so many moving parts, there was little room for error.

As the evening progressed, the office remained a bubble of activity in the otherwise quiet building. Jerry and Sandra were methodical, going through their checklists repeatedly, confirming and reconfirming details with each team involved in the operation.

At one point, Jerry stepped away from the screens to stretch his legs. He walked over to the window, where the first stars of the evening were beginning to appear. The calmness of the night sky was in stark contrast to the storm of activity inside. He allowed himself a moment to breathe, to feel the cool glass against his forehead, and then turned back to the task at hand.

Returning to his desk, Jerry dialed into a secure line to speak briefly with the leaders of the surveillance teams. "Stay alert and maintain radio silence unless it's critical," he instructed, his voice both firm and encouraging. "We depend on your eyes out there."

As the call ended, he looked over to Sandra, who was meticulously documenting their strategy. "We're as ready as we'll ever be," he stated, more to himself than to her.

Sandra looked up, her eyes tired but determined. "Yes, we are," she affirmed. "Let's catch these guys."

The office was quiet again, save for the soft tapping of keys and the occasional static from the radios. The readiness of the teams, the precision of their planning—it all culminated in this stretch of waiting, where patience was as crucial as any action they would undertake.

Finally, with their preparations complete, Jerry and Sandra gathered their notes and turned off the screens, plunging the room into semi-darkness. They left the office, the door clicking shut behind them, sealing off the hub of their strategic efforts.

The corridors of the police station were quiet as they made their way out, the weight of the impending operation hanging over them like a heavy cloak. Outside, the night had fully settled, the darkness complete except for the scattered lights of the city. They parted ways in the parking lot, each lost in their thoughts about the days ahead, the quiet of the night wrapping around them as they prepared to face what would come.

Chapter 6
The Stakeout

As dawn broke over Greendale, a thin mist hung low over the streets, lending an eerie quiet to the town. Jerry was already at his desk, the remnants of a hurried breakfast beside him, his eyes glued to the screens displaying the real-time feeds from the surveillance teams positioned along the anticipated route of the contraband shipment. Sandra was in the command center, coordinating with field units and ensuring all communication lines were open and secure.

Every officer involved in the operation was on high alert. The tension was palpable, each passing minute stretching longer as they awaited the signal that the shipment was on the move. Jerry's phone buzzed intermittently with updates from the field agents—still nothing significant to report.

The silence was suddenly broken by a crisp voice over the radio. "Eagle one to base, we have visual on the target vehicle. Approaching checkpoint delta."

Jerry's hand shot out to the radio. "Copy that, Eagle one. Maintain distance and keep visuals. Do not engage until we have confirmation of the cargo."

The response was immediate and affirmative. Jerry turned to another screen, pulling up the camera feed from checkpoint delta. A grainy image of a nondescript van appeared, moving steadily along the tree-lined road. It was alone, no convoy, which was unusual for a shipment suspected to be of high value.

Sandra's voice came through on the speakerphone, "Jerry, visuals on one vehicle only. Does that fit the profile of the operation we were expecting?"

"It's atypical," Jerry responded, his brow furrowed in concentration. "Keep eyes on it. It could be a decoy, or they might have changed tactics."

Minutes ticked by as they tracked the van's progress. The vehicle made no effort to divert from its path or speed, which only added to Jerry's suspicion. "All units, stay alert," he instructed. "We're not sure if this is what we think it is."

As the van neared the designated interception point, the lead surveillance unit prepared to discreetly follow it into the industrial area of Greendale, where the exchange was suspected to take place. Jerry coordinated with Sandra to ensure that SWAT teams were ready to move on his command.

"Base to Eagle one, prepare to initiate a soft stop at the next turnoff. We need to inspect that vehicle," came Sandra's directive.

The operation moved swiftly. The van was smoothly guided off the main road by unmarked police vehicles, its driver seemingly unaware of the orchestration around him until it was too late. Within moments, law enforcement had the van surrounded in a low-key but firm blockade.

Jerry arrived at the scene just as officers were cautiously approaching the vehicle. "Driver, step out of the vehicle with your hands visible," one of the officers called out, his voice calm but authoritative.

The driver complied, stepping out into the cool morning air, hands raised, confusion apparent on his face. He was quickly secured and read his rights while another team prepared to inspect the van.

Jerry watched closely as the doors to the back of the van were opened, revealing not the anticipated cache of weapons or drugs, but boxes of commercial electronics—nothing illegal, but potentially part of the smuggling operation they were investigating.

"Looks like commercial goods, but we'll need to verify every serial number against stolen property reports," Jerry said, turning to a nearby officer. "Let's get these back to the station for a thorough check."

As the van and its driver were taken into custody, Jerry stood back, watching the operation wind down. The mist had lifted, and the first rays of morning sun began to filter through the trees, casting long shadows across the road.

While this might not have been the full extent of what they had hoped to intercept, every piece of evidence was vital. As the officers wrapped up the scene, Jerry's thoughts were already turning to the next steps in their investigation. The quiet of the morning returned as they cleared the area, the day's early promise still hanging in the balance.

As the operation at the industrial area wrapped up, the confiscated electronics were carefully cataloged and loaded into police vehicles for transport back to the station. The driver, a man in his mid-thirties with a wary expression and nothing to say without his lawyer present, was also taken in for questioning. Jerry watched as the convoy prepared to leave, his mind analyzing every possible angle of what they had uncovered.

Back at the station, the mood was subdued. While the morning's efforts had yielded results, they were not the decisive breakthrough Jerry had hoped for. He returned to his office to sift through the latest reports and updates, trying to piece together how the mundane contents of the van fit into the larger puzzle.

Upon entering his office, Jerry found a report on his desk from the tech team. They had made progress on decrypting more of the communications. Pulling up the digital copies on his computer, Jerry scrolled through the intercepted messages, searching for any detail that might indicate the purpose of the intercepted shipment.

"Anything that can tell us if we're looking at the right shipments or just chasing shadows," Jerry murmured to himself, his eyes scanning the encryption-breaking summaries. The language of the messages was coded, but certain phrases stood out—terms that might refer to the electronic goods as a cover for something else, or perhaps a coded inventory.

A knock on the door pulled him from his concentration. It was Sandra, carrying a fresh cup of coffee and a notepad filled with her own notes.

"We're not finding any stolen property serial numbers matching those in the van," Sandra reported as she handed Jerry the coffee. "It seems legitimate, at least on the surface."

Jerry took a sip, considering this. "Thanks. It might be a front, or we might have spooked them into cleaning up their act for this shipment. Keep a team on the driver; he might still lead us somewhere."

"Will do," Sandra affirmed. "I'll also keep pressing the tech team. If these messages can give us a clearer picture, we might be able to anticipate their next move instead of reacting to it."

As Sandra left, Jerry turned back to his computer, opening a digital map that displayed the routes and known associates tied to the network. His finger traced along lines that connected various nodes—warehouses, drop-off points, and now this odd shipment of electronics. Each node was a part of the network, and each held potential clues to unlocking Marco's strategy.

The rest of the day was spent in detailed analysis. Jerry worked through lunch, barely touching his sandwich, as he cross-referenced the new data with ongoing investigations. He sent periodic updates to field agents, asking them to keep a watch on certain locations that might suddenly activate if the network felt compromised.

By late afternoon, a pattern began to emerge from the chaos. The electronics, while legal, were being moved through channels that had previously been used for smuggling contraband. This dual-use of logistics suggested a sophisticated level of operational security from Marco's network. They were hiding in plain sight, using legitimate business as a cover.

As the sun began to set, casting a golden glow through his office window, Jerry finally leaned back in his chair. The pieces were slowly coming together, revealing the complex web of Marco's organization. There was a long way to go, but each small revelation added to the bigger picture.

He made a few notes for the next day's tasks, then shut down his computer, the screen's light dimming as he stood and stretched. The office was quiet, most of the staff having left for the day. Jerry walked to the window, looking out over Greendale as it shifted from day to night. The streets were calm, the peaceful facade belying the undercurrent of criminal activity he was so deeply entrenched in uncovering.

With a final glance at the quiet town, Jerry grabbed his coat and turned off the lights, the office fading into darkness behind him as he stepped out into the evening, ready to face whatever challenges tomorrow would bring.

The next morning brought a crisp clarity to Greendale, the air fresh with the promise of early spring. Jerry arrived at the station before dawn, his mind already churning through the day's objectives. The first order of business was a debrief with his team and Sandra, who had gathered in the main conference room, their faces reflecting a mix of determination and the fatigue of long hours.

"Good morning, everyone. Let's get straight to it," Jerry began, his voice cutting through the low murmur of conversation. "The shipment we intercepted may not have been what we expected, but it's given us a new angle to explore. The legitimacy of these shipments could be a cover, a way to keep the operation under the radar."

Sandra nodded, her hands folded neatly in front of her. "That's our current theory. We're dealing with someone who knows how to hide in plain sight, using legitimate business operations to mask the illegal ones. It's clever, and it's effective."

"Do we have any leads on who might be orchestrating this from the legitimate side? Any connections to Marco that we can trace?" an officer asked, leaning forward in his seat.

"We're working on that," Jerry replied. "Our next step is to trace the origins of these electronics. Find out who's shipping them and where they're really going. There's a paper trail there—we just need to follow it."

"I've already started pulling records from the companies listed on the shipping labels," another officer chimed in. "It's going to take some time to sift through, but we should be able to find discrepancies or links to known associates of Marco."

"Good," Jerry said with a nod. "Keep me updated on any progress. Every little detail helps."

Sandra then took over the discussion. "In the meantime, we need to stay vigilant. I want increased surveillance on all known routes and check points updated daily. We can't afford to miss anything."

"Understood," came the collective response.

The meeting continued with each team member outlining their tasks for the day. Jerry listened intently, interjecting occasionally with directives or clarifications. Once the meeting was adjourned, he lingered to discuss specifics with Sandra.

"Sandra, how confident are you about our intel from the tech team? Are they close to cracking more of the encrypted messages?" Jerry inquired, his tone serious.

"They're making progress, but it's slow. The encryption is sophisticated, more so than we've seen before. It suggests professional involvement at a high level," Sandra explained, her eyes meeting Jerry's with a hint of concern.

"That fits with Marco's profile. He wouldn't risk amateur mistakes in communications," Jerry concluded. "Keep pressing them for results. Anything they can give us could be the key to unraveling this whole operation."

"I will," Sandra assured him. "And Jerry, make sure you're taking some time too. This case is a marathon, not a sprint."

Jerry smiled faintly, appreciating her concern. "I'll try, Sandra. But you know as well as I do, it's hard to step back when you're this close to breaking it wide open."

With a final nod, Jerry left the conference room and returned to his office. He spent the rest of the morning reviewing reports and making calls to enhance their operational intelligence. His focus was razor-sharp, each piece of information a potential stepping stone to the next breakthrough.

By mid-afternoon, the office buzzed with the energy of new information coming in. Reports from the tech team indicated potential breakthroughs in the decryption of key communications. Jerry felt a surge of adrenaline at the news, his instincts telling him they were on the brink of something significant.

The day waned into evening, and the stack of reports on Jerry's desk grew smaller as he worked through them. Outside, the sky turned a brilliant hue of twilight, the sun dipping below the horizon. The quiet of the evening settled around the station, a stark contrast to the flurry of activity within, where Jerry continued to piece together the complex puzzle that was Marco's network.

As the shadows lengthened and the office grew quiet with the departure of the day staff, Jerry remained hunched over his desk, surrounded by the soft glow of his desk lamp and the flickering screens of his computer. His focus was unwavering as he delved deeper into the intricate web of financial transactions and communication trails that threaded through the criminal network they were unraveling.

The office was silent except for the occasional crackle of the police radio and the steady hum of the air conditioning. Papers with scribbled notes, digital maps dotted with markers, and photographs of suspects and locations were spread out before him, each item a piece of the puzzle that slowly formed a clearer picture of the operation's scope and Marco's involvement.

Jerry's phone vibrated softly against the wooden surface of his desk, a message from the tech team signaling a breakthrough in decrypting the encrypted communications. With a mixture of relief and anticipation, Jerry opened the email, scanning the contents rapidly. The decrypted messages revealed plans for an upcoming transaction—a significant one, according to the details, scheduled to occur at a location that had not been under surveillance.

Immediately, Jerry reached for his radio, contacting Sandra to relay the information. "We've got a lead on a potential big move by Marco's group," he informed her, his voice steady despite the late hour.

"Understood," Sandra's voice crackled through the radio, alert despite the time. "I'll get teams mobilized to cover the location. Keep me posted on any more intel that comes through."

Acknowledging with a brief "Will do," Jerry turned his attention back to the screens. The next steps were crucial, and timing was everything. They needed to position their units strategically, ensuring they could intercept the transaction without alerting Marco's people.

For the next several hours, Jerry coordinated with various units, arranging for surveillance and interception teams to take their positions around the newly identified location. Maps were updated, routes were plotted, and every possible scenario was accounted for. The operation was a delicate dance of precision and adaptability, and Jerry was the conductor.

Throughout the night, Jerry monitored the progress of the teams as they moved into position. Reports came in regularly, each officer's voice a thread in the fabric of the operation. Jerry responded to each, his commands concise, ensuring that every detail was addressed.

As dawn approached, the operation was in full swing, with all teams reporting readiness. Jerry allowed himself a moment to breathe, stepping away from the desk to stretch his legs and refill his coffee cup. The station was still mostly quiet, the buzz of activity confined to the areas where officers coordinated their efforts.

Returning to his desk, Jerry watched the live feeds from the surveillance cameras, his eyes sharp for any sign of the transaction. The tension was palpable, even through the digital screens, as everyone awaited the moment of action.

Finally, as the first light of dawn tinted the sky with hues of orange and pink, movement on one of the screens caught Jerry's eye. Vehicles began to converge on the location, and figures started to disembark. Jerry's hand went to his radio, ready to give the command to move in.

The operation unfolded rapidly once initiated. Jerry directed the teams through their maneuvers, each movement bringing them closer to disrupting Marco's network. As the sun rose fully over the horizon, bathing the city in light, the culmination of their night's work became apparent.

With the suspects in custody and the evidence secured, Jerry finally leaned back in his chair, the adrenaline slowly ebbing from his veins. The morning had brought a significant victory, but the investigation was far from over. As the city woke up around him, unaware of the night's events, Jerry's mind was already turning to the next steps, the next leads to follow, and the relentless pursuit of justice that awaited.

Chapter 7
Inside the Lair

Chapter 7 of Jerry's relentless pursuit began under the stark fluorescent lights of the Greendale police station's main conference room, transformed into a hub of forensic activity. Boxes of evidence collected from the recent bust were being meticulously cataloged by a team of officers, each piece potentially a key to unlocking further secrets of Marco's expansive criminal network.

Jerry stood beside a large table covered with documents and electronic devices seized during the raid, his eyes scanning the material evidence as he spoke with Sandra, who was cross-referencing details on her laptop.

"Any luck matching the serial numbers from the electronics to reported thefts?" Jerry asked, picking up a tablet from the table and turning it over in his hands.

Sandra shook her head, her expression mirroring the frustration they both felt. "Not yet. It seems these items were clean, so to speak. But I'm running a second check through the national database just to be sure."

"That's thorough. Good. What about the financial documents? Anything that ties back directly to Marco?" Jerry set the tablet down, his gaze fixed on a stack of papers Sandra was working through.

"We've found several transactions that trace back to shell companies. I'm digging deeper to see if there's a direct link to Marco or any of his known associates," Sandra replied, tapping at her keyboard. "It's a tangled web, but there are patterns. It's just a matter of tracking them to their source."

Jerry nodded, his mind ticking through the implications. "Keep at it. Every bit of data could be the break we need. Have we heard back from the tech team on the rest of those encrypted messages?"

"They're still working on it. The encryption is more complex than anything we've seen before. But they're making progress," Sandra said, a note of hope threading through her words.

As they spoke, Officer Marla entered the room, her face brightening as she approached them. "Jerry, Sandra, we've got something," she announced, holding up a USB drive. "One of the laptops had this hidden in a false bottom in the case. Looks like it might contain financial records."

"Excellent find, Marla. Let's see if we can access the data," Jerry said, his interest piqued as he took the USB drive and handed it to Sandra.

Sandra inserted the USB into her laptop, her fingers deftly navigating the decryption software. After a moment of tense silence, folders appeared on the screen, each labeled with dates and cryptic names.

"Looks like we're in," Sandra murmured, opening the first folder to reveal a series of spreadsheets and documents.

Jerry leaned over to look, his detective instincts flaring as he pointed to one of the documents. "Check that one. It looks like a ledger. Might give us insight into how the money's flowing."

They scanned the document, finding detailed entries of transactions that spanned several months. The figures were significant, hinting at a large-scale operation.

"This could be it. This could be the financial backbone of the entire network," Jerry said, a trace of triumph in his voice.

Sandra nodded, her eyes not leaving the screen. "I'll pull these into our analysis software. If we can map out the transactions, we might be able to pinpoint where the money's going and, more importantly, where it's coming from."

As Sandra worked, Jerry paced slowly around the room, his mind racing with the possibilities now unfolding before them. Every document, every piece of data added to the mosaic they were piecing together, a clearer picture of Marco's operations and perhaps even the man himself.

Outside, the morning had shifted into afternoon. The police station was a hive of activity, every officer and staff member pulled into the orbit of the case that had consumed so much of their energy and resources.

Jerry stopped pacing and looked back at Sandra, who was still absorbed in her analysis. "Keep me posted on any new developments," he said, his tone a mix of command and encouragement.

"I will," Sandra replied, her focus unbroken.

Stepping out of the conference room, Jerry felt the weight of their discoveries. Each step was a step closer to dismantling Marco's network. As he walked down the corridor, his resolve deepened, ready to face the challenges that awaited.

Later that day, Jerry convened a small task force in a side office, the air thick with anticipation as they prepared to delve deeper into the financial web uncovered by Sandra's earlier analysis. The team, composed of forensic accountants and seasoned detectives, was buzzing with the potential of breaking open the financial structure of Marco's criminal enterprise.

"Let's go over what we've found so far," Jerry began, gesturing to the digital projector where a complex diagram of transactions and accounts was displayed. "Sandra, can you walk us through this?"

Sandra nodded, clicking to the first slide of her presentation. "We've identified several key accounts that appear repeatedly across the documents. These accounts tie back to shell companies, but they're cleverly disguised to look like legitimate businesses."

One of the detectives, a middle-aged man named Frank, leaned forward, squinting at the screen. "Have we been able to link any of these directly to Marco or is he still keeping his distance?"

"That's where it gets tricky," Sandra replied, shifting to another slide showing a network of transactions. "Direct links to Marco are still elusive, but we see his known associates cropping up around the fringes. I believe he's using them as buffers."

"So, he never touches the money directly," another detective, Elena, chimed in. "He's insulated. Smart. Makes pinning anything directly on him difficult."

"Exactly," Jerry said, picking up the thread. "Our best bet is to map out the flow of money and pressure those closest to him. If we can flip one of his associates, it could lead us straight to him."

"Speaking of associates," Frank said, tapping a pen against his notepad, "do we have any leads on who might be willing to talk? Anyone facing charges that might be motivated to cooperate?"

"There's a couple," Jerry responded, his gaze thoughtful. "I've asked Marla to pull up everything we have on them. Criminal histories, financial pressures, known weaknesses. We'll approach the most likely candidates first."

Sandra advanced the slides to a list of names. "These three here are the most connected and the most vulnerable. Two of them have significant gambling debts, and the third is facing possible charges in another jurisdiction. They might be open to making a deal."

"Good," Jerry nodded. "Let's start putting together a strategy for approaching them. We'll need to be careful not to spook them. If Marco gets wind of this, he'll tighten his circle even more."

The team spent the next hour strategizing, discussing potential approaches for turning Marco's associates. Each plan was meticulously crafted, considering all possible outcomes and reactions. The room was alive with the energy of collaborative problem-solving, a testament to the collective experience and determination gathered around the table.

As the meeting drew to a close, Jerry summarized their next steps. "We need to move quickly but cautiously. The moment we show our hand, we risk pushing Marco and his operation further underground. Sandra, keep digging into the financials. Frank, Elena, start putting together the dossiers on our potential cooperators."

"Will do, Jerry," Frank confirmed, gathering his notes.

"And I'll coordinate with the DA's office, see what kind of deals we might be able to offer," Elena added, her tone determined.

"Great work, everyone," Jerry concluded, standing to signify the end of the meeting. "Let's bring this home."

As the team dispersed, Jerry stayed back, reviewing the network of transactions on the screen once more. The complexity was daunting, but each connection they uncovered brought them closer to dismantling Marco's shadowy operations. His resolve was firmer than ever as he turned off the projector, the room dimming with the fading light of the screen. The quiet of the office was a stark contrast to the storm of activity that had just taken place, a brief respite as they prepared for the next phase of their investigation.

Jerry spent the rest of the afternoon in a solitary review of the potential leads and evidence that had accumulated over the past few weeks. His office, usually a hub of activity and collaboration, was now a quiet sanctuary of reflection and strategy. He pored over the financial documents and communications, each piece a breadcrumb on the trail leading to Marco and his hidden operations.

As he reviewed the evidence, the door to his office opened, and Sandra entered, carrying a stack of newly printed reports and a fresh cup of coffee for Jerry. She placed the reports on his desk with a slight thump, pulling up a chair next to him.

"Here are the latest intercepts from the communications surveillance," she said, flipping open the top folder to reveal a series of transcripts. "We might have something here."

Jerry accepted the coffee with a nod, his eyes scanning the first page of the transcript. "Anything jump out at you?" he asked, his voice low, the fatigue of the long days evident but his determination undimmed.

"A few more mentions of a big move planned for the end of the month," Sandra replied, pointing to a highlighted section of the text. "It's coded, but the context suggests they're moving more than just electronics this time. Could be what we've been waiting for."

"That's promising," Jerry murmured, making a note in the margin of the report. "We need to ensure our surveillance on their known routes is watertight. I don't want them slipping through our net this time."

"I'll double-check the assignments and make sure we have our best teams on it," Sandra assured him, her own resolve mirroring Jerry's.

The room fell into a comfortable silence, filled only by the soft rustling of papers and the occasional sip of coffee as they continued their review. After a while, Jerry leaned back in his chair, stretching his arms above his head.

"We're getting closer, Sandra. I can feel it," he said, more to himself than to her.

"We are," she agreed, closing the folder with a snap. "Marco's been careful, but he's not infallible. We'll catch him."

The conversation shifted then to logistical planning. They discussed coordination with other departments, the allocation of surveillance resources, and the setup of potential sting operations. Each decision was weighed carefully, the stakes too high for any oversight.

As the sky outside darkened, signaling the end of another day, Jerry and Sandra finalized their plans. They were a formidable team, their complementary strengths forming the backbone of the investigation.

Sandra gathered the folders, ready to leave. "I'll get these over to the tech team for one more pass before the morning. See if they can tighten up the timeline based on this new information."

"Thanks, Sandra. Let me know the moment you hear anything," Jerry said, standing to stretch his legs again. The long hours were taking their toll, but the progress they were making fueled him.

Sandra nodded, pausing at the door. "Will do, Jerry. See you bright and early."

With that, she left, and Jerry was once again alone in his office. He turned to look out the window, watching the quiet streets of Greendale. The town was peaceful, unaware of the machinations unfolding in its shadows. Jerry turned back to his desk, his gaze falling on the photos of suspects and maps lined with routes and notes.

The pieces were in place, and soon, he hoped, they would bring the entire operation crashing down. This thought comforted him as he finally turned off the lights and left the office, the halls of the station quiet and dim, echoing with the day's resolve.

The early hours of the next morning found Jerry already at his desk, the only illumination coming from his desk lamp and the computer screen. His concentration was absolute as he revisited the transcripts and reports from the previous day, looking for any detail that might have been overlooked. The quiet of the office at this hour was a stark contrast to the flurry of activity that would start in just a few hours as the rest of the team arrived.

A soft knock on the door broke his concentration. He looked up to see Marla, holding a steaming cup of coffee in one hand and a thick folder in the other.

"Morning, Jerry. Thought you might need a refill," she said, placing the coffee on his desk with a smile. She held up the folder. "And the tech team had a breakthrough night. They cracked another chunk of those encrypted messages."

"Perfect timing, Marla. Let's see what they've got," Jerry responded, his fatigue momentarily forgotten as he took the folder and began flipping through the pages.

As they reviewed the new information, Jerry's eyes narrowed. "This... this is significant. Look at this, Marla. Dates, times, locations—this could be the itinerary for their next major move."

Marla leaned over the desk, her finger tracing the lines of text. "It looks like they're planning something big for the end of the week. Multiple locations, all synchronized. This could be what we've been waiting for."

"We need to act on this," Jerry said, his mind racing through the logistics. "Coordinate with Sandra and get the surveillance teams briefed and in position by tonight. We can't give them any room to maneuver."

"I'm on it," Marla replied, her tone as determined as Jerry's. She paused at the door, turning back to him. "We're going to get them this time, aren't we?"

"We have to," Jerry said, his voice firm. "Too much is at stake."

As Marla left to carry out her tasks, Jerry took a moment to sip his coffee, staring out the window at the waking city. The weight of responsibility was heavy on his shoulders, but the progress they were making bolstered his resolve.

Later, as the morning progressed into a bustling hive of activity, Jerry convened a meeting with the task force. The room was filled with the key players of the operation, each aware of the critical phase they were entering.

"Based on the latest decrypted messages, we believe we have pinpointed the time and place of their next major operation," Jerry began, his voice capturing the room's full attention. "This is our best chance to intercept and dismantle a significant part of their network."

"We have teams ready to deploy to each location," Sandra added, her presence commanding as she detailed the strategic positions. "Each team knows their role, the backup plans, and what's expected of them. We can't afford any mistakes."

The room was tense with anticipation as they went over the final details. Officers double-checked their gear, reviewed maps, and went over communication protocols one more time. The air was thick with the urgency of the impending operation.

"Stay sharp, stay focused, and remember, we're all relying on each other," Jerry concluded, his gaze sweeping across the faces of his team. "Let's bring this home."

As the meeting broke up, the officers moved out, each to their respective assignments. Jerry stayed behind, his eyes on the screens displaying the locations they would be monitoring. The operation was in motion, each moment critical to its success.

Outside, the day was bright, but inside the command center, the mood was one of controlled intensity. Jerry remained at the helm, watching, waiting, ready to make the calls necessary to guide his team through the operation.

As the clock ticked down to the operation's commencement, the quiet before the storm was palpable. Jerry stood by, the fate of the operation—and potentially the case—hanging in the balance, his resolve as firm as ever.

Chapter 8
Unlikely Informant

The dawn of a critical day in the investigation broke over Greendale, its streets quiet, but the command center at the police station was a hive of activity. Jerry stood before a large digital map illuminated with various markers and routes, the focal point of the room. Around him, officers and specialists were poised at their stations, headsets in place, eyes fixed on screens. Sandra was coordinating with field units, her voice a constant presence over the comm system.

"Everything's in place, Jerry. Teams are on standby at all marked locations. We're ready to move on your command," Sandra reported, looking up from her workstation to meet Jerry's gaze across the room.

"Good. Keep everything tight. I want updates every five minutes," Jerry responded, his tone calm but firm, his eyes scanning the live feeds from the surveillance cameras positioned around the suspected meeting spots.

"Copy that," Sandra affirmed, turning back to her console. "Eagle team, confirm status."

"Eagle team in position. All quiet on the southern front," crackled the response through the speakers, the voice belonging to the team leader stationed at the most critical point.

Jerry nodded slightly, then shifted his attention to another screen showing drone footage. "Hawk team, report."

"Hawk team positioned. We have visual on two vehicles approaching the drop point. License plates match those on our watch list," another voice responded, the tone slightly tense with anticipation.

"Keep your distance. Let them make the first move," Jerry instructed, his fingers tapping rhythmically against the tabletop as he watched the vehicles come to a stop.

"Understood. Maintaining surveillance," the Hawk team leader replied.

As the operation unfolded, Jerry communicated seamlessly with his teams, his command clear and decisive. Sandra continued her coordination, ensuring that all moving parts of the operation were synchronized.

"Jerry, we have movement at location three. Looks like they're starting to unload," Sandra updated, her eyes not leaving the monitors as she relayed real-time movements.

"Confirm contents if possible. Falcon team, move in for a closer look but stay out of sight," Jerry directed, shifting his focus to another feed showing a group of men unloading boxes from a van.

"Falcon team moving in. We have a good vantage point," came the response, a slight rustle of movement audible even through the encrypted line.

Minutes ticked by like hours, each second stretched thin by the tension. Jerry continued to oversee the operation, his experience and instinct guiding the decisions that would hopefully lead to a significant breakthrough.

"Sandra, any update from Falcon team?" Jerry asked after a moment of waiting that seemed to drag on.

"They're in position now. Visual confirmation on the boxes... They're marked as electronics, but we're seeing additional security than usual. Something's not right," Sandra reported, frowning slightly.

"Could be a front. Keep watching. Any deviation from the plan, I want to know immediately," Jerry said, his gaze locked on the screen showing the Falcon team's feed.

"Will do. Falcon team, maintain visual. Do not engage unless absolutely necessary," Sandra conveyed the instructions, her voice steady.

As the operation continued, Jerry's communication with his teams became more sporadic, each update more crucial than the last. The morning light began to strengthen, casting long shadows across the city that mirrored the growing intensity within the command center.

"Jerry, Falcon team has visual confirmation. The boxes contain... wait, they're opening one," Sandra suddenly interjected, her voice sharp with urgency.

Everyone in the command center held their breath, waiting for the confirmation that would either escalate or de-escalate their response.

"It's confirmed. They're armed. Looks like high-caliber weapons," Sandra finally said, her tone grave.

"Alright. That's our cue. All teams, move in. Apprehend with caution," Jerry commanded, his voice resolute, the weight of the moment evident in his expression.

As the teams executed the arrest protocols, Jerry and Sandra monitored the feeds, ensuring the safety of their officers and the effectiveness of the takedown. The room was filled with the sounds of coordinated movement and focused commands, a symphony of law enforcement in action.

As the suspects were secured and the weapons confiscated, Jerry allowed himself a moment of muted relief. The operation was a success, but this was just the beginning of the end. The cleanup and subsequent investigations would take time, and the real work of dismantling Marco's network was still ahead.

As the dust settled on the successful operation, Jerry and Sandra convened in the debriefing room, where the atmosphere was one of cautious optimism mixed with the adrenaline of the morning's events. The room was lined with monitors, still displaying the various scenes of the operation as teams completed the securing of the locations and processed suspects.

"Great work today, Sandra. That was textbook," Jerry began, allowing a brief smile to cross his face as he sank into a chair opposite her.

"It was a team effort, Jerry. You orchestrated it flawlessly," Sandra responded, returning the smile with a nod of respect. She then flipped open her laptop, pulling up the preliminary reports. "We've got all suspects in custody and a significant haul of weapons. Plus, some of them are talking already. They're scared, and that's good for us."

Jerry leaned forward, intrigued. "Anything substantial from them yet?"

"A couple are hinting at bigger fish. They're being vague, but it's only a matter of time before one of them cracks. We'll keep the pressure on," Sandra said, scrolling through a digital dossier of the arrested individuals.

"That's promising. We need to leverage whatever fear they have. Push for details on the network, any higher-ups they're willing to name," Jerry suggested, his mind already racing through the possible interrogation strategies.

"Absolutely. I've got our best interrogators on it. They know how to make them talk," Sandra assured him, her tone confident.

Jerry's gaze drifted to the monitors, watching as the last of the field teams wrapped up their work. "This is a big win, but it's not the end. We need to use this momentum. Do we have anything that could lead us directly to Marco?"

Sandra sighed, tapping a few keys on her laptop. "Not directly. He's insulated himself well. But, with the evidence we've collected today and the statements we might get, I think we're getting closer than ever."

"We have to keep digging. Every piece of information is a potential lead. What about the financials? Anything new from the seized documents that could point us in the right direction?" Jerry inquired, his mind never straying far from the next step.

"We're still analyzing the latest batch. The forensic accountants are optimistic they'll find something we can use to trace back to Marco or at least to someone close to him," Sandra explained, her eyes scanning through an email update from the finance team.

"Good. Keep me updated. And let's make sure the evidence from today is secured and catalogued meticulously. I don't want any mistakes that could jeopardize the prosecutions," Jerry stated firmly, standing up to stretch his legs.

"Of course, I'll supervise that personally," Sandra replied, also standing. "And Jerry, try to get some rest. We both need to be sharp for what comes next."

Jerry nodded, knowing she was right, but feeling the weight of responsibility that made rest seem like a distant luxury. "I will. You too, Sandra."

As they left the debriefing room, their steps echoed in the quiet hall, each absorbed in their thoughts about the case. The day had brought them a significant victory, but the war was far from over. They walked back to their offices to regroup and prepare for the next phase of their investigation, driven by the knowledge that every successful operation brought them closer to dismantling Marco's network. The challenge was daunting, yet it was the fuel that drove them forward, each step a movement towards justice.

In the aftermath of the raid, the police station buzzed with activity as officers processed evidence and prepared reports. Jerry was in his office when Sandra entered, a folder in her hand and a look of cautious optimism on her face.

"Got a minute, Jerry?" Sandra asked as she stepped inside, closing the door behind her.

"Of course," Jerry replied, gesturing for her to sit. "What do you have?"

Sandra opened the folder, spreading several documents across Jerry's desk. "We've made some headway with the financial records we seized. It looks like we've traced a series of transactions that could lead us closer to Marco."

Jerry leaned forward, examining the documents closely. "Are you saying these transactions directly link to him?"

"Not directly to him, but to a couple of businesses known to be fronts for his operation," Sandra explained. "These records show a pattern of money transfers that coincide with other activities we've known about but couldn't prove until now."

"That's excellent," Jerry responded, his eyes still scanning the documents. "Have we been able to identify anyone new from this? Any other names popping up that we should be looking into?"

"There are a few. Most are probably just middlemen, but one name stands out — Vincent Marelli. Appears more than once, associated with larger transactions," Sandra said, pointing to a highlighted section on one of the pages.

"Vincent Marelli..." Jerry murmured, searching his memory. "I remember this name. He was flagged in a different investigation last year — nothing solid enough to hold onto then. Looks like we should pay him another visit."

"I agree. I think a closer look at Marelli could open up some new avenues for us," Sandra added, her voice filled with a renewed urgency.

Jerry nodded, picking up the phone to arrange a meeting. "I'll have Marla pull up everything we have on Marelli. Let's see if we can connect the dots that lead us back to Marco."

As Sandra was about to leave, Jerry stopped her. "How's the team holding up? It's been non-stop for weeks now."

"They're tired, but they're motivated. Today's win has given everyone a boost. But I'll make sure they all get some downtime soon. We can't afford burnout," Sandra assured him.

"Good, that's important," Jerry acknowledged, his concern for his team evident.

Later that afternoon, Jerry and Sandra convened a strategy meeting with key team members to discuss the potential implications of their new findings and how best to approach investigating Vincent Marelli.

"Here's what we know," Jerry began, addressing the room. "Marelli's transactions are significant, and they tie into the broader network we're unraveling. He's our best lead right now on getting to Marco."

"Plans for approaching Marelli?" one of the detectives asked.

"We do this carefully," Jerry outlined. "Surveillance first. We need to know his movements, who he meets with, and how he operates day-to-day. Marla, I want you on this. Gather as much intel as you can before we make a move."

"Understood," Marla responded, jotting down notes.

"And I'll coordinate with the DA's office to see what legal leverage we might have, including any search warrants or listening devices we might need," Sandra added.

The meeting continued with discussions on various surveillance techniques and coordination points, each team member assigned specific tasks to ensure a comprehensive approach to the investigation.

As the meeting wrapped up, Jerry stayed back to review the action plan once more. The next steps they were about to take could be decisive in penetrating Marco's operations. His determination was as strong as ever, tempered only by the complexity of the challenge ahead. With each piece of the puzzle that fell into place, the picture became clearer, and Jerry's resolve to see the case through to the end deepened. As he finally left the meeting room, his mind was racing with possibilities, each scenario playing out the next moves in the intricate dance of strategy and investigation.

The next few days saw Jerry and his team deep in the throes of surveillance operations focused on Vincent Marelli. Covertly, they monitored his movements, his interactions, and his business dealings, each piece of data meticulously logged and analyzed. Jerry spent long hours in the makeshift surveillance room, a bank of monitors displaying live feeds from cameras strategically placed to watch Marelli's known haunts and offices.

From the dimly lit room, Jerry watched as Marelli conducted his business with a calm demeanor, meeting various individuals who, to the untrained eye, appeared to be nothing more than business associates. However, Jerry knew better. Each handshake and each exchange was potentially a thread leading back to Marco, and he was determined to pull each one until the web unraveled.

Marla was frequently by his side, providing updates on the digital tracking of Marelli's phone and financial activities. "Transactions have increased in frequency over the last two days," she reported during one of her updates. "Looks like he's gearing up for something big."

Jerry nodded, his eyes never leaving the screens. "Keep an eye on any new names or accounts that come up. Anything out of the ordinary could be what we're looking for."

The operation was exhaustive and exhausting. The team rotated in shifts, but Jerry found himself present for most of them, his dedication a steady constant in the ebb and flow of the investigative tide.

On the third day, a breakthrough came. The team intercepted a phone call between Marelli and an unknown contact discussing a significant shipment due to arrive at the docks in two days' time. The conversation was cryptic, but the mention of "the usual precautions" and "ensuring the boss is happy with the delivery" was enough to pique Jerry's interest.

"This could be it," Jerry murmured to Sandra as they reviewed the intercepted call in his office. "If we can intercept this shipment, we might just catch the break we need to reach Marco."

"Let's make sure we have all hands on deck for this one. I don't want Marelli slipping through our fingers because we weren't prepared," Sandra responded, her voice tinged with both anticipation and caution.

Plans were drawn up quickly. Surveillance was increased, and preparations were made to intercept the shipment at the docks. Jerry coordinated with local authorities to ensure they had enough manpower and legal backing to act the moment Marelli showed up at the docks.

As the day of the operation dawned, Jerry was once again in the command center, his gaze fixed on the live feeds. The team was in place, hidden from view but ready to move on his command. The tension was palpable, each member of the team aware of the stakes.

Hours passed with little activity, and then, suddenly, a convoy of trucks turned into the dock. Jerry leaned forward, his focus sharpening. "That's our cue. Everyone, stay sharp."

The operation moved swiftly. As the trucks came to a stop and men began to unload, Jerry's team moved in, their approach coordinated and silent. Marelli was there, overseeing the operation. As he realized the police were closing in, his initial shock gave way to resignation.

The takedown was clean. Marelli and several of his associates were apprehended, and the shipment—full of contraband hidden amongst legitimate goods—was seized.

As the suspects were led away in handcuffs, Jerry allowed himself a moment of quiet satisfaction. This was a significant victory, but the true test was still to come—getting Marelli to talk and lead them to Marco.

Back at the station, as the evidence from the docks was being cataloged, Jerry watched the team at work. They were efficient, thorough, and driven, qualities that Jerry valued above all. The night was setting in, the office slowly emptying as another day of hard work came to an end. But for Jerry, the work would continue. He knew the battle was far from over, but every victory, no matter how small, was a step closer to the endgame. As he finally left the office, the corridors of the station were quiet, echoing with the day's achievements and the promise of more to come.

Chapter 9
A Deeper Conspiracy

As dawn crept over the horizon, casting a pale light through the blinds of Jerry's office, it found him still poring over the newly gathered evidence from the recent dock operation. His desk was buried under stacks of paperwork, digital devices, and photographs that captured the scope of the criminal network they were dismantling. Every document represented a thread in the intricate tapestry of organized crime that had infiltrated not just Greendale but extended beyond its borders.

With a steaming cup of coffee cooling unnoticed at his side, Jerry reviewed the list of items confiscated during the raid. The array of contraband was diverse, ranging from high-end electronics to unregistered firearms, each item cataloged meticulously by his team in the hours following the operation.

"Good haul," Sandra remarked as she entered the room, her eyes taking in the sprawl of evidence that Jerry was analyzing. "This should give us plenty to work with."

Jerry nodded, barely looking up from the manifest. "It's solid. But it's not just what we found—it's what it represents. We're getting closer, Sandra. I can feel it."

Sandra pulled up a chair, her demeanor serious. "I've scheduled interrogations for this morning. Marelli and two of his associates. We need to push hard, see if we can turn one of them."

"Agreed," Jerry responded, finally sitting back and taking a sip of his now lukewarm coffee. "Keep the pressure on Marelli. He's the key. If he decides to cooperate, he could lead us straight to Marco."

The morning light grew stronger, casting long shadows across the room that seemed to underscore the gravity of their conversation. Sandra stood, adjusting her jacket. "I'll make sure the interrogation team is prepped. We'll crack him, Jerry."

With a brief nod, Jerry watched her leave, then turned his attention back to the screens displaying various feeds from ongoing surveillance operations. Each feed was a window into the activities of the city as it woke up, oblivious to the undercurrents of crime that flowed beneath its everyday hustle.

Hours passed, and the office became a revolving door of officers bringing in reports, updates, and requests for decisions. Jerry handled each with a calm efficiency, his mind always returning to the larger picture. His phone buzzed with a text from Sandra: "Interrogation underway. Standing by for any breaks."

As midday approached, Jerry decided to step out of his office, needing to stretch his legs and clear his head. The corridors of the police station were busy with the day-to-day activities of law enforcement, but Jerry's presence seemed to bring a momentary calm as officers nodded respectfully to him.

He made his way to the observation room adjacent to the interrogation suites. Through the one-way glass, he could see Marelli, handcuffed and tense, sitting across from an officer. The interrogation was in full swing, the officer's voice firm but controlled. Jerry didn't need audio to know the pressure being applied; it was all in the body language, the intensity of the exchange.

Returning to his office, Jerry sat down and continued his review. The documents spread out before him contained potential leads, connections, and new avenues to explore. Each piece of evidence, each snippet of information was a potential key to unlocking the next level of the operation.

As the afternoon wore on, Jerry remained focused, his determination undiminished by the hours of meticulous work. The office grew quieter as evening approached, the bustle of the morning giving way to the more subdued tones of nightshift preparations.

The phone rang, breaking the calm. Jerry picked it up, his voice steady. "Maitland."

Sandra's voice came through, tinged with fatigue but underlined with excitement. "Jerry, we got something. Marelli's talking. He's ready to negotiate."

A surge of adrenaline shot through Jerry. "I'll be right there," he responded, his fatigue forgotten as he grabbed his jacket and headed out the door.

The evening was settling over Greendale as he made his way to the interrogation room, the weight of the case momentarily lifted by the prospect of a breakthrough. Each step Jerry took was fueled by the blend of persistence and anticipation that had defined his career—a career that now seemed poised on the edge of a defining moment.

Jerry entered the interrogation room with a palpable sense of urgency, his eyes quickly adjusting to the dim light as he spotted Marelli sitting across from Sandra. The suspect appeared worn down by the hours of questioning, his posture slumped, eyes weary yet alert. Jerry pulled up a chair next to Sandra, giving Marelli a measured look.

"Mr. Marelli," Jerry started, his voice even and controlled, "Sandra tells me you're ready to talk. That's good. It's in your best interest to cooperate."

Marelli rubbed his hands together nervously, his gaze shifting between Jerry and Sandra. "Yeah, I... I've been thinking. I don't want to go down for this—not alone."

"What are you offering, Vincent?" Sandra interjected, her tone firm but encouraging.

Marelli took a deep breath, exhaling slowly before responding. "I can give you names, places... things that'll help you get closer to Marco. But I need protection—witness protection. And I don't want any jail time."

Jerry nodded, understanding the stakes for Marelli. "We can work with that if your information checks out. You help us catch Marco, and we'll help keep you safe. But we need something concrete, Vincent. We need to know we can trust you."

Marelli licked his lips, considering his options momentarily before speaking up. "Alright. There's a shipment coming in—bigger than anything before. It's Marco's big play. I can tell you where and when."

Sandra quickly took notes, her expression intent. "Go on, we're listening."

"It's set for next Thursday, late night. Dock seventeen. It's not just goods this time. There's something else, something big. I don't know all the details, but it's enough to set Marco up for a long time," Marelli divulged, his voice a mix of fear and relief as he shared the information.

Jerry exchanged a quick glance with Sandra, both recognizing the potential breakthrough. "Anything else? Anyone else involved that we should know about?"

"There's a new guy, came in about a month ago. Goes by the name of Rickson. He's been running the logistics on this one. Heard he's close to Marco, real close," Marelli added, his eyes darting to the door as if expecting someone to burst through at any moment.

"Good, that's very helpful, Vincent," Sandra said, closing her notebook. "We'll take everything you've given us and verify it. If it checks out, we'll make arrangements for your protection."

Jerry stood, signaling the end of the meeting. "You've made the right choice, Vincent. Help us take down Marco, and you get a fresh start. We'll be in touch."

As they left the interrogation room, the weight of Marelli's revelations hung between Jerry and Sandra. They headed straight to Jerry's office to discuss the new leads.

"Dock seventeen, next Thursday. That gives us less than a week to prepare," Jerry pointed out, pacing slightly.

"We'll need to pull in additional resources, maybe even ask for federal assistance," Sandra suggested, already pulling up her phone to make calls.

"Agreed. And keep an eye on this Rickson character. He could be our direct line to Marco if we play this right," Jerry added, stopping by the window to look out at the city.

As the evening turned to night, the pieces of the puzzle began to fall into place, setting the stage for what could be the final act in their long investigation. Jerry felt a mix of anticipation and trepidation. The next few days would be crucial, not just for the case, but for everyone involved. The stakes were higher than ever, and as he looked out into the night, Jerry knew that the path ahead would test them all.

The command center was bustling with energy as Jerry and Sandra coordinated the extensive preparations for the operation at Dock Seventeen. With less than a week to act, every detail mattered, and the room was a hive of activity, filled with officers and agents moving briskly, phones ringing, and keyboards clacking.

"Okay, let's go through this one more time," Jerry said as he stood at the head of the conference table, looking over the assembled team. "We have credible intel on a major shipment coming in, potentially linked directly to Marco. This could be our chance to catch him red-handed."

Sandra, standing beside a digital map displayed on the screen, pointed to several key locations. "Based on Marelli's information, the shipment will arrive here, at Dock Seventeen. We'll have two teams in place. Team one will handle the initial interception. Team two will provide backup and secure the perimeter."

"Who's leading the teams?" asked Lieutenant Gomez, looking up from his notebook.

"Captain Rivera will lead team one. I'll be with team two," Sandra responded, marking the positions on the map with red and blue markers.

Jerry turned to the tech team at the back of the room. "What's the status on surveillance setup at the docks?"

"We've got cameras and mics installed around the dock area. Everything's feeding live to us here. We'll have eyes on the ground well before the shipment arrives," replied the head of tech operations, tapping away at his laptop.

"Good. I want updates every hour on that feed. Any changes, I want to know immediately," Jerry directed, his tone firm.

Sandra chimed in, "What about local PD and Coast Guard? We'll need them on standby for any spillover or if this goes waterborne."

"I've already got calls in to both. They'll be ready to mobilize at a moment's notice," Jerry assured her, then looked around the room, meeting the eyes of his team. "This operation hinges on precision and timing. We need to be airtight. No leaks, no slip-ups."

An officer raised his hand, a young detective who had been quiet up until now. "Sir, what's the ROE for this operation? Are we expecting armed resistance?"

Jerry nodded at the question. "Assume they are armed. However, engagement is only if necessary. The priority is to secure the shipment and apprehend the suspects without incident. But protect yourselves and your teammates first and foremost."

"Are we clear on Marelli's role during this?" another officer asked, looking concerned. "He's still a risk, even if he's cooperating."

Sandra responded, "Marelli will be in a safe house until the operation is over. He's under guard and won't be anywhere near the docks. We can't afford any complications from him."

Jerry glanced at his watch, noting the late hour. "Alright, let's wrap this up. Finalize your teams and gear up. We meet back here at 0400 for a final run-through. Rest up while you can. Tomorrow we bring this home."

As the team disbanded, heading off to prepare, Jerry lingered, reviewing the map and going over every possible scenario in his mind. Sandra stayed back, her expression thoughtful.

"You okay with how things are set up?" Jerry asked her quietly.

Sandra nodded slowly, her gaze fixed on the map. "It's solid, Jerry. If this goes according to plan, it could be the break we've been chasing. Just... it's been a long road."

"It has," Jerry agreed, his voice softening. "But one worth traveling. Let's see this through to the end."

The room slowly emptied, leaving Jerry and Sandra in the quiet aftermath of the strategic storm. They shared a look of mutual respect and understanding, aware of the challenges ahead but ready to face them. As they left the command center, the weight of the impending day was palpable, but so was the resolve that had brought them this far. They were ready to end this, once and for all.

The pre-dawn hours at Greendale's police command center were tense and expectant as Jerry and his team made their final preparations for the operation at Dock Seventeen. The team gathered for one last briefing, the room humming with the low murmur of focused conversation.

"Alright, everyone, this is it," Jerry began, his voice cutting through the chatter, commanding immediate attention. "In less than two hours, we execute the plan we've been preparing for all week. Every role is crucial, every action counts. Captain Rivera, status on team one?"

Captain Rivera, a seasoned officer with an authoritative presence, stood and addressed the room. "Team one is geared up and in position. We have visual on the dock entrance and are ready to intercept as soon as the target arrives."

"Excellent," Jerry nodded. "And team two?"

Sandra, overseeing the secondary team, replied, "Team two is on standby for perimeter security and to provide immediate support to team one if needed. All escape routes are covered."

Jerry glanced around, meeting the eyes of his team members. "Communications, ensure all lines are open and clear. No delays. We need instant relay of any changes on the ground."

The communications officer, a young woman with sharp eyes, confirmed, "All channels are tested and functioning. We have direct feeds from all surveillance points to your monitors."

Turning his attention to the logistics officer, Jerry asked, "All non-lethal measures prepared?"

"Yes, sir. We have tear gas and tasers, plus the K-9 units on standby," the officer responded.

Jerry's gaze then settled on the tactical lead, "And lethal force?"

"Only as a last resort, per your orders. All officers are briefed on engagement rules. Safety is our priority," the tactical lead affirmed.

"Let's keep it tight and clean. We're here to stop a major criminal operation and apprehend suspects, not to escalate unnecessarily," Jerry stated, the seriousness of the situation reflected in his tone.

Sandra added, "Remember, the goal is to capture these suspects for interrogation. We need what they know about Marco and his network."

An officer raised a question, "What's the call if the situation escalates unexpectedly?"

Jerry answered, "Follow the chain of command. If you're in doubt, hold position and call it in. We adapt in real-time, but we stick to the plan as much as possible."

Another officer, checking her gear, spoke up, "And if we encounter civilians?"

"Evacuate them safely. This is a controlled operation, but keep your eyes open. Civilians should not be anywhere near, but if you see anyone, it's your responsibility to ensure their safety," Sandra directed, her command clear.

Jerry took a deep breath, looking over his team, their faces set with determination. "This is more than just another bust. This is about protecting our city, dismantling a network that's endangered our streets. You are the best of the best; that's why you're here. Let's do this right."

Heads nodded, the room filled with a renewed sense of purpose as officers checked their equipment one last time.

"Teams, synchronize watches. We move at 0530. Check your gear, stay alert, and watch each other's backs," Jerry concluded, his voice imbued with confidence and resolve.

As the officers dispersed to their positions, Jerry and Sandra shared a brief look of mutual support. They then took their places at the command station, ready to oversee the operation. The screens in front of them showed live feeds from various cameras, the early morning stillness deceptive of the action that was about to unfold.

The minutes ticked down to go-time, each second heavy with anticipation. As the clock struck the hour, every officer was in place, every eye trained on their role, ready to execute the plan that would hopefully close a significant chapter in their fight against organized crime.

Chapter 10
Gathering the Troops

As the first light of dawn touched the edges of Dock Seventeen, the air was thick with tension. Jerry, positioned in the mobile command unit, watched the live feeds intently, each screen split into different angles covering every conceivable approach to the target area. Beside him, Sandra coordinated the communication with the various teams stationed around the perimeter.

"Team One, report status," Sandra's voice was crisp over the radio.

"Team One in position. No movement yet," Captain Rivera's voice responded, his tone steady.

"Visual on the dock is clear. Satellite feeds are live and showing no unexpected activity," added the tech officer, monitoring another array of screens.

Jerry leaned forward, his focus on a screen showing a thermal image of the warehouse. "Keep an eye on those back exits. We know they've tried to slip out the back in past operations."

"Roger that. Teams Two and Three have the exits covered," Sandra confirmed, marking notes on her digital pad.

Minutes passed with agonizing slowness, the operation teetering on the edge of action. Suddenly, a blip on one of the screens caught Jerry's attention. "Movement on the northeast side. Looks like a vehicle approaching."

"Got it," Sandra relayed. "Teams, be alert. Target vehicle is inbound."

The radio crackled with acknowledgments as all units tightened their focus. The vehicle, a nondescript cargo truck, rolled slowly towards the warehouse, its approach watched by dozens of eyes, both on the ground and through electronic surveillance.

"Let them start the unload. We need to catch them in the act," Jerry murmured, his eyes not leaving the screen where the truck had stopped, and figures began to disembark.

"Team One, hold position. Let them engage with the cargo," Sandra instructed quietly into her mic.

The tension was palpable as figures moved around the truck, opening the rear to start unloading boxes that, to the untrained eye, looked ordinary enough.

"Wait for my go," Jerry said softly, almost to himself, waiting for the moment when enough evidence could be visually confirmed to ensure the arrests would stick.

"Go," Jerry finally said after a tense few minutes, watching enough boxes being moved into the warehouse.

"Team One, move in. Apprehend all suspects. Team Two, secure the perimeter. Ensure no one leaves the scene," Sandra commanded, her voice firm and authoritative.

The operation burst into motion. Officers in tactical gear swiftly approached the suspects, their movements coordinated and silent until the last possible moment. The suspects, caught off guard, barely had time to react as they were efficiently detained.

"Team One has control of the scene. Suspects in custody. We're securing the cargo now," Captain Rivera reported back, the relief in his voice masked by professionalism.

"Excellent work. Begin processing the scene. I want everything cataloged before it goes back to the station," Jerry directed, already thinking ahead to the evidence processing and the interrogation of the suspects.

As Sandra coordinated the follow-up procedures, Jerry finally allowed himself to relax slightly, the initial part of the operation having gone off without a hitch.

"Looks like we got them with the goods in hand," Sandra said, turning to Jerry with a slight smile.

"We did. Good planning, good execution," Jerry acknowledged, returning the smile. "Let's hope this leads us straight to Marco."

Sandra nodded, her gaze turning back to the screens showing the teams at work. "This is a big win, Jerry. But it's not over yet."

"No, it's not," Jerry agreed, his mind already on the next steps. "Let's get everything back to the lab. I want reports on my desk as soon as they're available."

"Will do," Sandra confirmed, already dispatching orders through her headset.

As the dawn broke fully over the horizon, bathing the dock in the early morning light, the command unit was abuzz with the successful apprehension of the suspects. Jerry stood by the monitors, watching as his team efficiently wrapped up the operation, a mixture of satisfaction and resolve etched on his features. This was a significant victory, but the path ahead remained fraught with challenges.

The morning unfolded with the meticulous processing of the crime scene at Dock Seventeen. The warehouse, once a silent participant in illicit exchanges, was now alive with forensic teams and officers cataloging every piece of evidence. Jerry oversaw the operation, ensuring that each step was executed with precision.

"Make sure every box is opened and its contents verified," Jerry instructed a group of forensic technicians. "Photograph everything before you move it."

"Yes, sir," one of the techs replied, marking off the checklist on her digital tablet.

As the evidence was documented, Sandra approached Jerry, her expression one of focused concern. "We've secured the warehouse perimeter and initiated checks on all vehicles and containers in the vicinity. Everything's being brought in for a full sweep."

"Good. What's the status on the suspects?" Jerry asked, his gaze momentarily shifting to the line of handcuffed individuals seated under the watchful eyes of several officers.

"Detained and en route to the station for questioning. I've arranged for separate interrogation rooms; we'll start peeling back their stories as soon as they're processed," Sandra explained, her voice steady despite the complexity of the situation.

Jerry nodded approvingly. "Prioritize anyone who looks like they might fold under pressure. We need actionable intelligence if we're going to leverage this against Marco."

"Understood," Sandra confirmed, then hesitated slightly before adding, "Jerry, there's also this..." She handed him a small, sealed evidence bag containing a flash drive. "Found hidden in a false compartment within one of the crates."

Jerry examined the bag closely. "Have it analyzed immediately. It could contain anything from financial records to shipping logs that might lead us directly to Marco."

"I'll get our tech team on it as soon as we're back at the station," Sandra assured him, making a note on her tablet.

As they spoke, the operation continued around them. Officers moved back and forth, carrying evidence bags and equipment, while techs worked their scanners and cameras, documenting the scene.

Jerry's walkie-talkie crackled to life. "Base to Commander, the last of the cargo has been secured and cataloged. Ready for transport."

"Proceed with transport. Ensure tight security all the way to the evidence lock-up," Jerry responded, clipping the walkie-talkie back onto his belt.

Turning back to Sandra, he continued their earlier conversation. "Once we have everything back at the station, I want a preliminary report on my desk. Anything that stands out, I need to know—immediately."

"Will do, Jerry. I'll oversee the transport myself and make sure the interrogations begin as soon as the suspects are ready," Sandra replied, her tone matching the gravity of their task.

As the sun climbed higher, casting stark shadows across the busy dock, the scope of their operation became ever clearer. Every officer, every technician, played a vital role in the intricate ballet of law enforcement unfolding under Jerry's command.

Before leaving the scene, Jerry took one last look around the now-quiet warehouse. "This was well-executed today, Sandra. Thanks for your sharp oversight," he acknowledged, his voice carrying a slight edge of fatigue.

Sandra smiled, a brief flash of camaraderie passing between them. "We're a good team, Jerry. Let's bring this home."

With a nod, Jerry signaled that it was time to leave. They walked back to their vehicles, the weight of the day's success tempered by the knowledge of the challenges that lay ahead. As they drove away from Dock Seventeen, the site receded into the background, but its significance in their ongoing battle against organized crime remained at the forefront of their thoughts. Each step forward was a step closer to their ultimate goal: dismantling Marco's network and restoring peace to the streets of Greendale.

Back at the station, Jerry and Sandra convened in the main briefing room, surrounded by officers and specialists busily preparing for the next phase of the operation. The room was abuzz with activity, with officers updating logs and techs processing digital evidence as quickly as they could.

"Let's go over what we have so far," Jerry started, addressing the room. "I want to make sure nothing slips through the cracks. Sandra, status on the evidence processing?"

"Most of the physical evidence from the docks has been cataloged and is undergoing detailed examination. The tech team is currently prioritizing the flash drive we found. They're trying to break the encryption," Sandra reported, flipping through her digital tablet to bring up the latest updates.

"And the suspects?" Jerry asked, his gaze sharp and focused.

"Interrogations have begun. We've separated the ones we believe might cooperate from the hardened elements. Initial reports suggest a couple are ready to talk, possibly in exchange for deals. I'll know more within the hour," Sandra answered.

Jerry nodded, then turned to address the tech officer in charge of the digital evidence. "What's the status on cracking that flash drive? Anything we can use?"

The tech officer, a young woman with a keen eye for detail, responded promptly. "We're making progress, sir. The encryption is sophisticated, but we're getting through. Should have something actionable soon, hopefully."

"Keep me posted. Every minute counts," Jerry emphasized, his expression serious.

Turning his attention back to Sandra, he continued, "Once we have the information from the flash drive, I want a meeting with the DA. If the suspects start talking and we can match their stories with hard evidence, we might just be able to roll this up all the way to Marco."

"Understood," Sandra replied. "I'll arrange for the DA to be on standby. Also, surveillance on the known associates from the flash drive—if we find any names—is already being set up."

"Good. Let's keep the pressure on," Jerry said, walking over to a large map on the wall, dotted with various markers. "We need to anticipate Marco's moves. He's going to know we're closing in soon, if he doesn't already."

As they strategized, an officer approached with a phone in hand. "Commander, tech team has an update. They want you on the line."

Jerry took the phone, listening intently as the head of the tech team relayed their findings. "We've accessed some of the files. There's a list—names, dates, possibly routes for other operations. Looks like we hit the jackpot."

"That's excellent news," Jerry responded, a hint of relief in his tone. "Compile everything and send it to my station. I'll review it with Sandra, and then we decide our next move."

Handing back the phone, Jerry turned to Sandra, his strategy already forming. "Once we have that list, we cross-reference everything. Names, known associates, anything that ties these operations together. We might finally be able to draw Marco out."

"Agreed," Sandra said, her focus matching Jerry's. "I'll get the interrogation team to press harder with the new info. If any of those names come up, we'll have corroboration for the DA."

As the meeting wrapped up, the team dispersed, each member with clear tasks and renewed urgency. Jerry and Sandra remained behind, reviewing the digital map and planning their next moves.

"This could be the break we've been waiting for," Jerry mused aloud, his eyes tracing the lines and connections on the map.

"It could be," Sandra agreed, her tone cautious yet optimistic. "But let's not celebrate yet. There's still a lot to do."

Jerry nodded, his gaze firm and determined as they returned to their workstations. The possibility of finally dismantling Marco's network was within reach, and neither of them was willing to let it slip through their fingers. As they dove back into the cascade of tasks, the station hummed around them, a symphony of law enforcement working tirelessly to restore order and justice.

Later that evening, as the last streaks of sunlight faded from the sky, Jerry and Sandra sat together in the dimly lit operations room, surrounded by monitors displaying maps and data feeds. The room buzzed with the residual energy of the day's frenetic activities, yet a semblance of calm had begun to settle as they approached the potential culmination of their case.

"Have you seen this latest from the tech team?" Jerry asked, sliding a tablet across the table to Sandra. "They've decrypted more of the flash drive. It includes detailed schedules and contacts that corroborate the suspect's stories."

Sandra scanned the document quickly, her eyes flickering with recognition and anticipation. "This is solid, Jerry. With this, we can not only support the current charges but also expand our investigation. There are names here linked to other major players, possibly even Marco directly."

Jerry nodded, his expression resolute. "That's what I was thinking. We need to start coordinating with the other agencies listed here. Some of these operations cross state lines."

"Already on it," Sandra responded, tapping her phone to life. "I've set up calls with the FBI and the DEA for tomorrow morning. They've been tracking a couple of these names from a different angle."

"That's perfect. The broader we can cast this net, the better," Jerry agreed. He paused, then added, "How are the preparations for the DA meeting going? We need all this ironclad if we're going to make it stick legally."

Sandra looked up from her notes, a slight smile playing at her lips. "We're well-prepared. I've compiled a summary of all the evidence, including witness statements and this new data from the tech team. The DA will have everything they need to proceed."

"Good work," Jerry said, leaning back in his chair. "This case... it's one of the biggest we've tackled. I know it's been a marathon, but we're nearing the finish line."

"It's been more than a marathon, Jerry," Sandra chuckled, her fatigue evident but her spirit undiminished. "But you're right. We're close now."

The conversation shifted slightly as Jerry looked around the room, taking in the stacks of papers and the blinking lights of the computers. "Once this is over, what's next for you, Sandra? This case has consumed so much of our lives."

Sandra sighed, her gaze turning thoughtful. "A vacation might be nice. Somewhere quiet. Then, it's back to the grind. There are always more cases, more puzzles to solve."

Jerry smiled. "You deserve that break. We both do. Maybe I'll finally take that fishing trip I've been putting off for years."

"That sounds perfect, Jerry. Just make sure you actually go this time," Sandra teased, her tone lightening the mood.

Their laughter was a brief respite from the gravity of their work. As it faded, Jerry stood, stretching his limbs tiredly. "I'm heading out soon. Tomorrow's going to be another long day. Make sure you get some rest too, Sandra."

"I will, Jerry. See you in the morning," Sandra replied, gathering her things.

As Jerry walked to the door, he turned back briefly. "We're doing good work, Sandra. Thanks for being on this journey with me."

"Anytime, Jerry. It's what we do," Sandra called out as he exited the room.

The night outside was quiet as Jerry made his way to his car. The streets of Greendale were peaceful, but the work he and his team had done today would ripple through the city in ways most would never see. As he drove home, the weight of the day began to lift slightly, replaced by the quiet satisfaction of a job well done and the anticipation of the final act yet to unfold.

Chapter 11
Undercover Night

In the subdued light of early morning, Jerry and Sandra found themselves once again in the operations room, now transformed into a strategic hub for what could be the final push in their extensive investigation. The walls were lined with monitors displaying various data feeds, and a large table was strewn with documents and digital devices.

"Today's the day, Sandra. How are we on final preparations?" Jerry asked, his voice low but clear, as he glanced at the array of screens.

"We're set. The DA is on board with all the charges, and the FBI and DEA have confirmed their involvement based on the names and connections we uncovered," Sandra responded, her tone professional but tinged with anticipation. "They're ready to move as soon as we give the go-ahead."

"That's excellent news," Jerry replied, rubbing his hands together in a rare display of nervous energy. "What about the local teams? Are they in position?"

"Yes, everyone's where they need to be. The surveillance teams reported in not ten minutes ago; all clear and holding positions," Sandra confirmed, checking off points on her digital planner.

Jerry nodded, then shifted the conversation. "And the evidence—everything's been double-checked? The last thing we need is a technicality messing this up."

"Triple-checked, Jerry. Every 'i' dotted, every 't' crossed. This case is airtight," Sandra reassured him, her confidence bolstering his own.

"Good. Good." Jerry paused, looking over the evidence one more time. "Once we start this, there's no going back. You ready for this?"

"As ready as we'll ever be," Sandra replied, a slight smile breaking through. "It's been a long road, but we're finally here. Let's bring Marco down."

Jerry smiled back, then picked up a walkie-talkie. "All teams, this is Commander Maitland. Stand by for go on my mark."

The room fell silent, the tension palpable as they awaited his command. After a moment that felt much longer than it actually was, Jerry spoke into the walkie-talkie again. "Execute Operation Endgame. Go, go, go!"

As the teams moved out, Jerry and Sandra monitored their progress, watching the live feeds closely. Each team was a moving piece in a well-oiled machine, their movements precise and calculated.

"Team One reports they're in position," Sandra relayed, her eyes not leaving the screen.

"And Team Two has eyes on the target. They're moving in now," she continued, her voice steady despite the adrenaline surely coursing through her.

"Excellent. Keep me posted on any changes," Jerry said, his focus total as he watched the operation unfold. "Any word from the DA?"

"Just in now, they're ready to process any arrests we make today. They've got the paperwork all prepared," Sandra responded, her efficiency a calming force in the storm of activity.

"Perfect," Jerry replied. Then, more quietly, "You know, whatever happens today, I just want to say—it's been an honor, Sandra."

Sandra turned to look at him, her expression earnest. "The honor's been mine, Jerry. We've been through the wringer, but I wouldn't have wanted to do this with anyone else."

Their moment of reflection was brief, as a voice crackled through the walkie-talkie. "Commander, Team Two has Marco in custody. I repeat, Marco is in custody."

A collective breath seemed to be released throughout the room. Jerry let out a long, slow exhale, feeling the weight of months of hard work finally culminating in this singular moment.

"Bring him in. Make sure he's secure," Jerry instructed, his voice a mixture of relief and command.

As they awaited Marco's arrival, Jerry and Sandra prepared to face the next phase of their journey: prosecution and trials. But for now, they allowed themselves a moment to appreciate the victory, a testament to their dedication and resolve. As the first hints of dawn turned into morning, Greendale began to wake up, unaware of the monumental efforts that had taken place to ensure its safety. Jerry and Sandra remained vigilant, ready to tackle whatever challenges might come next, but today they had won a significant battle.

As Marco was escorted into the interrogation room under heavy guard, the atmosphere at the station was a mix of triumph and tense expectation. Jerry, standing beside Sandra, watched through the one-way glass as Marco was seated, handcuffed, at the table.

"This is a big moment, Jerry. Are you ready to handle this, or do you want me to take the lead on the questioning?" Sandra asked, her gaze fixed on Marco, who sat calmly, almost defiantly.

"I'll take the lead. You back me up," Jerry decided, taking a deep breath to steady himself. "Let's remind him why he's here."

They entered the room, and Jerry took a moment to size up Marco, who looked back with a cool, measured stare. "Marco, you're in a lot of trouble," Jerry began, sitting across from him. "But you already know that, don't you?"

Marco smirked slightly, "I've been in trouble before. Doesn't seem to stick."

"It'll stick this time," Sandra chimed in, her voice firm. "We have enough to put you away for a long time."

Jerry leaned forward, placing a folder on the table, filled with evidence and photographs. "We've been building a case against you for months. We have your transactions, your associates, and now, we caught you red-handed today."

Marco glanced at the folder but remained silent, his demeanor unreadable.

"You can make this easier on yourself, Marco," Jerry continued, watching for any sign of weakness. "Help us understand your network. Who else is involved? How far does this go?"

Marco scoffed, leaning back in his chair. "And what do I get in return? A pat on the back and a lighter sentence?"

"We can negotiate terms, but only if you cooperate fully. Help us clean up the streets," Sandra offered, her tone slightly softer, trying a different angle.

"Streets? You think this is about the streets?" Marco laughed coldly, shaking his head. "You have no idea what you're dealing with, do you?"

Jerry's eyes narrowed, "Try us. Give us something to work with, Marco."

After a moment's hesitation, Marco leaned forward, his voice low. "If I talk, I need full immunity and protection. And not just for me, for my family too."

"That can be arranged, but we need verifiable information, Marco. No games," Jerry replied, sensing the shift in their conversation.

Marco nodded slowly, considering his options. "Alright. I'll talk. But remember, you asked for it. This goes deeper than you think."

Sandra quickly interjected, "Start from the beginning, Marco. We're listening."

Marco began to outline his network, starting with the local operations and gradually revealing connections that spanned across states and even international borders. Jerry and Sandra listened intently, taking notes, occasionally asking for clarifications.

As the interrogation continued, Jerry felt a mix of satisfaction and disbelief at the depth and complexity of Marco's revelations. The pieces of the puzzle were finally falling into place, painting a picture larger and more intricate than they had anticipated.

"We'll need to verify all of this," Jerry said as Marco finished, the weight of the information heavy in the room.

"Verify it then," Marco replied, a tired resignation in his voice. "You'll see. I'm just a piece of a bigger puzzle."

With that, the interrogation concluded. Jerry and Sandra stepped out of the room, leaving Marco under guard. They exchanged a look, a silent agreement on the enormity of what they had just learned.

"We have a lot of work ahead of us," Sandra said, her voice a mix of awe and determination.

"Yes, we do," Jerry agreed, feeling both the thrill of the chase and the burden of the road ahead. As they walked back to their offices to begin the next phase of their investigation, the station buzzed around them, unaware of the seismic shifts occurring within its walls. The day was far from over, and the real work was just beginning.

After the extensive interrogation with Marco, Jerry and Sandra returned to the operations room to process the flood of information they had received. The room, usually abuzz with activity, seemed to quiet just a touch as they entered, the gravity of their investigation palpable in the air.

"Let's start mapping this out," Jerry said, gesturing to the large digital screen at the front of the room. He began to input the details Marco had provided, each piece adding to a complex web of connections and locations that sprawled across the screen.

Sandra, reviewing the notes they had taken, cross-referenced the names and places with their existing databases. "Some of these names are coming up in other cases," she noted. "Looks like Marco wasn't exaggerating about the reach of his network."

Jerry paused, absorbing the scale of the operation they were uncovering. "This is bigger than we thought. We're going to need to coordinate with federal agencies if we're going to make a dent here."

"I'll start putting together a task force," Sandra offered, already drafting a list on her tablet. "We'll need our best people on this, plus support from the FBI and maybe even Interpol."

Jerry nodded in agreement, his mind racing through the logistics. "Make it happen. And get the DA on the line too; we need to make sure our legal bases are covered with this kind of inter-agency involvement."

As they worked, the door to the operations room opened and Lieutenant Gomez entered, a folder of reports in hand. "Got the latest from the tech team," he announced, handing the folder to Jerry. "They've confirmed some of the financial trails Marco mentioned. Looks like we can tie these back to several big players."

"That's excellent," Jerry responded, flipping through the reports. "Add this to our evidence board. Every bit helps."

Sandra looked up from her work, her face set in a determined expression. "Once we get the task force up and running, we'll need to start hitting these leads hard and fast. Surprise is going to be key in shaking up this network."

Jerry closed the folder, his gaze meeting Sandra's. "Agreed. We've got momentum now; let's not waste it."

The work continued into the evening, with Jerry and Sandra orchestrating a multitude of tasks: setting up meetings, coordinating with other agencies, and planning the steps forward. The room buzzed with renewed energy as the scope of their task expanded, the team motivated by the breakthroughs and the challenges ahead.

At one point, Jerry stepped aside, taking a moment to view the full evidence board they had compiled. It was a tapestry of crime and collusion that had, until recently, been hidden in the shadows. Now, it was laid bare, ready to be dismantled piece by piece.

Sandra joined him, her arms crossed as she took in the board. "We're going to take down one of the biggest criminal networks this city has seen," she said, not just as a statement of intent, but as a promise.

"Yes, we are," Jerry agreed, his voice firm. "And when we do, we'll make sure they don't just rebuild. We're going to change the game."

As they turned back to their desks, the work ahead seemed daunting, but for the first time in a long time, it also felt entirely achievable. The night grew deeper as they planned their next moves, the city outside unaware of the fight being waged on its behalf. But inside the operations room, the commitment was clear: they would see this through, no matter what it took.

As evening deepened into night, Jerry and Sandra remained in the operations room, surrounded by the glow of computer screens and the constant hum of activity. They were finalizing the strategic plan for the newly formed task force that would tackle the sprawling criminal network Marco had unveiled.

Sandra was on a call with an FBI liaison, her tone both firm and diplomatic. "We appreciate the FBI's readiness to assist on this. Yes, we'll share all relevant data by tomorrow morning and expect your analysts to help us pinpoint potential international links."

Jerry, meanwhile, was reviewing a digital map littered with pins and notes. He looked up as Sandra ended her call and approached the table. "How did it go with the FBI?"

"They're on board and ready to assign resources. They understand the scale of what we're dealing with," Sandra replied, updating the task force file on her laptop.

"Good. We'll need all the help we can get," Jerry said, zooming in on a section of the map. "I've been looking at the transport routes Marco mentioned. There's a pattern to the timing and security measures they use. We might be able to intercept another shipment."

Sandra leaned over the map, tracing the routes with her finger. "Let's set up surveillance on these points. If we can catch them in the act again, it will bolster our case and possibly lead us to more key players in the network."

"Agreed. I'll have Gomez coordinate the surveillance teams and make sure they're equipped for a long stakeout," Jerry decided, making a note in his digital planner.

As they worked, an officer entered the room with a printout. "Commander, we've got the preliminary forensics back on the items from the last raid."

Jerry took the printout, scanning the contents. "Anything stand out?"

"A couple of the weapons had serial numbers that match those reported stolen from military facilities. It's a big link. This isn't just organized crime; it's national security level," the officer reported, his tone serious.

"That escalates things," Sandra noted, her brow furrowing. "We need to notify Homeland Security. This could help strengthen the inter-agency collaboration."

"I'll handle the Homeland Security call. Could you follow up with the DA? Make sure they're aware of this development," Jerry asked, already reaching for his phone.

"Will do," Sandra confirmed, stepping aside to make the call.

The operations room had become a strategic nerve center, with every call and report shaping the course of their extensive investigation. As the night wore on, Jerry and Sandra continued to direct the flow of operations, their focus unwavering.

At one point, they paused, taking a brief moment to regroup. Sandra glanced at Jerry, who was staring thoughtfully at the map. "You ever think we'd get this deep?" she asked.

"Hope for the best, plan for the worst," Jerry responded, giving her a wry smile. "But honestly, no. This is bigger than anything I've handled before."

"It's a good thing we're in it together, then. Couldn't ask for a better partner in this," Sandra said, returning the smile.

"Yeah, same here," Jerry agreed, then turned back to the map. "Let's keep pushing. The more we uncover, the safer the streets will be."

As they resumed their work, the room filled again with the low buzz of activity. The night outside was dark and quiet, but inside, every light was on, every screen active, every officer and agent moving with purpose. The fight against the criminal network was far from over, but with every piece of evidence, every strategic decision, they were closing in, dismantling the shadows piece by piece.

Chapter 12
Alliances Tested

Jerry and Sandra continued their late-night vigil in the operations room, surrounded by the hum of activity as reports and updates streamed in from various teams. The weight of their responsibilities seemed to deepen with each new piece of intelligence they gathered, yet the clarity of their mission kept them focused.

Sandra looked up from her laptop, catching Jerry's eye. "The DA's fully briefed on the military-grade weapons involvement. They're pushing for maximum charges based on national security threats, and they want us to proceed with rounding up the higher-ups identified from Marco's intel."

"That's exactly the leverage we needed. With the stakes raised, we might shake loose some of the more reticent players in this network," Jerry responded, leaning back in his chair momentarily before turning his attention back to a secure email he was composing.

"And Homeland Security is stepping up their involvement. They're sending an analyst team first thing in the morning to review our findings and coordinate on the national security elements," Sandra added, updating the task force coordination log.

"Perfect," Jerry nodded. He paused, then added, "How are we handling the media? This is going to blow up once it hits the press."

"I've got our PR team drafting statements as we speak. They're emphasizing the cooperation between agencies and the significant blow we've dealt to organized crime," Sandra explained, her eyes scanning a draft on her tablet.

"Good. Keep it tight. We don't need the media circus to complicate things further," Jerry said, his tone indicating his concern over public exposure complicating their operations.

As they discussed their strategy, an officer approached with a phone in hand. "Commander, it's Agent Clarkson from the FBI. He's got an update on the inter-agency task force."

Jerry took the phone, his expression turning serious. "Clarkson, what's the status?"

"Jerry, we've got green lights across the board. The task force is officially operational. We've also flagged several accounts for freezing, based on the financial trails your team uncovered," the agent reported.

"That's excellent news. We're synchronizing our raids for tomorrow. Expect updates from our end by noon," Jerry replied, his mind already racing through the logistics of the coordinated raids.

"Understood. We're all in. See you on the ground, Jerry," Agent Clarkson said before ending the call.

Jerry handed the phone back to the officer and updated Sandra. "It's all coming together. Tomorrow's actions will likely determine the next phases of our operation."

Sandra nodded, her expression determined. "I'll finalize the raid schedules and ensure all team leaders are crystal clear on their objectives. We can't afford any missteps."

"Let's also make sure all evidence handling protocols are double-checked. I don't want a single piece of this slipping through due to procedural errors," Jerry added, his voice firm.

"Already on it. I've scheduled a final review of all protocols for first thing tomorrow," Sandra assured him.

They worked well into the night, finalizing every detail, double-checking every document, and rehearsing every scenario. As dawn approached, the first hints of light began to filter through the blinds, casting long shadows across the room that had become their fortress during these critical hours.

"Get some rest, Jerry. Tomorrow's a big day," Sandra finally said, her voice softening a bit.

Jerry gave a tired smile. "You too, Sandra. We'll need to be sharp."

They left the operations room together, the corridor outside deserted at this early hour. The quiet of the building was a stark contrast to the storm of activity inside their operation center. As they parted ways, each felt the weight of the impending day—a day that might well define their careers and the safety of their city.

As the sun rose over Greendale, casting a golden glow on the city, Jerry and Sandra stood in the bustling operations room, now the heartbeat of an unprecedented city-wide crackdown on the criminal network they had been unraveling for months. Today's raids were the culmination of all their efforts, and the air was charged with a palpable sense of urgency and expectation.

"Teams are in position, Jerry. We're ready to move on your command," Sandra reported, her voice steady despite the high stakes. She held a radio in one hand, coordinating closely with the units stationed across the city.

Jerry nodded, his gaze fixed on the large digital map displaying the locations of today's targets. "Let's do this clean and by the book. We can't afford any slip-ups. Give the signal."

Sandra lifted the radio to her mouth, her voice resolute as she transmitted the order. "All units, this is command. Execute Operation Dawn. Go, go, go!"

As they watched the live feeds from body cams and drones, images flickered across the screens, showing SWAT teams moving swiftly and silently into position. The choreography of law enforcement was precise, each movement practiced and perfect.

"Bravo team is in," one of the tactical coordinators reported over the radio. "Entry secured, no resistance."

"Charlie team to command, we have secured the eastern warehouse. Found significant amounts of contraband. Proceeding to secondary search," another voice crackled through.

"Keep the updates coming," Jerry said, his focus unwavering as he monitored the progress of each team. "Sandra, make sure the evidence teams are ready to move in as soon as the locations are secured."

"They're already briefed and on standby," Sandra confirmed, her eyes never leaving the screens. "Forensic units will follow closely to ensure proper collection and documentation."

The operation unfolded rapidly, with reports flowing into the command center. Each successful breach added another piece to the vast puzzle they had been piecing together.

"Command, this is Delta team. We've encountered resistance at the north dock. Need backup," a strained voice suddenly announced, breaking the rhythm of positive reports.

"Response team two, you are clear to assist Delta team. Exercise caution," Jerry commanded, his voice calm but firm.

As the backup team moved in, Jerry and Sandra exchanged a brief look of concern but remained focused on managing the operation.

Minutes later, the tension broke slightly. "Delta team reporting, situation under control. One suspect detained, others in flight but being pursued."

"Good recovery," Jerry responded. He then turned to Sandra. "Let's make sure medical is on standby; I don't want any injuries going untreated."

"Already done. Medical units are at all major raid sites," Sandra assured him, her efficiency a calming force amid the chaos.

As the morning progressed, more units reported in with their status. The majority were successful, with dozens of suspects detained and crucial evidence secured. Each successful report brought them closer to dismantling the network that had plagued Greendale for so long.

Sandra, updating a digital log of all the morning's activities, finally allowed herself a moment to speak her mind. "Jerry, this is a major win. It's a good day."

"It is," Jerry agreed, allowing himself a rare smile. "But we'll need to keep the momentum going. The follow-up on this will be crucial. We've got to process all the evidence correctly and prepare for the trials."

"Absolutely," Sandra nodded. "I'll start coordinating debriefs for all units. We need to capture everything while it's fresh."

The command center remained active, the air still buzzing with residual adrenaline as the first rays of sunlight turned into the bright light of day. Jerry and Sandra continued to oversee the wrap-up of the morning's raids, their thoughts already turning to the next phases of their investigation. They knew the battle was far from over, but today, they had struck a significant blow against the darkness that had once seemed untouchable.

Late into the evening, the operations center continued to hum with the subdued buzz of ongoing work. Jerry sat at his desk, surrounded by stacks of paperwork and multiple computer screens, each displaying streams of data from the day's successful raids. His focus was on consolidating the information into a comprehensive report that would be crucial for the ongoing investigations and upcoming prosecutions.

Across the room, Sandra was coordinating with the forensic teams, ensuring that the evidence collected was being processed accurately and efficiently. Her voice, firm and authoritative, occasionally broke the room's steady murmur as she confirmed the receipt of digital forensics results and the proper storage of physical evidence.

"Jerry, the preliminary forensics on the hard drives we seized today are in," Sandra called across the room, her tone hinting at the significance of the findings.

Jerry looked up, his eyes weary yet alert. "Anything we can use immediately?"

"Some interesting financial records that could tie several loose ends in our case against the network's financial structure," she replied, walking over to hand him a printed summary.

He scanned the document quickly, his mind adept at catching crucial details even after hours of relentless focus. "This could help us map out the rest of their operations. Good work. Make sure the team keeps digging into this tonight. We need everything they can extract by tomorrow."

Sandra nodded and returned to her station, her steps purposeful. As she departed, Jerry turned his attention back to his screens, where he was reviewing surveillance footage that might provide additional leads on the suspects who had managed to evade capture during the day's raids.

The room was a capsule of concentrated effort; every officer and analyst there was committed to their task, aware of the stakes involved. Jerry's leadership had fostered a sense of shared purpose that permeated the space, binding the team together in their common goal.

After some time, he stood and stretched, his body stiff from hours of sitting. He walked over to the large map on the wall, tracing routes and marking points of interest with a digital pen. Each mark represented a piece of the larger puzzle, a node in the vast network they were dismantling.

As he worked, an officer approached tentatively, holding a report. "Commander, the latest intel from our informants suggests there might be a meeting tomorrow between some of the remaining network members, possibly to discuss their next moves."

"Where?" Jerry asked without turning, his attention still partially on the map.

"An abandoned industrial site on the outskirts of town. It's secluded, which fits their pattern when under pressure," the officer detailed, handing over the report.

"Set up surveillance. Use only our most trusted team; I don't want this getting out. If this meeting happens, it could be our chance to catch more of them red-handed," Jerry directed, his mind already racing through the logistics necessary to manage such an operation discreetly.

"Understood, Commander. I'll handle it personally," the officer assured, already moving to carry out the orders.

As the officer walked away, Jerry finally paused, allowing himself a moment to feel the weight of the day's achievements. They had struck a significant blow against the network, but the battle was ongoing. The possibility of intercepting another major meeting was an opportunity he could not ignore.

Returning to his desk, he sat down to finish his reports, his eyes occasionally drifting to the live feeds from the surveillance cameras set up around the city. The night was far from over, and neither was their vigilance. As the clock ticked deeper into the night, the operations center remained a beacon of light and activity, a testament to the relentless pursuit of justice that drove Jerry and his team forward. Each piece of information, each strategic decision, brought them closer to their ultimate goal, and despite the late hour, the resolve within the room never wavered.

As the night wore on, Jerry convened a final briefing with Sandra and key team leaders in the operations center to discuss the potential meeting of network members they expected to intercept the next day.

"Alright, let's walk through the plan step by step," Jerry started, his voice clear and assertive, setting the tone for the urgent meeting. "We have a potential gathering of high-value targets. This might be our chance to cripple the network further. Sandra, you've been coordinating the setup. What's the status?"

Sandra, looking over her notes and digital maps, responded, "Surveillance is already in place around the suspected meeting site. Two undercover teams are positioned to observe without being noticed. We're keeping it tight, minimal personnel to avoid spooking them."

Jerry nodded, processing the information. "Good. We need eyes on who attends and what they transport. Any identification of key players or materials could be critical. What's the approach if they spot our surveillance?"

"We pull back immediately," Sandra said firmly. "The goal is to gather intelligence, not to engage. If they suspect they're being watched, they might go deeper underground, and we lose our advantage."

"Exactly," Jerry agreed. "Now, if they proceed with the meeting and we confirm the identities and gather sufficient evidence, what's our move?"

"We wait for your signal," one of the team leaders interjected. "Once we have confirmation from you, we move in swiftly to detain them. All teams are prepped for rapid deployment."

"And the legal prep? We need to ensure any actions we take are covered," Jerry inquired, looking towards the officer responsible for liaising with legal advisors.

"All warrants are secured, and legal is on standby throughout the operation," the legal officer confirmed. "We have the green light for detainment based on probable cause from the intel gathered tonight and previous operations."

Jerry gave a satisfied nod. "Keep them on speed dial. We might need quick clarifications depending on how things unfold."

Turning his attention back to the broader strategy, Jerry continued, "Let's talk contingency. Sandra, if things escalate beyond our control, what's our backup?"

Sandra glanced at her digital device before answering, "We have tactical support on standby a few blocks away. Non-lethal options are prioritized, but they're equipped for any necessary escalation. Medical units are also prepped to move in if needed."

"Good, let's keep it clean and controlled," Jerry emphasized. "We're walking a tightrope here. The right information could dismantle what's left of this network, so precision is key."

The room absorbed his words, each member aware of the stakes.

"Lastly, communication during the op needs to be crystal clear. Use coded signals, and keep radio chatter to a minimum," Jerry concluded, his gaze sweeping across the faces of his team. "We can't afford any mistakes. Everyone needs to know their role and execute flawlessly."

"Understood, Commander," came the unified response from the team.

"Alright, get some rest," Jerry said, standing up to signal the end of the briefing. "We have a big day ahead. Let's make sure it counts."

As the team dispersed, Sandra lingered to speak with Jerry. "You think they'll show?" she asked, a trace of concern in her voice.

"They're desperate, and they need a new plan. They'll show," Jerry responded confidently, though the weight of uncertainty was never far from his mind.

With a final nod to Sandra, Jerry left the room to prepare for the next day's crucial operation. As he walked through the quiet corridors of the station, his resolve hardened; they were close to a decisive victory, and he could feel the tide of battle shifting in their favor. The night might have been drawing to a close, but the fight was far from over.

Chapter 13
The Heist Begins

Dawn was just breaking, casting a pale light over the city as Jerry arrived at the operations center. He found Sandra already there, coordinating last-minute details with the surveillance teams.

"How are we looking?" Jerry asked as he approached Sandra, who was monitoring the live feeds from the undercover teams positioned near the industrial site.

"We have visual on the site. No activity yet, but our teams are in place and ready," Sandra reported, her eyes scanning the screens. "Everything's quiet for now."

Jerry nodded, taking a moment to survey the setup. "Keep me updated on any movements. And remind everyone, we need solid evidence and visuals before we make any moves."

"Understood," Sandra responded, then switched her radio to address the teams. "All units, this is command. Maintain stealth. No engagement until we have confirmation of the targets and their activities."

As she set down the radio, one of the surveillance officers called out, "We have a vehicle approaching the site. Looks like one of the known associates' cars."

"Let's see who's inside. Get the camera on that vehicle," Jerry instructed, leaning closer to the monitor displaying the feed.

The camera zoomed in as the car slowed near an entrance of the dilapidated warehouse, its license plate matching one from their watchlist. The car stopped, and two figures stepped out, scanning the area cautiously.

"Recognize them?" Jerry asked, his voice low.

"One looks like Thompson. He's been on our radar for smaller deals, but we suspected he was connected deeper," Sandra identified the first man.

"And the other?"

"New face, possibly the contact Marco mentioned last week. We'll need to get a clear ID," Sandra said, making a note on her pad.

"Keep an eye on them. Let's find out what they're here for," Jerry stated, watching as the two men entered the warehouse.

The team waited in silence, the tension mounting with each passing minute. Sandra continued to relay instructions, ensuring the surveillance was uninterrupted.

After several minutes, Jerry broke the silence. "Any movement inside, or are they still just setting up?"

"Cameras inside show they've met with two more individuals. Looks like a handover of some sort," another officer monitoring a different set of feeds reported.

"Can we get audio?" Jerry questioned, trying to gauge the situation fully.

"Working on it, but it's tough. The warehouse isn't ideal for acoustics, especially with the minimal prep time we had," Sandra explained.

"Keep trying. Any information on what they're handing over?" Jerry pressed, needing more to make a move.

"Looks like documents and a laptop. Hard to say for sure from this distance," the officer replied, adjusting the controls to try and zoom in further.

"Documents could be key. We need that laptop," Jerry mused aloud, considering their options.

"If we go in now, we risk spooking them before we gather enough evidence," Sandra cautioned, aware of the operation's delicate balance.

"I agree. Let's hold back until we see how this plays out. But be ready to move on my command," Jerry decided, his gaze fixed on the unfolding scene.

As they waited, the tension in the room was palpable. Each officer was alert, ready to act on Jerry's word. The surveillance continued to feed live images, capturing every movement inside the warehouse.

"We're close, Sandra. This could be what we need to tie all the loose ends," Jerry whispered, almost to himself, his focus never wavering from the monitors.

"Yes, we are," Sandra affirmed quietly, equally engrossed in the operation's critical phase. They both knew the importance of the next few hours, the potential to finally dismantle the network that had eluded them for so long.

As the sun rose higher, casting its light into the dark corners of the warehouse on the screens, Jerry and Sandra prepared for whatever came next, ready to end the long chase.

The surveillance continued as Jerry and Sandra watched the figures inside the warehouse through the grainy feed of the hidden cameras. The tension in the operations room was palpable; each officer ready to move at Jerry's command, yet under strict orders to hold until the signal was given.

"Looks like they're packing up," an officer monitoring the video feed reported. "Seems like the meeting's winding down."

Jerry leaned closer to the monitor, trying to discern the details of the objects being handled. "Can we confirm they're taking the laptop with them?"

"It appears so. One of the new faces just placed it in a briefcase," the officer responded, adjusting the focus.

"Okay, that's our cue. We can't let that laptop leave the site. It likely contains crucial data," Jerry decided, turning to Sandra. "Prepare teams

Alpha and Bravo for a soft breach. I want them in quietly—no sirens, no noise."

"Understood," Sandra replied, immediately relaying the orders through her radio. "Alpha, Bravo, you are green for a soft breach. Enter quietly, minimal force, secure the laptop and any documents."

As the teams moved out, Jerry kept his eyes glued to the screen, watching for any change in behavior that might indicate the suspects were aware of the impending breach. "Let them think they're clear, then move in. Timing is crucial here."

The minutes stretched out, each second ticking by with excruciating slowness as they waited for the teams to report their positions. Finally, the radio crackled to life.

"Alpha in position. No visibility on the suspects from our angle," the team leader reported.

"Bravo in position. We have a visual on two suspects heading towards the exit with the briefcase," another voice added.

"Bravo, take point. Alpha, back them up. Wait for my signal," Jerry instructed, his voice calm but firm.

"Waiting on your go," Bravo's leader responded.

Sandra glanced at Jerry, her expression a mix of anticipation and anxiety. "This is it."

Jerry didn't take his eyes off the screen. "Now, Bravo. Go now."

The footage from Bravo's body cam showed the team moving swiftly, yet silently, towards the exit where the suspects were about to leave. The door swung open unexpectedly, startling the suspects just as the officers revealed themselves.

"Police! Drop the briefcase and step away from it!" the lead officer commanded, his voice authoritative and clear.

The suspects froze, clearly caught off guard. One of them slowly set the briefcase down, raising his hands in surrender, while the other seemed to hesitate.

"Both of you, hands up and turn around slowly," the officer continued, the situation under control as Alpha team moved in to assist.

Jerry watched as the suspects complied, the officers quickly moving to handcuff them and secure the briefcase. "Good work, Bravo, Alpha. Secure the suspects and bring everything in. Great job."

Sandra let out a breath she seemed to have been holding. "That went smoothly. Hopefully, the contents of that laptop are worth the risk we took."

"We'll know soon enough," Jerry said, finally allowing himself a moment to relax. "Let's get that laptop to tech analysis immediately."

As the operations room buzzed with the aftermath of the successful intervention, Jerry and Sandra started organizing the debrief and evidence processing. The morning's work was far from over, but they had secured a potentially pivotal victory.

"Let's keep the momentum going," Jerry said, his voice a mixture of fatigue and resolve. "Every piece of evidence brings us closer to dismantling this network for good."

Sandra nodded, her determination reflecting Jerry's. "We'll break them down, piece by piece."

As they prepared for the next steps, the operations room continued to be a flurry of activity, with everyone focused on their tasks. The sense of teamwork was palpable, each member playing a part in the intricate dance of law enforcement that Jerry and Sandra orchestrated. They knew the job was far from done, but today, they had struck a significant blow against their adversaries.

After the successful interception at the warehouse, the focus shifted to the analysis of the seized laptop, which was now in the hands of the tech team at the police station. The operations room, still buzzing with the morning's adrenaline, gradually calmed as officers and specialists began the meticulous process of documentation and evidence handling.

Jerry stood beside the tech team's workstations, watching as the lead analyst, a young woman named Lisa, booted up the laptop. She navigated through several security protocols, her fingers moving deftly across the keyboard.

"Any luck cracking it?" Jerry asked, his voice low, mindful of the tension that lingered in the room.

"We're through the initial security. Starting the deep dive now. It could take some time, depending on what we find," Lisa responded without looking away from the screen.

"Keep me posted. Anything you can get could be crucial," Jerry said, then turned to leave Lisa to her work, his confidence in her abilities clear.

He moved over to where Sandra was coordinating the incoming reports from the various teams involved in the morning's operations. She looked up as he approached, her face reflecting both fatigue and satisfaction.

"How are we doing on the debriefs?" Jerry asked.

"Progressing. Teams are reporting in detail. No major injuries, and all suspects are accounted for," Sandra replied, marking off notes on her digital tablet.

"Good. Let's make sure those reports are thorough. We'll need all the details we can get for the prosecutions," Jerry instructed, his gaze scanning the room.

As the hours passed, the operations room transformed into a hive of quiet activity. Officers and analysts worked on their respective tasks, piecing together the evidence that would build the case against the network.

Jerry returned to Lisa's workstation periodically, checking on the progress. On one such visit, he found her more animated, a sign that she had found something significant.

"We've got something. Looks like encrypted files, but I managed to access them. There's a trove of communications here, some directly mentioning Marco and several high-value targets," Lisa reported, her eyes alight with the thrill of the discovery.

"Excellent work, Lisa. Can you pull all references to those names? We need to know who else is in the network and any planned activities," Jerry asked, his interest piqued by the breakthrough.

"Already on it. I'll compile a report and have it on your desk within the hour," Lisa confirmed, turning back to her screens, her focus renewed.

Jerry nodded his approval and walked back to Sandra, who was monitoring the flow of information from the various departments.

"Lisa's cracked the laptop. She's pulling out names and plans now. It looks like we might have enough to expand our targets," he shared quietly with Sandra.

"That's what we needed. I'll alert the task force. It's time to start planning the next round of raids," Sandra said, her voice steady, already sending out the necessary communications.

As the day wore on, the station remained a center of unrelenting diligence. Every officer, every analyst contributed to the unfolding case, their collective efforts slowly untangling the vast web of criminal activity that had once seemed indomitable.

Outside, the city carried on, unaware of the monumental efforts being made on its behalf. Inside, Jerry and Sandra continued to steer the course of the investigation, their resolve unshaken by the enormity of the task. Each piece of evidence, each successful decryption, added to their momentum.

By the time evening approached, the operations room had collected a substantial amount of actionable intelligence. Jerry and Sandra reviewed the new data, planning their next moves, aware that each decision could lead to significant breakthroughs.

The day had brought them closer to dismantling the network than ever before. As they prepared to leave for the night, the weight of their achievements hung in the air, mixed with the anticipation of what was yet to come. Their path forward was clear, and as they stepped out of the operations room, the silent corridors of the station echoed with the promise of continued pursuit, the drive to restore peace and order never ceasing.

As evening settled over Greendale, the operations room at the police station still buzzed with activity. Jerry and Sandra convened in Jerry's office to map out their strategy based on the day's discoveries. The walls of Jerry's office, covered with whiteboards and maps, reflected the complex web of the criminal network they were dismantling.

"Based on Lisa's findings, we have potential leads on two more high-value targets," Jerry said, pointing to the names scribbled on the whiteboard. "These could be key players in the network's hierarchy."

Sandra, reviewing the list, added, "We need to prioritize these leads. If we move quickly, we can prevent them from going underground. Have we got enough to bring them in?"

Jerry nodded, flipping through a dossier. "We do. Between the communications Lisa decrypted and the evidence from today's raids, we can get warrants by tomorrow morning."

"Good. I'll coordinate with the task force to prepare for these arrests. Timing will be crucial," Sandra stated, typing notes into her tablet.

Jerry looked over the map, tracing routes with his finger. "Let's make sure we have surveillance teams on them tonight. I don't want them slipping through our fingers."

"I'll have the surveillance units notified and in position within the hour," Sandra assured him, her efficiency a constant in the midst of chaos.

As they strategized, an officer knocked and entered Jerry's office, holding a report. "Commander, we've just received confirmation from forensics. The documents recovered today are linked directly to several unsolved cases across the state."

"That's excellent," Jerry responded, taking the report and quickly scanning it. "This could be the break we've been looking for in those cases. Make sure copies of this report get to the respective departments first thing tomorrow."

"Will do, Commander," the officer replied, stepping out as quickly as he had entered.

Turning back to Sandra, Jerry said, "This ties up a lot of loose ends for us and other jurisdictions. It could lead to a significant reduction in their operations statewide."

"Absolutely," Sandra agreed, her mind already on the broader implications. "The impact of today's work is going to be felt far beyond Greendale."

As they continued to plan, Jerry's phone rang. He answered, listening intently, then responded with a firm, "Understood. Keep me updated," before hanging up.

"That was the chief. He's fully backing our push on these new leads. He also wants us to prepare a comprehensive briefing for the mayor tomorrow. There's going to be a lot of public interest once this hits the news," Jerry informed Sandra.

"We should highlight the inter-agency collaboration and the breakthroughs in forensic technology that led to today's successes," Sandra suggested, already considering the angles for the briefing.

"Good point. Let's include that," Jerry agreed. "Also, emphasize the community impact. It's important the public knows the significance of what we're doing."

The meeting continued as they refined their action plan for the following day. With each decision, the path forward became clearer, each strategy more defined.

Finally, as the sky darkened outside, signaling the end of a long day, Jerry and Sandra wrapped up their planning session. "We've made more progress today than in the last six months. Let's keep the momentum going," Jerry said, a slight weariness in his voice.

"We will, Jerry. Let's meet first thing in the morning to finalize the details for the upcoming operations," Sandra proposed, gathering her notes and standing up.

"See you then," Jerry replied, giving Sandra a nod of appreciation for her relentless dedication.

As Sandra left, Jerry took a moment to look out his office window, reflecting on the day's victories and the challenges ahead. The city lights flickered below, a reminder of the lives they were working to protect. With a deep breath, he turned back to his desk, ready to prepare for another day of strategic decisions and leadership, driven by the commitment to restore peace and order to the streets of Greendale.

Chapter 14
Chaos Ensues

As the new day dawned in Greendale, the police station was a hive of activity. Jerry was already in his office, pouring over the latest updates from the overnight surveillance teams. The room was cluttered with coffee cups and case files, evidence of the long hours spent in pursuit of justice. Sandra entered, her expression serious, carrying a thick folder under her arm.

"Morning, Jerry. I've got the updates from last night's surveillance. Looks like our targets are still in the dark about our moves," Sandra said, handing him the folder.

Jerry skimmed the contents quickly. "Good. Any movements?"

"Minimal. One of the targets met with an unknown individual late last night, but we've got it on video. We're enhancing the images to get an ID," she replied, leaning against the side of his desk.

"Keep me posted on that. Any lead is crucial at this point," Jerry said, setting the folder down and looking up at Sandra. "What's the status on the task force?"

"They're assembled and ready. We've briefed everyone on the potential risks and the importance of this operation. They're prepared for a full-scale mobilization once we confirm the operation's go," she updated, her tone reflecting the gravity of their undertaking.

"That's good. I want to avoid any hitches. Let's make sure our communication lines are secure and open," Jerry stressed, his mind already running through potential scenarios.

"I've triple-checked everything. We're as ready as we can be," Sandra assured him, her confidence bolstering his own.

Jerry nodded and stood, walking over to the large map pinned to his wall, dotted with various markers and notes. "Today could be a turning point for us. We need to be precise, Sandra. Every step must be calculated. We can't afford to tip them off."

"I agree. The element of surprise is our best advantage," Sandra said, joining him at the map. "Once we move, it needs to be decisive and swift."

They reviewed the map in silence for a moment, each marker representing a piece of the larger puzzle they were painstakingly assembling. The network they were dismantling was extensive, but they were now closer than ever to its core.

"Let's go over the entry points again. I want to make sure we have all exits covered. No one gets out without our say-so," Jerry directed, pointing to several critical locations on the map.

Sandra pulled up some notes on her tablet. "All exits will be manned, and we have sniper teams on standby. Additionally, our air support will provide real-time updates from above."

"Excellent," Jerry responded, satisfied with the arrangements. "What about the DA? Are they prepped for the influx of cases if today goes as planned?"

"They're ready. I spoke with the assistant DA this morning. They have a team standing by to process any arrests we make today," Sandra replied.

Jerry took a deep breath, the weight of their responsibilities momentarily pressing down on him. "We're making a significant move against some very dangerous people, Sandra. It's going to get more intense from here."

Sandra met his gaze, her eyes steady. "We knew this day would come. We're ready, Jerry. This team is the best I've worked with. We'll handle whatever comes our way."

"Thanks, Sandra. That means a lot," Jerry said, giving her a small, appreciative nod. "Let's get to the briefing room. I want to give one last talk to the team before we go."

As they left Jerry's office, the corridor was bustling with officers gearing up for the day. The air was filled with a sense of urgency, but also an undercurrent of determination. Today's operations could indeed tip the balance in their favor, and everyone at the station felt the momentum building.

Together, Jerry and Sandra walked toward the briefing room, ready to face the day's challenges head-on, each step forward a testament to their dedication to their duty and the city they were sworn to protect. The morning's light streamed through the windows, casting long shadows behind them as they moved, a visual reminder of the darkness they were striving to bring into the light.

The briefing room was filled with the tense energy of anticipation as Jerry and Sandra entered. Members of the task force, all clad in tactical gear, turned their attention towards them, awaiting the final directives before moving out. Jerry stood at the forefront, a projector illuminating the details of their operation on the screen behind him.

"Today, we dismantle a major part of the network that has plagued our city," Jerry began, his voice resonant, instilling a sense of purpose in everyone present. He walked them through the map displayed on the screen, pointing out locations and strategies, his demeanor calm yet commanding.

Sandra took over to detail the operational specifics—timing, signals, and communication protocols. Each officer listened intently, understanding their individual roles in the day's complex choreography. She emphasized the need for precision and caution, reminding them of the non-lethal priorities unless absolutely necessary. The room was filled with a focused silence, the kind that spoke of professionals well-versed in their duties, bracing for the challenges ahead.

Once the briefing concluded, the officers began to disperse, moving towards their designated vehicles. Jerry took a moment to speak individually with several team leaders, offering last-minute advice and reassurances. Sandra, meanwhile, coordinated with the communications team to ensure all channels were open and clear, double-checking every frequency and encryption.

As the teams set out, Jerry and Sandra returned to the operations room, where multiple screens displayed live feeds from drones and body cams.

They settled into their chairs, their eyes rarely blinking as they monitored each movement, each transition from point to point.

The city outside was beginning to wake up, oblivious to the significant law enforcement operation unfolding. In contrast, the atmosphere in the operations room was a blend of high alert and procedural calm. Every officer and analyst knew their role, the room humming with a controlled, efficient energy.

Jerry's focus was unyielding as he watched a team approach one of the high-priority targets. His hand was steady on the radio, ready to give orders or change plans at a moment's notice. Sandra kept detailed logs of the operation's progress, her proficiency ensuring that nothing was missed.

Hours passed, the tension occasionally broken by updates through the radio. "Alpha team in position," "Bravo has visual," "Charlie encountering light resistance"—each report a crucial piece of the ongoing tactical puzzle. Jerry responded to each with concise commands, his experience guiding the operation with precision.

Outside, the sun climbed higher, casting stark shadows across the buildings of Greendale. Inside, the dimly lit operations room served as a stark reminder of the day's gravity. Each feed on the monitors, each piece of intercepted communication, added layers to their understanding of the network they were dismantling.

By mid-morning, several key arrests had been made, and important evidence had been secured, each success a testament to the meticulous planning and execution of Jerry, Sandra, and their team. They remained vigilant, aware that the operation was far from over, but each victory brought a quiet sense of accomplishment.

In the operations room, the steady hum of machinery and low murmur of voices continued as Jerry and Sandra prepared for the next phase. The city was now fully awake, its residents unaware of the significant blows being dealt against the criminal elements within their midst.

Jerry glanced briefly at Sandra, a mutual recognition of their progress passing silently between them. They turned back to their screens, their commitment unwavering, ready to face whatever the operation would bring next. As the day wore on, the operations room remained a beacon of determination and resolve, a central point from which the safety of the city was being quietly, effectively secured.

By early afternoon, the operation had advanced significantly, with several key arrests and the seizure of crucial evidence. Jerry and Sandra reconvened in the operations room, alongside key team members, to assess the status and plan the subsequent moves.

"We've made good progress," Jerry stated, looking around at the assembled team. "But we can't let up. We need to press our advantage while we have the momentum."

Sandra nodded, adding, "The arrests this morning have already caused ripples. We're seeing some movement within the network—perhaps attempts to regroup or move resources."

Jerry focused on the live feeds and reports coming in. "Have we been able to track any of these movements?"

"We have a few leads," one of the analysts interjected, handing Jerry a tablet displaying a map with various markers. "Based on the latest communications intercepts, we believe they might be trying to consolidate their remaining assets at a few key locations."

"Let's make sure we're on top of these. Assign surveillance teams to monitor these areas. I don't want anyone slipping through our net," Jerry directed, his tone indicating the urgency of the situation.

Sandra was already coordinating the necessary resources. "I'll redirect some of our units to cover these locations. We'll maintain a tight perimeter and keep a low profile—we don't want to spook them until we're ready to move in."

"Exactly," Jerry agreed, examining the tablet further. "What's the status of the evidence processing? Anything else we can use to tighten the screws?"

"We're still cataloging some of the material seized this morning, but we've found more encrypted data that could be promising," an evidence technician reported. "We're running it through decryption now. We should have something by the end of the day."

"Keep me updated on that. Every piece of information is crucial," Jerry responded, handing back the tablet.

As they discussed their next steps, Sandra's phone buzzed. After a quick glance at the screen, she looked up with a new intensity. "That was the DA's office. They're starting to prepare the cases based on the arrests and evidence we've provided. They want to ensure we have everything buttoned up for a solid prosecution."

Jerry nodded his approval. "Good. Let's make sure our reports are detailed and our evidence chain is unbreakable. We've got the upper hand now; let's not give them any room to maneuver legally."

"I'll oversee the finalization of the reports personally," Sandra assured him. She then turned to the team. "Everyone, let's stay sharp. We're doing great work here, but it's not over yet."

The team members acknowledged with nods and murmurs of agreement, each returning to their tasks with renewed vigor. Jerry and Sandra took a moment to review the broader strategy, ensuring they were not missing any angles.

"Once we crack that encrypted data, we might need to move quickly. Be prepared to adjust our tactics on the fly," Jerry reminded Sandra.

"I'll have contingency plans ready," Sandra replied, always one step ahead in planning.

The operations room remained active as the day progressed into evening. Updates continued to flow in, and each new piece of information added depth to their understanding of the network they were dismantling.

Outside, the city carried on, most of its residents oblivious to the critical work unfolding within the police station's walls. Inside, the light waned as the sun set, but the screens and monitors cast a constant glow, illuminating the faces of Jerry, Sandra, and their team as they continued their vigilant watch over Greendale.

As the night deepened, so did their resolve, each aware that the successes of the day were merely steps towards a larger goal. They remained ready to adapt, to confront whatever challenges might arise, driven by a shared commitment to see the operation through to its end.

By early afternoon, the operation had advanced significantly, with several key arrests and the seizure of crucial evidence. Jerry and Sandra reconvened in the operations room, alongside key team members, to assess the status and plan the subsequent moves.

"We've made good progress," Jerry stated, looking around at the assembled team. "But we can't let up. We need to press our advantage while we have the momentum."

Sandra nodded, adding, "The arrests this morning have already caused ripples. We're seeing some movement within the network—perhaps attempts to regroup or move resources."

Jerry focused on the live feeds and reports coming in. "Have we been able to track any of these movements?"

"We have a few leads," one of the analysts interjected, handing Jerry a tablet displaying a map with various markers. "Based on the latest communications intercepts, we believe they might be trying to consolidate their remaining assets at a few key locations."

"Let's make sure we're on top of these. Assign surveillance teams to monitor these areas. I don't want anyone slipping through our net," Jerry directed, his tone indicating the urgency of the situation.

Sandra was already coordinating the necessary resources. "I'll redirect some of our units to cover these locations. We'll maintain a tight perimeter and keep a low profile—we don't want to spook them until we're ready to move in."

"Exactly," Jerry agreed, examining the tablet further. "What's the status of the evidence processing? Anything else we can use to tighten the screws?"

"We're still cataloging some of the material seized this morning, but we've found more encrypted data that could be promising," an evidence technician reported. "We're running it through decryption now. We should have something by the end of the day."

"Keep me updated on that. Every piece of information is crucial," Jerry responded, handing back the tablet.

As they discussed their next steps, Sandra's phone buzzed. After a quick glance at the screen, she looked up with a new intensity. "That was the DA's office. They're starting to prepare the cases based on the arrests and evidence we've provided. They want to ensure we have everything buttoned up for a solid prosecution."

Jerry nodded his approval. "Good. Let's make sure our reports are detailed and our evidence chain is unbreakable. We've got the upper hand now; let's not give them any room to maneuver legally."

"I'll oversee the finalization of the reports personally," Sandra assured him. She then turned to the team. "Everyone, let's stay sharp. We're doing great work here, but it's not over yet."

The team members acknowledged with nods and murmurs of agreement, each returning to their tasks with renewed vigor. Jerry and Sandra took a moment to review the broader strategy, ensuring they were not missing any angles.

"Once we crack that encrypted data, we might need to move quickly. Be prepared to adjust our tactics on the fly," Jerry reminded Sandra.

"I'll have contingency plans ready," Sandra replied, always one step ahead in planning.

The operations room remained active as the day progressed into evening. Updates continued to flow in, and each new piece of information added depth to their understanding of the network they were dismantling.

Outside, the city carried on, most of its residents oblivious to the critical work unfolding within the police station's walls. Inside, the light waned as the sun set, but the screens and monitors cast a constant glow, illuminating the faces of Jerry, Sandra, and their team as they continued their vigilant watch over Greendale.

As the night deepened, so did their resolve, each aware that the successes of the day were merely steps towards a larger goal. They remained ready to adapt, to confront whatever challenges might arise, driven by a shared commitment to see the operation through to its end.

Chapter 15
Aftermath

As evening approached, the operations room at the Greendale Police Department was awash in a soft glow from the overhead lights, casting long shadows that stretched across the floor and up the walls. The room was quiet except for the low hum of computers and the occasional murmur of officers discussing their next moves. Jerry and Sandra were seated at a central table, surrounded by monitors showing maps and live feeds from surveillance cameras.

Sandra broke the silence, looking up from a laptop screen filled with streams of data. "We've just received confirmation from the tech team. The data from the laptop we seized has been fully decrypted. It's more extensive than we initially thought."

Jerry leaned forward, his interest piqued. "What have we got?"

"Banking transactions, communication logs, even blueprints for what looks like a distribution center they were planning to set up in the next few months," Sandra detailed, scrolling through the documents. "This will give us enough to expand our investigation and possibly bring down more players in the network."

"Excellent," Jerry replied, his eyes scanning the documents Sandra was referring to. "We need to get this over to the DA and the task force planning team as soon as possible. Have we linked any of these documents to our existing cases?"

Sandra nodded. "Yes, several of the communications directly tie back to unsolved cases and known suspects. It's going to strengthen our position considerably."

The room's doors opened, and a junior officer stepped in, holding a stack of reports. "These are the latest updates from the field teams," he said, placing them on the table. Jerry and Sandra each took a stack and began to sift through them, marking key information and setting aside documents for further review.

As they worked, the clock on the wall ticked forward, marking the passage of time in the quiet room. The focus was intense as they correlated new data with ongoing cases, piecing together a broader picture of the criminal activities they were trying to stop.

"We're making significant headway," Jerry finally said, looking over at Sandra. "Today's operations have not just disrupted their current activities but have given us a foothold to prevent future ones."

Sandra, who had been meticulously organizing the evidence for presentation, looked up. "Yes, and the impact will be long-term. We're not just cutting off the head of the snake. We're dismantling the entire organism."

Their conversation was interrupted by the return of the junior officer. "Commander, Detective Mira on line two. She says it's urgent."

Jerry picked up the phone. "Mira, what's the situation?"

After listening for a moment, Jerry's expression grew serious. "Understood. Secure the scene; I'll send additional units." Hanging up, he turned to Sandra. "That was Mira. They stumbled upon another stash house while following up on one of the leads from the laptop. It's bigger than we thought."

Sandra immediately took action, grabbing her radio. "I'll coordinate the units. The more we uncover tonight, the less they have to regroup."

As Sandra dispatched the necessary forces, Jerry stood, stretching his legs, his mind clearly processing the day's events and the information still coming in. "Every piece brings us closer," he muttered, more to himself than to anyone else.

Returning his focus to the tasks at hand, Jerry continued to work well into the night alongside Sandra and their team. Their dedication was a testament to their commitment to the safety and security of Greendale. They were determined to ensure that the efforts of the day would not be in vain, laying the groundwork for further actions that would continue to dismantle the criminal network they had fought so hard to uncover.

As dawn crept over Greendale, the early morning light filtered through the blinds of Jerry's office, casting long, thin shadows across the room cluttered with evidence files and coffee cups from the night's endeavors. Outside, the city was waking up, the streets slowly coming to life as people began their daily routines, oblivious to the monumental efforts that had transpired through the night within the walls of the police station.

Jerry, looking weary yet resolute, sat at his desk reviewing the latest updates from the overnight operations. Each report detailed further successes: more arrests, additional evidence secured, and deeper insights into the criminal network that had once seemed impenetrable. The room was quiet, save for the soft clicking of a keyboard as Sandra updated the case files with the latest findings.

"Jerry," Sandra finally said, breaking the silence, "the task force did an exceptional job last night. We've dismantled significant portions of their operations."

Jerry nodded, his eyes not leaving the report he was reading. "Yes, they did. But we need to keep the pressure on. We can't afford to let up now."

He stood, stretching his back, feeling the toll of the long hours. Moving over to the map on the wall—a map now dotted with various colored pins representing different aspects of their operation—he traced a line connecting several key locations they had targeted. The visual representation of their progress was impressive, a clear sign of how far they had come since the beginning of this ordeal.

The clock on the wall ticked steadily, marking the passage of time as Jerry and Sandra planned their next steps. They were deep in the process of strategizing their approach to the remaining suspects and securing the evidence for prosecutions.

"Today, we start digging into the financials that were uncovered from the laptop," Jerry decided, his voice determined. "If we can link the money trail directly to the higher-ups, it could lead to more indictable offenses."

Sandra, who had been meticulously organizing the digital evidence, nodded in agreement. "I'll coordinate with the financial crimes unit. They have the expertise to decipher the complex networks we're seeing."

As the morning progressed, the operations room began to fill with other officers and specialists, each person contributing to the flurry of activity. Phones rang, radios crackled with incoming communications, and computers beeped as emails and reports flowed in. The dynamic was a well-oiled machine, each part working in sync under Jerry and Sandra's guidance.

During a brief moment of downtime, Jerry looked out his office window, watching the city come alive. His thoughts turned to the people they were working so hard to protect, the unseen impact of their efforts to ensure safety and security. It was a heavy responsibility, but one he and his team were fully committed to.

Returning to his desk, Jerry continued to work through the logistics of their next operations. Each decision was critical, each movement calculated. The success of their ongoing efforts to dismantle the criminal network depended on their continued vigilance and precise execution.

Sandra joined him with a new stack of reports, her expression serious but hopeful. "These just came in. More good news. Several more assets have been frozen, and we've got potential leads on two more associates."

"Excellent," Jerry responded, taking the reports from her. "Let's review these and prepare for the next briefing. The team needs to be aware of these developments."

As they settled down to review the new information, the room once again filled with the sound of their collaborative efforts. The work was far from done, but with each report, each piece of evidence secured, they were one step closer to their goal. The morning light grew brighter, illuminating the path they were paving towards a safer city, their resolve as strong as ever.

By mid-morning, the atmosphere in the briefing room was thick with anticipation as Jerry and Sandra prepared to update the entire task force on the latest developments and strategize the day's objectives. The team, a mix of local police, federal agents, and specialists, filled the room, ready with notepads and digital devices.

"As you all are aware, our efforts over the last 24 hours have been tremendously successful," Jerry began, his voice carrying a mix of authority and gratitude. "We've dismantled several key components of the network, and thanks to your hard work, we are seeing the dominoes fall."

Sandra stepped up to the projector, switching the display to a series of charts and graphs. "Let's talk specifics. Based on the data we've decrypted, we've identified two more high-ranking members of the network. Here are their profiles and last known locations." The screen displayed photos and detailed information about the targets.

"Surveillance teams have been monitoring these individuals since early this morning," Sandra continued. "We believe they might be attempting to flee the city, considering the heat we've put on their operations."

Jerry took over, pointing to a map on the screen with several marked areas. "Our plan today is to intercept these individuals before they can make any moves. Alpha team, you'll take the north side. Bravo, you're on the south. We've got all exits from the city covered."

One of the team leaders raised his hand. "Do we have any intelligence on whether they're armed, or if they have security with them?"

"Good question," Jerry responded. "Our intel suggests they may be traveling lightly to avoid drawing attention. However, assume they are armed for your safety. Non-lethal force is preferred, but protect yourselves."

Sandra chimed in, "We also have information that they might be trying to destroy evidence. Digital forensics, you need to be ready to recover any data you can from their devices. Time is of the essence."

A digital forensics officer nodded, replying, "We've prepped our mobile units for rapid data recovery. We can process scenes on-site if necessary."

Jerry looked around the room, meeting the eyes of his team. "This is a critical moment for us. The actions we take today could very well determine the outcome of this entire operation. I need everyone to be on their game."

"Are there any particular concerns regarding the public areas? Some of these locations are pretty crowded during the day," another officer asked, scanning the marked map.

"That's a valid concern," Sandra acknowledged. "We've coordinated with local businesses and security where possible to minimize any risks to civilians. Our approach needs to be discreet but decisive."

Jerry concluded, "Keep communications open, and report any deviations from the plan immediately. We need to be flexible and ready to adapt to any situation."

As the briefing wrapped up, the team members began to disperse to their assignments, each person clear on their role and the day's high stakes.

Sandra pulled Jerry aside as the room cleared. "We've covered all angles, but I've got that knot in my stomach that says this isn't going to go down easily."

Jerry gave a wry smile, his experience telling him she might be right. "In our line of work, that feeling means you're ready. Let's stay sharp and see this through."

With a nod to each other, they left the briefing room to oversee the operation from the command center. Today's actions would be crucial, and both Jerry and Sandra were poised to lead their team through whatever challenges came their way. As they stepped into the corridor, the weight of responsibility was palpable, but so was the determination to succeed.

The command center was abuzz with activity as Jerry and Sandra monitored the operation's progress, their eyes flicking between the various screens showing real-time data and locations of the task force teams.

"Alpha team, report status," Jerry spoke into the microphone, his voice steady amid the background noise of communications and coordinations.

"Alpha team in position. Target spotted entering the designated café. We have visual confirmation and are prepared to intercept on your command," came the crisp reply over the radio.

"Maintain surveillance. Do not engage until Bravo team is in position," Jerry directed, glancing at Sandra who was coordinating with another team.

Sandra, just finishing her call, updated Jerry, "Bravo team is delayed by traffic but should be in position within minutes. They're taking a secondary route to avoid alerting the target."

Jerry nodded, replying to the team, "Alpha, hold position. Bravo is en route. We need full containment before we make a move."

Switching to a different channel, Jerry then checked in with another unit. "Charlie team, anything to report?"

"Charlie team here. We've got eyes on the second target. He's still at his residence. Looks like he's packing up, might be preparing to move out soon," the officer on the other end reported.

"Keep a watchful eye. Let me know if he leaves the premises," Jerry ordered, then turned to Sandra. "We need to ensure no one slips through. These are high-priority targets."

"Understood," Sandra acknowledged, her fingers swiftly moving over her tablet to send instructions. "I'm sending Delta team to assist Charlie. If our target moves, they'll be ready to intercept."

The tension in the room was palpable as everyone waited for the precise moment to act. Jerry's experience had taught him that timing was crucial in operations like these. Too early, and they risked everything falling apart; too late, and the targets could vanish.

Sandra's voice broke his concentration, "Bravo team is now in position. We're ready to proceed."

"Alpha, Bravo, you are clear to engage. Apprehend the targets with minimal disruption," Jerry commanded, his gaze fixed on the live feeds showing the teams moving discreetly into action.

The operation unfolded quickly. On the screen, Jerry and Sandra watched as Alpha team members converged on the café. The footage showed them entering calmly, blending with the crowd before closing in on their target.

"Target in custody," the leader of Alpha team soon reported, "No incidents. The café was secured, and the suspect was cooperative."

"Excellent work, Alpha," Jerry responded, a hint of relief in his voice.

Turning to another screen, Sandra pointed out, "Charlie team is moving. The second target is leaving his residence now."

Jerry switched to monitor that operation. "Delta, move in. Assist Charlie with the apprehension."

As the teams executed the arrest, the coordination was seamless. Within moments, the radio confirmed, "Second target in custody. We're heading back now."

Jerry leaned back for a moment, allowing himself a brief exhale. "Both targets secured, Sandra. Let's start processing and debriefing right away."

Sandra nodded, already typing up the orders. "I'll arrange for transport and make sure the interrogation rooms are prepped."

As the immediate tension eased, the command center began to quiet down, officers starting to debrief and wrap up their roles. Jerry stood, stretching slightly, his mind already on the next steps.

"We'll need to comb through the evidence they had on them, see if there are any more links we can trace," he mused aloud.

Sandra agreed, "Absolutely. Every bit of information is crucial."

The room continued to buzz with a quieter energy, the success of the day's operations marking a significant victory. But both Jerry and Sandra knew their work was far from over. There were more leads to follow, more pieces of the puzzle to put together. They returned to their tasks, the city outside moving past another day, largely unaware of the critical work being done on its behalf.

Chapter 16
A Cat's Loyalty

As the day wound down, the sun began to set over Greendale, casting a golden hue through the windows of the police station's operations room. Jerry and Sandra remained at the helm, overseeing the meticulous process of consolidating the day's achievements. Their focus was unwavering as they reviewed arrest reports, surveillance footage, and seized evidence, ensuring every detail was accounted for.

Outside, the bustling city started to quiet, but inside, the energy was still palpable. Officers and analysts worked diligently, their efforts synchronized like a well-oiled machine. The room buzzed with the low hum of conversation and the occasional beep of incoming data, signs of an operation that was far from over.

Jerry stood by a large digital display, reviewing the encrypted files recovered earlier in the day. His expression was one of concentration as he cross-referenced the newly uncovered information with existing case files. He was methodically piecing together the network's hierarchies and financial pathways, each discovery a potential lead to further dismantle the criminal operations.

"Any updates on the decryption progress?" Jerry called out to a tech analyst working at a nearby station.

"We've cracked another layer. It looks like we've got a series of transactions that might expose additional assets hidden by the network," the analyst replied, turning his screen so Jerry could see the flow of illicit funds.

"Excellent. Document everything. I want a full report by tomorrow morning," Jerry instructed, his voice carrying a mix of satisfaction and resolve.

Sandra, meanwhile, was on a call, coordinating with federal agencies to share the latest intelligence. Her conversations were precise, ensuring that the information flowed seamlessly between different jurisdictions involved in the broader investigation. She ended her call and approached Jerry with an update.

"We've got the green light to proceed with the federal task force. They're bringing in additional resources to help with the follow-up investigations," she reported, her tone indicating the importance of this support.

"That's great news," Jerry responded, nodding in approval. "Let's make sure our teams are prepped for joint operations. I don't want any missteps."

As they planned their next actions, other team members began to compile evidence packages, each labeled meticulously and ready for the prosecutors. The legal implications of their findings were significant, and there was a collective understanding of the need for thoroughness in every aspect of their preparation.

The operations room gradually quieted down as officers completed their assignments for the day. Some discussed their next shifts, while others debriefed and shared insights from the field. Despite the late hour, the dedication was evident; everyone understood the stakes and the impact of their work.

Jerry finally stepped away from the digital display, his mind still racing with the details of the case. He glanced around the room, seeing the signs of a day's hard work on everyone's faces. He made his way to Sandra, who was organizing the final reports on her desk.

"We've done good work today," Jerry said to Sandra, allowing a moment of reflection amidst the relentless pace.

"We have," Sandra agreed, looking up from her papers with a tired but satisfied smile. "But tomorrow, we go again. There's still a lot to do."

Jerry acknowledged with a nod. "We'll be ready."

As they gathered their belongings and prepared to leave, the operations room was dimming, the screens casting a soft glow in the quiet space. The challenges they faced were ongoing, but Jerry and Sandra, along with their team, were resolute. They exited the room, the door closing softly behind them, the echoes of the day's successes lingering in the air, a silent testament to their commitment and the promise of continued vigilance.

In the operations center, Jerry and Sandra stood before a bank of monitors, each showing different angles and locations, as their teams positioned themselves based on the morning's brief. The atmosphere was tense, but controlled, a testament to the experience and focus of the assembled law enforcement personnel.

"Team Delta, what's your status?" Jerry asked into the radio, his eyes fixed on a screen displaying a grainy feed of an industrial area.

"Delta in position, no sign of the target yet. We're camouflaged and waiting for further movement," came the static-filled reply.

Sandra, holding a tablet and scrolling through digital maps, updated Jerry on another operation. "Alpha team reports they have visual confirmation on one of the targets. They're observing until we give the go-ahead to intercept. They're in a public space, so the team is being extra cautious to avoid any collateral."

"Understood, keep them on a tight leash, Sandra. We can't afford a scene," Jerry responded, his voice calm but firm.

He then switched channels. "Bravo team, report."

"We're at the secondary location. It seems quiet, but we're set up and ready," the team leader from Bravo responded, the sound of slight wind distortion coming through.

"Good. Maintain position and stay alert. Any changes, I want to know immediately," Jerry instructed, then turned to Sandra. "How are we coordinating the asset freezes? Any word from the financial unit?"

"The banks are cooperating. Freezes are being implemented as we speak. It should start impacting their operations by midday, squeezing them further," Sandra replied, her focus on a list of account numbers and corresponding actions.

"Perfect. That might stir the hornet's nest. Be ready for any reaction," Jerry said, a strategic glint in his eye.

Suddenly, an alert came through on one of the screens. "Sir, we have movement at the industrial site. Looks like several individuals are exiting a building. Possible target sighting," an analyst pointed out urgently.

Jerry quickly moved to view the screen. "Delta team, you seeing this?"

"Affirmative, we have eyes on three individuals matching the descriptions. Preparing to engage on your command," Delta team's leader responded, readiness evident in his tone.

"Wait for my confirmation. Sandra, can we confirm these are our targets via drone visuals?" Jerry asked, turning to Sandra who was already on it.

"Drone is overhead. Zooming in for facial recognition," she confirmed, then after a tense pause, "Confirmation received. Those are our targets."

"Delta team, you are clear to engage. Remember, we need them in one piece, no unnecessary risks," Jerry commanded, watching the live feed intently as the team moved in with precision.

The operation unfolded smoothly on the screen. The suspects, surprised but compliant, were quickly detained by Delta team, who handled the situation with professional ease.

"Targets secured, no casualties. We're preparing for extraction," the Delta team leader reported back, a note of satisfaction in his voice.

"Excellent work, Delta. Bring them in. And good job coordinating the visuals, Sandra," Jerry said, relief mixed with commendation in his tone.

Sandra nodded, her attention still partially on her tablet. "I'll inform the interrogation unit to prepare. We'll need to debrief them as soon as they arrive."

As they awaited the return of Delta team, Jerry and Sandra reviewed the next steps. "Once we have the suspects in custody, we need to press them for information. Today's operations might give us the leverage we need to break them."

Sandra agreed, "Absolutely. The sooner we integrate this with the financial data, the clearer the picture we'll have of the entire network."

The center remained abuzz with activity, but there was a palpable sense of achievement as each team's success was reported. Jerry and Sandra continued to monitor and coordinate, their expertise guiding the operations towards a comprehensive crackdown on the criminal network that had once seemed untouchable. As each report came in, the puzzle pieces fell into place, painting a picture of victory through vigilance and strategic planning.

As the day progressed into the afternoon, the operations center maintained a steady rhythm of activity. Jerry and Sandra, deeply involved in overseeing the processing of the newly detained suspects, coordinated closely with different departments to ensure the integration of all new intelligence into the broader case.

Jerry glanced at the array of monitors displaying various feeds from around the city and turned to a nearby officer. "Have all the detainees been brought in for processing?"

"Yes, sir. All targets from today's operations are now in custody and are being processed. Interrogations will begin within the hour," the officer confirmed, checking off items on his digital pad.

"Make sure those interrogations are thorough. We need to exploit every piece of information they can give us," Jerry instructed, his tone serious as he considered the implications of their morning's success.

Sandra, meanwhile, was liaising with the forensics team. "How are we doing on the analysis of materials seized today?"

"We're making good progress," replied the head of the forensics unit, who had approached with a preliminary report. "We've recovered documents and digital media that could further expose network connections. Also, the initial scans of the financial records are uncovering some promising leads."

"Excellent. Keep me updated on any developments, especially anything that can tie the loose ends of the network's operations," Sandra responded, her mind already tracing the potential threads the new evidence could unravel.

As they spoke, Jerry walked over to the large glass board used to map out the criminal network. He marked several new connections based on the morning's arrests, his marker squeaking slightly as he drew lines connecting various aliases and locations.

"This is coming together, Sandra. Look at how the pieces are fitting," Jerry said, stepping back to view the entire board.

Sandra joined him, her eyes scanning the network they had outlined. "It's intricate, but you're right. Today's operations have added another layer of depth to our understanding. I think we'll see the domino effect soon enough."

"I hope you're right. We need to keep up the momentum," Jerry mused, his gaze lingering on the board.

The two of them then moved to a quieter corner of the room, where they could discuss their next steps without interruption. "We need to decide on our approach for the next few days. With the assets frozen and these key players in custody, the network will be scrambling," Jerry said thoughtfully.

Sandra nodded in agreement. "We should monitor all known associates. Any unusual activity could lead us to other parts of the network trying to reorganize or recover."

"Exactly my thought. Let's increase surveillance and also press our informants for any new information. Anything that can give us an advantage," Jerry added.

Their conversation was interrupted by an update from one of the surveillance teams. "Commander, we've noticed increased activity at one of the secondary locations we've been monitoring. Looks like some members are trying to retrieve something."

Jerry's expression hardened. "Keep an eye on them. Do not engage unless absolutely necessary. Gather as much information as you can and report back."

"Understood, Commander," came the reply.

As the afternoon wore on, the operations center did not slow down. Officers and analysts continued their work, processing the influx of data and coordinating further actions based on the evolving situation.

Jerry and Sandra, though weary from the day's efforts, remained vigilant, their commitment unwavering as they navigated the complexities of dismantling a major criminal network. Each development, each piece of intercepted communication, and every report that came in was another step towards their goal.

Outside, the light began to fade as evening approached, casting long shadows across the operations center. Inside, the light of screens illuminated the determined faces of Jerry, Sandra, and their team as they continued their vigil, the weight of their responsibility as palpable as ever.

As evening set in, Jerry and Sandra remained ensconced in the operations center, surrounded by the soft glow of computer screens and the low murmur of ongoing communication. Their day had been long, yet the necessity of their mission kept them anchored to their posts, reviewing the outcomes of their efforts and planning the next steps.

"Let's review the status from today's interrogations. What have we learned?" Jerry asked, his voice carrying a mix of fatigue and anticipation.

Sandra, scanning through a digital report, responded, "The interrogations have been quite productive. One of the suspects has confirmed the existence of another storage location, potentially holding more evidence critical to our case."

"That's a significant breakthrough," Jerry acknowledged, his interest piqued. "Have we mobilized a team to secure that location?"

"Yes, I've dispatched Team Echo to handle it. They're en route now and should be there within the hour," Sandra confirmed, her efficiency evident in her swift organization.

"Good. What about financial ties? Any luck tracing the flow of money?" Jerry continued, his focus shifting to the broader implications of their findings.

"The financial unit has made some headway. They've traced several transactions to offshore accounts, which seem to be the primary funding source for the network. We're coordinating with international authorities to freeze those assets," Sandra reported, detailing the complex web of financial transactions they were attempting to unravel.

Jerry nodded approvingly. "That's crucial. Cutting off their funding will cripple their operations significantly. Keep pushing on that front."

As they discussed, an officer approached with an urgent update. "Commander, Team Echo has arrived at the storage location. They've encountered resistance. Requesting further instructions."

Jerry's expression turned serious. "Tell them to hold their position and maintain surveillance. We can't afford a firefight. We'll reinforce them if necessary."

"Understood, Commander," the officer replied, swiftly relaying the instructions.

Sandra looked at Jerry, concern etched on her face. "This operation is turning out to be larger than we anticipated. Every move we make seems to uncover more layers."

"It's the nature of these networks. They're deep-rooted and widespread. But every piece of the puzzle we uncover leads us closer to dismantling them completely," Jerry said, his tone resolute.

"True. Once we secure this new location, I think we'll gain enough leverage to pressure more members of the network into cooperating," Sandra speculated, her strategic mind already planning several moves ahead.

Jerry glanced back at the live feeds displaying Team Echo's progress. "Let's hope so. In the meantime, we need to ensure our teams are safe and that we gather as much evidence as possible. This could be the break we've been waiting for."

"Absolutely. I'll coordinate with logistics to ensure Team Echo has everything they need for a prolonged operation, just in case," Sandra said, already typing away on her tablet to arrange the necessary support.

The room remained tense with anticipation as they monitored the ongoing operation. Jerry and Sandra continued to direct their teams with precision, their experience and dedication evident in every decision they made.

As the night deepened, the stakes of their operation became even clearer. The network they were up against was formidable, but the resolve of Jerry, Sandra, and their entire team was stronger. They were determined to see this through, to restore safety to the streets of Greendale and dismantle the criminal enterprise that had taken root in their city.

Outside, the darkness of night enveloped the city, but inside the operations center, the light never dimmed, symbolizing the continuous vigilance of those committed to protecting and serving. Jerry and Sandra remained at their posts, their focus unwavering, as they prepared for whatever challenges lay ahead in their unrelenting pursuit of justice.

Chapter 17
Questioning

Dawn was breaking, casting a soft, diffused light over the city of Greendale. In the operations center of the police station, the overnight shift was winding down as Jerry and Sandra prepared to hand over to the morning crew. Despite the early hour, the two were methodically reviewing the events of the past night, their faces illuminated by the glow of computer screens.

Jerry leaned back in his chair, rubbing his tired eyes. He and Sandra had spent the entire night coordinating a series of raids and managing the flow of information that streamed in non-stop. The room was quieter now, the bustling activity of the night having tapered off into a subdued murmur.

"Any updates on the Echo team's situation at the storage location?" Jerry asked, his voice a bit hoarse from hours of command.

"They've secured the area. No further resistance encountered. They found a cache of documents and some electronic devices that could be crucial," Sandra replied, scrolling through the latest reports on her tablet. She looked up, her eyes serious but satisfied. "The forensic team is already on it. They're hopeful about retrieving valuable data."

Jerry nodded, processing the information. "That's good. That's very good. We'll need to debrief them as soon as they're back. Set up a meeting for when I'm back on shift."

"I will," Sandra assured him. She paused, then added, "The financial team also made some progress. They've traced more of the funds back to a couple of shell companies. It's convoluted, but they're unwinding it."

"That's what we need—more links to follow. We're unraveling this network strand by strand," Jerry murmured, a trace of exhaustion mingled with resolve in his tone.

The morning light grew stronger, signaling the start of another day. Jerry stood, stretching his limbs which were stiff from sitting too long. He walked over to a large wall map dotted with various colored pins, each representing different aspects of their ongoing operations. His hand hovered over the map, tracing the connections they had uncovered so far.

"We're making real progress," Jerry said, almost to himself. "But there's still so much to do."

Sandra joined him by the map, her gaze following his. "We are," she agreed. "Every arrest, every piece of evidence—it all adds up. We're getting closer to the core of this thing."

Jerry turned to her, his expression one of weary gratitude. "Your work has been invaluable, Sandra. Couldn't have done it without you."

"Same here, Jerry. It's been a long haul, but we're getting there," Sandra replied, offering a tired smile.

As they reviewed their next steps, the morning shift began to trickle in, each officer ready to take over and continue the work that had been so meticulously laid out by Jerry and Sandra. The changeover was smooth, a testament to the well-oiled machine that the Greendale Police Department had become under their watch.

Before leaving, Jerry took one last look around the operations center. "Keep me updated on any developments," he instructed the incoming shift supervisor.

"Will do, sir," the supervisor responded, nodding with respect.

With that, Jerry and Sandra gathered their belongings and headed towards the exit. The weight of their responsibilities lingered, but so did the satisfaction of knowing they were making a difference. They stepped out of the operations center, leaving behind the buzz of activity, ready to catch a few hours of rest before returning to continue their relentless pursuit of justice.

The city outside was waking up, unaware of the battles fought in its name throughout the night. Inside, the police station remained a beacon of vigilance, ready to face whatever challenges the new day might bring.

After a few hours of much-needed rest, Jerry returned to the station, feeling somewhat rejuvenated but still carrying the weight of the ongoing investigation. As he stepped back into the operations center, he was met by a flurry of activity. Sandra was already there, coordinating with different units, her focus as sharp as ever.

"Jerry, you're back," Sandra greeted him, her tone reflecting a mix of relief and urgency. "We've had some developments while you were away."

"What's happened?" Jerry asked, quickly slipping back into his role.

"The forensic team managed to recover data from the devices we seized last night. They've found detailed communications between the suspects and someone we haven't identified yet. It looks like this person could be a key player," Sandra explained, handing him a tablet with the recovered messages displayed.

Jerry scanned the messages, his brows furrowing as he absorbed the information. "This could be big. Do we have any leads on this new person?"

"Not yet, but I've asked the intelligence team to prioritize finding them. Based on these messages, it seems this individual is coordinating much of the network's activities from behind the scenes," Sandra replied, her fingers tapping rapidly on her own device as she sent out further instructions.

"We need to identify and locate them as soon as possible," Jerry said decisively. "Let's set up a task force specifically for this. The sooner we bring this person in, the closer we get to dismantling the whole network."

"I agree. I'll organize the task force and pull in our best people. We'll need all the expertise we can get," Sandra responded, already thinking through the logistics.

As they strategized, an officer approached with a phone in hand. "Commander, Detective Mira on the line. She says it's urgent."

Jerry took the phone. "Mira, what's the situation?"

After listening for a moment, Jerry's expression became serious. "Understood. Keep everything on lockdown until I get there." He hung up and turned to Sandra. "There's been a break-in at one of our evidence storage facilities. It's possible they were trying to retrieve or destroy evidence."

"That's a direct hit on our operations. We can't let this slide," Sandra said sharply, her mind racing with the implications.

"We won't," Jerry assured her, his jaw set. "I'm heading there now to assess the damage. Organize a security review of all our facilities. I want to know how they breached our protocols."

"Will do. I'll also enhance our surveillance on all known associates. If they're getting desperate, they might make more mistakes," Sandra proposed, her demeanor all business.

"Good thinking," Jerry nodded in approval. "Keep me updated, and let me know the moment you have anything on this unknown player."

As Jerry prepared to leave, he paused, reflecting on the severity of the breach. "This shows just how deep we're in, Sandra. They wouldn't risk exposure unless it was critically important. We're on the right track, but today's breach is a stark reminder of the dangers we face."

Sandra met his gaze, her resolve clear. "We'll tighten our security, Jerry. And we'll catch whoever is responsible. They've shown their hand, now we'll show them ours."

With a nod, Jerry left the operations center, headed for the compromised facility. The challenge was significant, but so was their determination. As he drove, the stakes of their investigation were clearer than ever. Not just for the integrity of their case, but for the safety of everyone involved. They were in a pivotal phase of their operation, and every action from here on out would count more than ever.

Arriving at the compromised evidence storage facility, Jerry was met with a scene of controlled chaos. Police tape cordoned off the area, and officers moved about, securing the scene and gathering evidence of the break-in.

Detective Mira approached Jerry as he stepped out of his car, her face a mix of frustration and determination.

"Jerry, glad you're here. We've got a situation," Mira began, leading him through the facility's main entrance. "Looks like they knew exactly what they were after. Went straight for the locked evidence from last week's raids."

"What's the extent of the damage?" Jerry asked, surveying the disarray within the facility.

"They managed to breach one of our secure storage rooms. Several items are missing, including documents and a couple of hard drives we seized. We're still taking inventory," Mira explained, her tone reflecting the severity of the loss.

Jerry frowned, processing the information. "Any leads on how they got in? This place was supposed to be secure."

"We're reviewing security footage now. Initial indications suggest they had inside knowledge. They bypassed key security protocols with precision," Mira responded, her voice tense as she handed Jerry a tablet showing the preliminary security footage.

"This complicates our position," Jerry noted, watching the footage. "We need to assume there's a leak somewhere or that our security measures are being countered effectively. I want a full review of all personnel who had access to this facility."

"Already on it," Mira assured him. "And we're tightening security across all our storage sites."

Jerry nodded, handing back the tablet. "Good. Let's keep this breach contained. I don't want word of this getting out and compromising our entire operation."

"We're doing our best to lock it down," Mira confirmed. She paused, then added, "What are your orders regarding the investigation into this breach?"

"Prioritize it. Use every resource we have. Whoever did this is directly connected to the network we're dismantling. It's crucial we find out how they knew about this facility and what exactly they've taken," Jerry instructed, his resolve firming.

Mira nodded in agreement. "I'll get our best detectives on it. We'll find the breach and plug it."

As they spoke, another officer approached, offering Jerry a list of the items confirmed missing so far. Jerry scanned the list, his mind already racing with the implications of each missing piece.

"We can't let this set us back. Continue with the operations as planned, but increase our caution. And keep me personally updated on any progress with this breach," Jerry said, handing back the list.

"You'll be the first to know," Mira promised, a determined glint in her eye.

Jerry took a final look around the facility, the gravity of the situation weighing heavily on him. "This is a setback, but it's not the end. We've faced challenges before. We'll handle this, and we'll come out stronger."

With a final nod to Mira, Jerry left the facility, heading back to the operations center. His mind was occupied with the breach, but also with the broader picture of their ongoing battle against the network. Every step they took seemed to reveal more about the depth and complexity of the criminal activities they were up against.

Back at the station, Sandra awaited updates, ready to adjust their strategy as needed based on Jerry's report. The battle was far from over, and every piece of information, every setback, and every victory brought them closer to their ultimate goal of dismantling the criminal network that had embedded itself so deeply in Greendale.

Back at the operations center, Jerry convened an emergency meeting with Sandra and the senior members of their team to address the security breach and to reinforce their strategy moving forward. As they gathered around the large conference table, the atmosphere was tense but focused.

"Let's go over what we know," Jerry started, looking at each member of the team. "The breach was targeted and sophisticated. They knew exactly what they were after, which suggests insider knowledge or a significant reconnaissance effort."

Sandra, who had been coordinating the responses since Jerry's departure, chimed in, "We've tightened security at all our facilities, and I've initiated a sweep for any bugs or surveillance devices in our offices. We're not taking any chances."

"Good. What about the missing items? Do we have a full list yet?" Jerry asked, his voice steady but concerned.

Mira, who had just joined the meeting, responded, "We've completed the inventory. The missing items include key documents and two encrypted hard drives that were part of the evidence against the network's financial operations. It's a significant loss."

Jerry's expression hardened. "We need to assume that anything on those drives will be compromised. Sandra, alert the financial crimes unit. They need to anticipate moves by the network to protect their assets."

"I'm on it," Sandra said, already typing out the instructions on her laptop.

"And what are we doing about the potential for an insider being involved?" Jerry's gaze swept across the room, meeting the eyes of his team members.

"I've ordered background checks to be re-run on everyone who had access to the evidence room," Mira replied. "We're also reviewing all recent communications and access logs."

"Let's go deeper than that," Jerry insisted. "Check financial records for unusual activity, social media for any indirect communications that might have been missed initially. We need to know if we're dealing with a mole or if our security protocols were simply outmatched."

Sandra added, "I suggest we also increase our surveillance on known associates of the network. If there's chatter about the breach, we need to intercept it."

"That's a good call," Jerry agreed. "Let's make sure our intel teams are prioritizing any leads that could point us to how our security was breached."

As they delved deeper into their strategy session, the team worked with a renewed sense of urgency. Each member was tasked with specific follow-ups, ensuring no detail was overlooked.

"How are we handling communications about this breach? We can't afford any leaks or misinformation getting out," Jerry queried, aware of the potential fallout.

"We're keeping it under wraps for now," Sandra reassured him. "Only this team and those directly involved in the recovery efforts know the full extent of what's happened."

Jerry nodded, satisfied with her response. "Keep it that way. The last thing we need is panic or rumors undermining our efforts."

As the meeting drew to a close, Jerry looked around the table at his team, their faces set with determination. "This breach is a setback, but it's also a reminder of the stakes we're dealing with. We're up against a sophisticated enemy, but we have the skills and the will to beat them. Let's get back to work and show them just how resilient we are."

With a collective nod, the team dispersed, heading back to their respective duties. Jerry and Sandra lingered for a moment, reviewing their notes.

"We've got our work cut out for us," Sandra said, a hint of resolve in her tone.

"We always do," Jerry responded, a slight smile breaking through his otherwise stern demeanor. "Let's get to it."

As they left the conference room, the weight of the task ahead was clear, but so was their resolve to overcome any challenge. The operations center, a hub of constant activity, was ready for whatever would come next, driven by a shared mission to protect and serve.

Chapter 18
Community Response

In the early hours of the morning, Jerry stood in the shadow-draped office of the Greendale police department, a buzz of anticipation setting the scene. Across from him, Sandra leaned against the cool metal of her desk, phone in hand, coordinating with units spread across the town. Whiskers, ever vigilant, sat at Jerry's side, his ears twitching at the faint sounds of radio chatter that filled the air.

"Looks like everything's in place for tonight's operation," Sandra began, her voice a mix of determination and fatigue. "The units are all briefed, and we've got eyes on every possible exit point. No way they're slipping through our fingers this time."

Jerry nodded, his gaze fixed on a large map pinned to the wall, dotted with various markers and notes. "Good. We need a tight net tonight. Any word from the tech team? Are the surveillance feeds holding up?"

"They're stable for now. I had them do a double check on all the equipment. We can't afford a glitch, not tonight," Sandra replied, scrolling through updates on her tablet.

"I appreciate your thoroughness, Sandra. It's crucial that we maintain control of the situation. We've come too far to let anything slip now," Jerry said, his voice steady, revealing his veteran resolve.

"That's the plan, Jerry. And speaking of plans, have you gone over the final details with the task force leaders?" Sandra asked, looking up from her tablet.

"Yes, I've just finished the last briefing. Everyone knows their role and what's expected of them. We're ready," Jerry confirmed, giving Whiskers a gentle pat on the head, signaling the calm before the storm.

Sandra let out a deep breath, the weight of their responsibility momentarily acknowledged in the quiet between them. "This operation could really change things for Greendale. We're finally going to clean up the streets, once and for all."

"That's the goal. And after tonight, we'll have the upper hand. We can start pushing back harder," Jerry said, his tone infused with a hint of optimism.

"Just make sure we keep things clean and by the book, Jerry. I don't want us to get overzealous and trip over our own feet in the process," Sandra cautioned, her eyes sharp.

"Don't worry, Sandra. We're going to handle this the right way, like we always do," Jerry assured her, his confidence unshaken.

As they finalized their preparations, the soft glow of dawn began to seep through the blinds, casting long shadows across the room. The quiet moment was a stark contrast to the impending action, a fleeting pause in their relentless pursuit of justice.

"Alright, let's get to our positions. It's almost time," Sandra said, stepping away from the desk, her expression shifting back to the task at hand.

Jerry nodded, standing up, his figure tall and commanding. Whiskers stood alongside him, his loyal companion in the many battles they faced together. Together, they moved towards the door, ready to step into the fray once more, under the ever-watchful eyes of the rising sun.

The dimly lit streets of Greendale hummed with the quiet tension of an impending storm as Jerry and Sandra stationed themselves in the mobile command center parked discreetly by the edge of the designated operational zone. The center was alive with the soft beeping of monitors and the crackling of radio communications.

"Check in with all units, Sandra. Make sure everyone is alert and in position," Jerry instructed, his eyes scanning the live feeds from various surveillance cameras set up around the area.

Sandra picked up the radio, her voice calm and authoritative. "This is command to all units, report your status."

One by one, the units responded, their voices crackling through the radio. "Alpha team in position," "Bravo team ready," "Charlie team on standby," they reported systematically.

"Looks like everyone's set. How are you holding up, Jerry? It's going to be a long night," Sandra asked, turning to look at him, a slight concern in her tone.

"We're doing what needs to be done, Sandra. It's not just another operation; it's about setting things right," Jerry replied, his gaze never leaving the monitors. "Keep an eye on the northern checkpoints. I have a feeling that's where we'll see the most action."

"Will do. I've got the thermal imaging up and running on screen four. We'll see them coming," Sandra said as she adjusted the settings on a nearby monitor, bringing up a heat map of the area.

As they focused on the screens, a sudden alert came from one of the surveillance teams. "Command, this is Delta team. We have movement in sector three. Multiple figures, possibly armed."

Jerry straightened up, his focus intensifying. "Delta team, maintain visual but do not engage. Sandra, can we get a drone over there?"

"Already on it," Sandra responded swiftly, her fingers flying over the controls to redirect a drone to the specified location. "You'll have eyes on the situation in two minutes."

"Good. Let's not take any unnecessary risks. We need a visual confirmation before any engagement," Jerry stated, watching as the drone feed came live on the screen, showing several shadows moving through an abandoned warehouse lot.

The next few minutes were tense, with both Jerry and Sandra watching the situation unfold. The figures were cautious, moving with a clear purpose, their actions captured in real-time by the overhead drone.

"Looks like they're heading towards the eastern exit. Beta team, be ready to intercept," Jerry commanded into the radio, his voice calm but firm.

"Command, Beta team copies. We're positioned and ready," came the reply, the team's readiness palpable even through the static of the radio.

As the figures approached the exit, the night erupted into sudden chaos. The suspects made a break for it, their quick movements kicking up dust and debris.

"Engage with caution, Beta team. Use of force only if absolutely necessary," Jerry ordered, his eyes glued to the screen as the team moved in.

The operation was swift, with precision that spoke of extensive training and preparation. Within moments, the suspects were subdued and detained, their attempted escape thwarted by the coordinated efforts of Jerry's team.

"Subjects in custody, command. Waiting for further instructions," Beta team reported, their tone professional and controlled.

"Excellent work, Beta. Hold your position and await transport for the detainees. Sandra, let's make sure these guys are processed quickly. We need to find out what they were after," Jerry said, a hint of relief in his tone as the immediate danger passed.

Sandra was already on the radio, coordinating the next steps. "Transport is en route, ETA five minutes. I'll inform the processing unit to be ready."

As the adrenaline of the moment subsided, Jerry and Sandra allowed themselves a brief moment to breathe. The night was still young, and more challenges awaited, but the success of their operation so far bolstered their resolve.

"We're doing good, Sandra. Let's keep the pressure on and wrap this up without any more surprises," Jerry said, his confidence in their operation evident.

"Agreed," Sandra replied, her eyes already scanning the monitors for any new developments. "Let's bring this home, Jerry."

With renewed focus, they turned their attention back to the array of screens, ready to guide their teams through the rest of the night's operations. The city of Greendale was quiet above, unaware of the silent battles being fought in its shadows.

The operation was winding down, but the night was far from over. Jerry and Sandra, still stationed in the mobile command center, were meticulously going through the aftermath of each team's engagement. The constant hum of radio chatter filled the small space, blending with the occasional beep of incoming data.

"Jerry, all teams are reporting in. All suspects detained tonight are secured and en route to processing," Sandra announced, her eyes never leaving the multiple screens that displayed various angles of the operation areas.

Jerry, rubbing his tired eyes, responded, "That's excellent to hear. Have there been any complications or injuries reported?"

"Nothing major on our side. A few scrapes and a twisted ankle for one of our officers, but that's about it. The suspects didn't go down without a fight, but our teams handled it well," Sandra updated, her voice a mixture of relief and pride.

"Good, good. How about the evidence? Did we recover everything we expected to find?" Jerry inquired, his focus shifting to the broader implications of tonight's successes.

"Yes, the preliminary reports look promising. We recovered a significant amount of digital media and documents from the locations. It appears they were trying to destroy some of it as our teams moved in, but we got there in time," Sandra explained, flipping through digital tabs to review the detailed list.

"That's a crucial win for us. Make sure the tech team prioritizes the examination of that media. Any intel on their next moves or contacts could help us preempt their strategies," Jerry stated, thinking ahead to the next phase of their investigation.

"I'll push that through first thing. Also, the interrogation teams are ready. They're waiting for your go-ahead to start with the suspects," Sandra mentioned, her tone indicating the preparedness to move quickly.

"Let's not waste any time then. Begin the interrogations as soon as they're processed. And Sandra, ensure those are conducted thoroughly. We need to squeeze out every bit of information they have. No stone goes unturned," Jerry ordered, his strategic mind mapping out the possible leads from the suspects' testimonies.

"Understood, Jerry. I'll supervise the initial rounds myself. We'll handle this by the book but with all the urgency it demands," Sandra assured him, her demeanor serious and determined.

"Excellent. And keep me updated on any breakthroughs or if there are any shifts in their behavior. Any sign of them cracking or willing to cooperate more fully can be critical," Jerry added, his experience showing in his attention to detail.

"Will do. I'll be on it personally," Sandra replied, already organizing her notes and preparing to move out.

Jerry paused, his gaze lingering on the screens showing the now quiet operation sites. "Sandra, tonight's operation... it was textbook. Your planning and execution were impeccable."

Sandra smiled slightly, appreciating the acknowledgment. "Thank you, Jerry. But it was a team effort. We have a good crew here. Dedicated."

"Yes, we do. And it's nights like these that remind me just how important each member of our team is. Let's make sure to commend them for their efforts," Jerry said, feeling a deep sense of camaraderie and pride in his team.

"I'll make sure of that. They deserve recognition," Sandra agreed, her respect for her team evident in her voice.

As the first light of dawn began to seep through the edges of the command center's windows, Jerry and Sandra prepared to transition operations back to the station. The city of Greendale was waking up, oblivious to the intense night of work that had just transpired under its very nose.

"Let's wrap this up and head back. We've got a lot to process and even more to prepare for the coming days," Jerry said as he started to gather his things.

"Right behind you, Jerry," Sandra responded, shutting down systems and securing confidential information.

Together, they stepped out of the command center, ready to face the challenges of a new day after a night of significant victories. The quiet of dawn was a brief respite, a calm before the storm of activity that awaited them at the station.

Back at the police station, Jerry and Sandra convened in the central briefing room, still energized by the night's outcomes. Around them, the room buzzed with officers updating records and discussing the next steps. The walls, plastered with maps and photos, bore testament to the depth and complexity of their ongoing operations.

"Alright, let's debrief while everything is fresh," Jerry started, addressing the room. "I want reports from all team leaders. Let's start with Alpha team. What's your status?"

"Alpha team secured all designated targets without significant issues. All suspects from our list are in custody. We encountered minor resistance but managed to control the situation quickly," reported the Alpha team leader, a seasoned officer with a no-nonsense demeanor.

"Good work. Bravo team, your report?" Jerry continued, his gaze sharp and focused.

"Bravo team here. We managed to recover most of the intended materials from the second location. However, one of the suspects managed to destroy some documents before we could apprehend him. We're currently sorting through what we salvaged to see if anything can be reconstructed," the Bravo team leader explained, showing a hint of frustration.

"That's unfortunate, but good job on managing to salvage what you could. Every piece counts," Jerry acknowledged, then turned to the Charlie team. "Charlie, what do you have for us?"

"Charlie team had a clean sweep. No casualties. We captured some key electronic devices and have already sent them to the tech team for immediate analysis. We also intercepted communications that could lead us to additional members of the network," detailed the Charlie team leader, her voice crisp and efficient.

"Excellent. That could be a game-changer. Make sure those devices are handled with priority. Any break in their communications could give us more leverage," Jerry directed, his mind already racing through the possibilities.

Sandra, who had been taking notes, chimed in. "I've arranged for round-the-clock shifts on tech analysis. We're not letting anything sit unattended. Jerry, we should also consider tightening security around our storage facilities. Last night's breach was a wake-up call."

"Agreed. We'll discuss the security measures in a moment. First, let's finish up with Delta team. Status?" Jerry shifted his attention to the last team.

"Delta team executed the arrest of three high-priority targets. We had a bit of a chase with one, but no injuries to report. All targets are being processed, and preliminary interrogation has started," reported the Delta team leader, a young officer with a commendable track record.

"Well done, everyone. Your efforts last night were critical. Sandra is right, though. We need to tighten our security. I don't want a repeat of last night's breach. Let's go over our current protocols and see where we can make immediate improvements," Jerry stated, shifting the meeting towards security.

Sandra took over, outlining potential security enhancements. "We need to increase surveillance at all key points. I suggest we implement double verification for accessing sensitive areas and consider external audits of our systems."

"That sounds like a solid start. Let's put those measures in place as soon as possible. Also, increase random checks and sweeps for bugs or unauthorized devices in all our offices and facilities," Jerry added, his tone indicating the urgency of these measures.

As the meeting drew to a close, Jerry looked around at his team, feeling a profound sense of pride and responsibility. "We've made great strides, but the road ahead remains challenging. Let's stay vigilant and keep pushing forward. Great work, everyone."

The team nodded, their expressions a mix of fatigue and determination, ready to continue the fight. Sandra stayed back as the room cleared, looking over her notes.

"Jerry, once we implement these security upgrades, I think we should run a full simulation to test them. We can't afford any weak links," she suggested, already planning the next steps.

"Let's set that up. Good thinking, Sandra. We're only as strong as our weakest point," Jerry agreed, ready to take on whatever challenges lay ahead.

Together, they left the briefing room, stepping back into the bustling environment of the police station, their resolve to protect and serve Greendale as steadfast as ever.

Chapter 19
Repairing Bonds

The morning in Greendale was unusually crisp, signaling the changing seasons. At the police station, Jerry and Sandra sat in the recently secured conference room, a large whiteboard filled with names and connections standing as a silent testament to the intricate web they were untangling.

"Look at this," Jerry said, pointing to a cluster of names on the board, his finger tracing the lines connecting them. "Last night's operations gave us the leverage we needed. This node here," he tapped on a name, "seems to be the key to understanding the larger structure."

Sandra leaned in, examining the board closely. "Yes, I see. If we can crack this part of the network, we might be able to unravel the whole thing. The interrogations from last night have already started to bear fruit."

"Exactly. What did the suspects reveal? Anything we can use to push deeper?" Jerry asked, his eyes not leaving the board.

"Some. Most are still holding back, but we've managed to confirm a few suspicions about the hierarchy. Also, one of them mentioned a location that hasn't come up in our investigations before," Sandra replied, flipping through her notebook to find her notes.

"A new location? That could be significant. Have we sent a team there yet?" Jerry's voice was tinged with both curiosity and urgency.

"Not yet. I wanted to cross-verify the information first. There's a chance it could be a decoy, meant to throw us off. But I agree, it's worth a look," Sandra suggested, her instincts as a detective shining through.

"Set up surveillance on that location. Keep it low-key for now. If it looks like there's substantial activity, we'll consider a raid," Jerry decided, nodding thoughtfully.

Sandra made a note on her digital tablet. "I'll arrange that. Also, the financial analysis team has made some progress with the data we recovered from those hard drives. It looks like we might be able to track down some of their funding sources."

"That's crucial. If we can choke off their funding, it might just starve them out," Jerry remarked, a strategic gleam in his eyes. "How solid is the financial data?"

"Pretty solid. There are layers of shell companies, but our team is good. They're peeling it back, transaction by transaction," Sandra explained, her respect for the team's skills evident in her tone.

"Keep pushing on that front. Every dollar we tie up is one less they can use against us," Jerry instructed, his voice firm.

"Understood," Sandra acknowledged, then shifted slightly in her chair. "Jerry, once we have more concrete information from the new location and the financial tracks, how do you want to proceed?"

"We'll need to be strategic. Gather all the intel, and then we hit them hard and fast. This isn't just about taking down a few key players anymore; it's about dismantling the entire network," Jerry outlined, his determination clear.

Sandra nodded in agreement. "It's a big puzzle, but we're starting to see the big picture. With each piece we place, we get closer."

"The key is to maintain our momentum and keep the pressure up. They're already feeling the pinch; let's turn it into a chokehold," Jerry said, standing up to add another piece of information to the board.

As they continued to strategize, the early morning light began to fill the room, casting long shadows that danced across the floor with the movement of the clouds outside. The day was beginning in earnest, and with it, another round in their relentless pursuit of justice. The city of Greendale was counting on them, and they were not about to let it down.

Later that afternoon, Jerry and Sandra gathered in the surveillance room, where multiple screens displayed live feeds from the new location that had been mentioned during the interrogations. They were joined by a team of analysts who monitored every movement captured by the hidden cameras.

"Anything unusual so far?" Jerry inquired, his gaze fixed on a screen showing the exterior of a nondescript warehouse.

"Not much. There's been some minor activity, a few individuals coming and going, but nothing that screams 'major operation' yet," one of the analysts reported, adjusting the focus on one of the cameras.

"Keep an eye on anyone who spends significant time there or shows up repeatedly. They might be cautious because they suspect we're onto them," Sandra suggested, leaning closer to a different screen displaying a zoomed-in view of the warehouse entrance.

"I've set alerts for any recognized faces from our database. If anyone linked to our existing cases shows up, we'll know immediately," another analyst chimed in, tapping away at her keyboard.

"Good thinking," Jerry nodded approvingly. "How about the traffic? Anything out of the ordinary?"

"We've tagged a couple of vehicles that appeared more than once. Running them through the system now to see if they're registered to any known associates or shell companies we've been tracking," the first analyst replied.

"That could give us the break we need. Keep me posted on that," Jerry said, his voice tense with anticipation.

Sandra, meanwhile, was reviewing a digital map dotted with various points of interest. "If we link any of those vehicles to this location, it might be enough to get a warrant. We need something concrete to move forward."

"I agree. It's all about connecting the dots. Every little detail could be the key," Jerry mused, his eyes never straying far from the screens.

Just then, a soft ping sounded from one of the computers. An analyst perked up, eyes scanning the incoming data. "We have a hit. One of the vehicles that showed up twice is registered to a shell company that popped up in our financial trails."

"That's excellent," Jerry said, stepping closer. "Can we get a warrant based on this?"

"It's a strong lead. I'll compile the request and run it through legal. We should have something solid to go on by tomorrow," Sandra responded, already pulling up the necessary forms on her tablet.

"Perfect. Let's keep this momentum going. Every step forward is a step closer to shutting them down," Jerry stated firmly.

Sandra nodded, her focus sharp. "I'll handle the warrant. In the meantime, let's not take our eyes off this place. Anything can happen."

The room fell into a routine hum of activity as each member of the team continued their surveillance and data analysis. Jerry and Sandra stood side by side, watching the screens, knowing that each passing moment could bring the breakthrough they needed.

"This is it, Jerry. I can feel it. We're on the verge of something big," Sandra said quietly, her intuition on high alert.

"I hope you're right, Sandra. For Greendale's sake, I hope you're right," Jerry replied, his voice a mixture of hope and the heavy burden of responsibility.

They continued to watch, the weight of their mission hanging in the air, palpable and pressing. The surveillance room, with its flickering screens and constant murmur of voices, was the focal point of an intense and sprawling investigation that reached deep into the shadows of the city. As they stood vigilant, the line between night and day blurred, time marked only by the slow progress of their pursuit of justice.

In the confines of the bustling police station, Jerry and Sandra regrouped in the strategy room, the walls plastered with maps and evidence photos. The day had been long, but the mood was one of cautious optimism as they prepared to delve deeper into the network they were untangling.

"Sandra, do you have the warrant?" Jerry asked, starting the conversation with a key concern as he sipped from a cup of strong coffee.

"Yes, it came through an hour ago. We're clear to proceed with the raid first thing in the morning," Sandra replied, placing a stack of documents on the table. "All teams are briefed. I've triple-checked the entry points and potential escape routes. We're not giving them any room to breathe."

"Excellent. And what about the backup? I don't want any surprises," Jerry said, his experience dictating his thoroughness.

"We've got units on standby, and I've coordinated with the state police for additional manpower. They'll be out of sight but close enough to support if things get hairy," Sandra explained, her strategic planning evident in her detailed preparation.

"That's good to hear. Now, tell me about the intel updates. Anything new from the surveillance feeds?" Jerry asked, leaning over the table to look at some maps detailing the targeted location.

"The last 24 hours have been quiet. Too quiet, if you ask me," Sandra noted, her intuition tinged with suspicion. "It's possible they know we're coming."

Jerry nodded, his face set in a grim line. "We anticipated they might catch on. That's why we're moving fast. The longer we wait, the more time they have to dismantle their operation and disappear."

"Exactly," Sandra agreed, checking her digital device for any last-minute communications. "On another note, the tech team cracked another layer of encryption on the hard drives we seized. They've uncovered a series of transactions that tie back to our mystery player. Looks like we're on the right track."

"That's a significant breakthrough. Good work pushing the tech team. Have we managed to trace where those transactions lead?" Jerry inquired, his interest piqued.

"We're still working on that. The trail leads overseas, so it's complicated, but I have our best financial analysts on it," Sandra said, her determination to untangle the web evident.

"We need that information, Sandra. If we can figure out where the money's going, we might be able to predict their next move," Jerry emphasized, understanding the critical nature of financial intelligence in their line of work.

"I know, Jerry. I'm on it," Sandra reassured him. "Now, regarding tomorrow's operation, I suggest we go in at dawn. Less foot traffic and the cover of early morning will give us the element of surprise."

"Agreed. Let's make sure everyone's on the same page tonight. I don't want any miscommunication during the raid," Jerry stated, the weight of command heavy on his shoulders.

"Understood. I'll hold a final briefing before we head out. Everyone will know their roles," Sandra confirmed, her competent leadership providing a solid foundation for their plans.

As they finalized their strategy, the clock on the wall ticked steadily, marking the late hour. The station was quieter now, the hustle of the daytime shift replaced by the low murmur of night operations.

"We've got a big day ahead, Sandra. Let's make sure we end this chapter for good," Jerry said, a mix of hope and determination in his voice.

"We will, Jerry. We're ready," Sandra replied, her confidence a steady beacon in the complex storm of their investigation.

With their plans set, they gathered their papers and prepared to leave the strategy room. The morning would bring challenges, but Jerry and Sandra were ready to face them head-on, driven by a shared commitment to safeguard their city and bring down the criminal network that threatened its peace.

The predawn hours in Greendale were quiet and dim, the streets empty except for the occasional early riser starting their day. At the police station, Jerry and Sandra, along with their assembled task force, geared up for the operation that lay ahead. The air was thick with tension and anticipation as they reviewed their final plans.

Jerry checked each member of the team, ensuring their readiness. "Remember, we need to be precise and controlled. No unnecessary risks," he instructed, his voice low and steady under the hum of the operation center's activity.

Sandra, clad in tactical gear, double-checked her communications equipment. "All teams are synced. We'll have eyes on the ground and from the air. Everything's set for your go, Jerry."

With a nod, Jerry glanced at the large digital clock on the wall. It was nearly time. He turned to face the team, who looked back at him with a mix of resolve and readiness. "This is what we've prepared for. Let's dismantle this network and protect our city."

As the clock ticked closer to the hour, they loaded into the armored vehicles, the soft clatter of gear and the muffled sounds of boots on pavement filling the early morning air. The convoy moved out, silent and swift, blending into the still-dark streets towards their target location.

The ride was tense, each member of the team lost in their thoughts, mentally rehearsing their roles. Sandra monitored the communications, her expression focused and sharp, occasionally issuing quiet confirmations back to Jerry, who kept a vigilant watch over the progression of their units.

Upon arrival, the team deployed with practiced efficiency, surrounding the designated warehouse that had been under surveillance for the past few days. The stillness of the morning was punctured by the soft commands issued via radio, each team member moving into position with deliberate care.

Jerry and Sandra took a moment to survey the scene from their command post, a discreet spot that offered a clear view of the warehouse entrance. Sandra handed Jerry a pair of binoculars, and he scanned the area, his eyes catching every detail.

"Perimeter is secure," came the report over the radio. "Ready to breach on your command."

Jerry handed the binoculars back to Sandra and picked up the radio. "Proceed with the breach. Remember, secure and contain. I want a clean operation."

As the go-ahead was given, the silence of the early morning was shattered by the precise execution of the breach. The doors to the warehouse were swiftly and quietly opened, and the entry teams moved in. Within moments, the radio crackled with updates.

"Main area clear. Moving to secondary."

"Suspects in custody, no resistance."

"Secure the evidence, check for any traps or hidden compartments," Jerry instructed, his voice calm, his demeanor that of a seasoned leader overseeing a critical operation.

Inside the warehouse, the teams worked quickly to secure every piece of potential evidence, documenting and tagging items as they went. Sandra coordinated the effort, ensuring that each unit was thorough and that all protocols were followed.

As the operation wound down, the first light of dawn began to touch the sky, casting a pale blue over the scene. The warehouse, once a node in a sprawling criminal network, was now under control, its secrets ready to be laid bare by the police force.

Back at the command post, Jerry and Sandra reviewed the preliminary reports. The operation had been a success, and while there was still much to do, this victory was significant. They shared a brief look of mutual respect and understanding. They had taken a crucial step towards dismantling the network, protecting their city from the shadows that had lurked within it. As the city awoke, unaware of the night's events, Jerry and Sandra prepared to continue their work, driven by the duty to serve and protect.

Chapter 20
A New Normal

The aftermath of the successful raid lingered in the air at the police station as the morning rolled in. Jerry and Sandra, along with their key team members, gathered in the main conference room, maps and digital screens displaying the newly seized evidence and suspect profiles. The room buzzed with a sense of achievement, yet the weight of the ongoing investigation kept everyone grounded.

"Let's start with the evidence," Jerry said, addressing the room while pointing towards the screens displaying items recovered during the raid. "What do we have that can directly link the suspects to the higher echelons of the network?"

Sandra, organizing the digital files on her tablet, responded, "We've managed to secure several encrypted devices that I believe contain substantial communications between our local suspects and the upper levels. The tech team is working on cracking the encryption as we speak."

"That's critical. We need that information to map out the next layer of this network," Jerry replied, his eyes scanning the evidence photos. "What about financial documents? Any luck tracing the money flow?"

"We did find some ledgers and digital records. Preliminary analysis suggests they were moving large sums through shell companies. It's a complex web, but our financial analysts are on it. We should have a clearer picture by the end of the day," Sandra explained, her tone reflecting the urgency of their task.

"Good. Keep pressing on that front. The financial trail could lead us directly to the masterminds," Jerry noted, shifting his attention to the team leaders gathered around the table.

One of the team leaders, a seasoned detective, chimed in. "We've also taken several suspects into custody who we believe are mid-level managers within the organization. Interrogations are underway, and we're hoping to flip at least one of them to get more direct information."

"That's promising," Jerry said with a nod. "Make sure those interrogations are thorough. Use everything we've got to leverage them. We need insiders who are willing to talk."

"Absolutely, we're on it," the detective assured him, ready to get back to work.

Sandra added, "I've scheduled a debrief with all units involved in the raid. We need to ensure every piece of information is shared and analyzed. Sometimes, the smallest detail can be the key to breaking a case wide open."

"Let's make that a priority. Coordination and communication must be flawless," Jerry emphasized, looking around at his team. "This is a pivotal moment in our investigation. We've got the momentum now, and we can't afford to lose it."

As they wrapped up the meeting, each member of the team knew their roles and the high stakes involved. They dispersed with a renewed sense of purpose, heading to their respective tasks with determination.

Sandra lingered for a moment, reviewing her notes. "Jerry, we're getting close. I can feel it. This could be the breakthrough we've been waiting for."

Jerry, gathering his own notes, agreed, "Yes, we are close. But let's stay sharp. Overconfidence can lead to mistakes, and we can't afford any."

With a mutual nod of understanding, they left the conference room to continue their work. The station buzzed with activity, a hive of dedicated professionals working tirelessly. Outside, the city went about its day, largely unaware of the intricate battle being waged within the walls of the police station to keep its streets safe. As Jerry and Sandra moved through the corridors, their resolve was clear—they would see this through, no matter what it took.

The morning progressed swiftly at the Greendale Police Station as Jerry and Sandra delved deeper into the layers of evidence uncovered from the raid. In the subdued light of the evidence room, they worked side by side with forensic analysts, piecing together digital trails and paper trails that crisscrossed and tangled like the web of a meticulous spider.

The room, usually silent except for the occasional hum of machinery, was today filled with the low, intense murmur of officers and specialists discussing their findings. Charts adorned the walls, each one representing connections and flows of money, contacts, and communications that painted a complex picture of criminal enterprise.

Jerry, focused intensely on a series of encrypted emails that had just been decrypted, found the thread he had been hoping for—an exchange that hinted at a much larger and more organized operation than they had first anticipated. It referenced dates and transactions that aligned suspiciously with known criminal activities across the state.

Sandra, meanwhile, was absorbed in a ledger filled with coded entries. Her patience and keen eye for detail slowly unraveled the codes, revealing a ledger of payments that corresponded to suspicious imports flagged at the port last year. The names associated with these entries were pseudonyms, but the amounts and dates provided a tangible link to known suspects.

As they worked, the occasional exchange of information between them was terse and to the point, reflecting the urgency of their task.

"Jerry, look at this entry. Does the date March 22nd mean anything to you?" Sandra asked, her voice low as she pointed to a heavily annotated page in the ledger.

Jerry looked up from his screen, his mind racing through the timeline they had constructed. "Yes, that was the date of the first major shipment interception. It's the same day referenced in these emails. It can't be a coincidence."

"Exactly my thought. It's too direct to ignore. We need to cross-reference this with the shipping logs," Sandra replied, already pulling up the relevant files on her tablet.

The morning wore on, and the pieces of the puzzle began to fit together with increasing clarity. Each document, each decrypted message added depth to their understanding of the network. It was evident that they were dealing with an organization that had its tentacles deep in various illegal activities, each meticulously documented in their own cryptic way.

The work was meticulous and demanding. The room was filled with the soft clicking of keyboards, the occasional beep of a machine confirming a match, and the rustle of papers as files were consulted and notes taken. The concentration was palpable, each member of the team aware of the importance of their findings.

By late morning, they had compiled a preliminary report that outlined the connections between the suspects, the financial transactions, and the illicit activities. This report would serve as the basis for the next series of raids and investigations, aimed at dismantling the remaining structures of the network.

As they prepared to brief the rest of the team, Jerry and Sandra shared a moment of quiet acknowledgment of the progress they had made. The work was far from done, but they had uncovered vital information that brought them closer to their goal.

Stepping out of the evidence room, they were met with the hustle and bustle of the station, a stark contrast to the concentrated silence they had left behind. The city outside moved unknowingly above the undercurrents of the battle being waged in its depths. Jerry and Sandra, their resolve fortified by the morning's successes, were ready to take the next steps, knowing that each piece of evidence brought them closer to restoring peace to the streets of Greendale.

Late in the afternoon, Jerry and Sandra convened a meeting in the large briefing room filled with the core investigative team. They prepared to outline the connections and strategies identified from the morning's work, knowing that these would guide the next phases of the operation.

"Let's bring everyone up to speed," Jerry began, standing in front of the room where maps and diagrams were displayed prominently. "The evidence we've been analyzing has given us new insights into the organizational structure and the financial underpinnings of this network."

Sandra took over with a clicker in hand, pointing to a chart on the screen. "We've broken down the financial transactions into categories. These appear to be directly linked to specific criminal activities, including smuggling and bribery. The patterns were encrypted, but thanks to our tech team, we've managed to decode a significant portion."

One of the lead analysts chimed in, "The patterns aren't just random. There's a schedule and a system to their madness. For instance, large payments coincide with incoming shipments that we suspected were carrying contraband. It's all there, timed almost to the day."

Jerry nodded, absorbing the information. "Good work on that. It gives us a predictive edge. We can anticipate their moves and intercept more effectively. What about the personal communications? Anything that can lead us to higher-ups not yet in our net?"

Sandra switched to another slide showing intercepted messages. "Yes, several communications mention a figure known only as 'The Accountant.' We believe this person is key to the financial operations, possibly even the architect of their laundering schemes."

"Have we identified this Accountant?" Jerry asked, his interest piqued.

"Not yet," Sandra admitted, "but the clues suggest they're not just operating locally. We might be dealing with someone with international connections, which complicates things."

Jerry leaned forward, his hands clasped. "International or not, we need to find out who this person is. Their knowledge could unravel the entire network. I want surveillance increased on all known contacts. Someone must be in touch with this Accountant."

An operations officer spoke up, "We'll need to coordinate with international law enforcement for that. If this person is overseas, we're going to hit a lot of red tape."

"Start the process," Jerry directed firmly. "The sooner we start, the sooner we get through that tape. Sandra, keep pushing on the financial angle. It's our strongest lead right now."

Sandra nodded, already listing next steps in her notebook. "I'll also have the team enhance the analysis of past transactions. There might be overlooked patterns that could point us directly to 'The Accountant.'"

"As for the rest of you," Jerry continued, addressing the room, "maintain pressure on all fronts. Surveillance, analysis, field ops—stay sharp. We're making progress, but this is far from over."

The team members nodded, each visibly refocused by the meeting's revelations. They understood the stakes and the importance of their roles in the intricate dance of investigation and enforcement.

"Any questions?" Jerry looked around the room, ready to clarify or expand on any point.

One junior analyst raised a hand. "How are we ensuring our own security? After the last breach, it's clear they're not just going to sit back."

Sandra answered, "We've upgraded our systems and protocols. Plus, we're conducting internal reviews more frequently. Trust is good, but verification is better."

"Exactly," Jerry affirmed. "Stay vigilant, everyone. Now, let's get back to it. Every second counts."

The meeting adjourned with a renewed sense of urgency. Team members dispersed to their respective tasks, each piece of the puzzle they worked on bringing them closer to the heart of the shadow that had loomed over Greendale. Jerry and Sandra remained briefly, reviewing their notes.

"We're on the right track, Sandra. Keep the pressure high," Jerry said as they prepared to leave the room.

"We will," Sandra assured him, determination in her stride as they left the briefing room to continue their day—a day of relentless pursuit in the shadowy world of crime fighting.

As the sun began to set over Greendale, casting long shadows across the bustling police station, Jerry and Sandra found themselves back in the surveillance room, surrounded by the glow of multiple screens. The day had been long, but the air was still charged with a palpable sense of anticipation.

"Let's review what we've gathered today," Jerry suggested, his voice carrying a quiet intensity as he looked over the monitors.

Sandra, who was cross-referencing a digital document with the images on the screen, responded, "We've made significant headway. The patterns in financial transactions have given us a clearer picture of how deep this network runs. It's more extensive than we initially thought."

"Have we pinpointed any new transactions that might lead us directly to 'The Accountant'?" Jerry asked, focusing intently on a graph displayed on one of the screens.

"Yes, we have a few leads. There were several high-value transactions that didn't fit the usual pattern," Sandra replied, pulling up a detailed spreadsheet. "Look here and here," she pointed, "these transactions are anomalies. They're much larger and linked directly to an offshore account that was only briefly mentioned in one of the decrypted emails."

"That could be our in," Jerry noted, leaning in closer to examine the details. "Have we managed to trace where these transactions originated from?"

"Not completely, but we're getting there. The financial team managed to track down a possible intermediary—a shell company based in Luxembourg. It seems to be a key piece in their operation," Sandra explained, highlighting the company's name on her tablet.

"We need to dig deeper into that lead. It could open up a whole new angle for us. What about the local operations? Any movements there that we should be aware of?" Jerry inquired, his mind already racing through the implications.

"The surveillance teams reported less activity than usual. It's like they're laying low, probably sensing that we're onto them. But we did catch a few of our known suspects meeting at one of the warehouses we have under watch," Sandra reported, switching the screen to show CCTV footage of the meeting.

"Keep a constant watch on that warehouse. If they're meeting there, it's important. It might even be the next point we hit," Jerry decided quickly, his decision-making sharp and focused.

"Already done. I've increased surveillance and have a response team on standby in case they start moving anything substantial," Sandra affirmed, updating the surveillance schedule on her tablet.

"As for the anomalies in the transactions, I want daily updates. Any slight change, any new transaction, I want to know immediately," Jerry continued, his strategy clear in his directive.

"You'll have it. I've set up alerts for any activity involving those accounts. We'll catch it the moment it happens," Sandra promised, her dedication evident.

"Good," Jerry said with a nod. "We're closing in, Sandra. I can feel it. This network won't know what hit them."

Sandra smiled slightly, her fatigue masked by the adrenaline of their progress. "Yes, we are. And when we do hit them, it'll be with everything we've got."

As they prepared to wrap up for the evening, Jerry paused, looking around the surveillance room filled with officers and analysts diligently monitoring every screen. "Let's keep up the pressure. Great work today, everyone. Let's bring this home."

With a final review of the screens, Jerry and Sandra left the room, their steps echoing softly in the corridor. The station quieted down as night fully descended, but the work never truly stopped. In the darkened corners of the city, in the glow of computer screens, the battle against the shadows continued, relentless and unwavering.

Chapter 21
Reflections

As the first light of dawn began to streak across the sky, Jerry and Sandra reconvened in the main strategy room of the police station, where the walls were lined with maps and photos of suspects and locations. Both looked weary but determined, ready to push forward in their relentless pursuit of the criminal network.

"Let's get straight to the point," Jerry said as he sipped his morning coffee, the steam curling up into the cool air of the room. "What's the status on the Luxembourg connection? Any breakthroughs with that shell company?"

Sandra, who was flipping through her tablet, looked up. "Yes, we've made some progress overnight. Our counterparts in Luxembourg have been cooperative. They've confirmed the company is a front and have frozen its assets. We're digging into the transactions to trace them back to our main suspects."

"That's excellent news," Jerry responded, his eyes lighting up with a mix of relief and anticipation. "It could lead us directly to the higher-ups. Have we managed to get any closer to identifying 'The Accountant'?"

"Not directly," Sandra admitted, her fingers pausing on the screen. "But the freeze on the Luxembourg accounts has stirred up some chatter. We intercepted a few panicked communications this morning. They're feeling the pressure."

"Good. Let's use that. Increase surveillance on all known associates. If they're scrambling, they might slip up," Jerry strategized, his mind racing through potential scenarios.

"I've already instructed the surveillance teams to do just that. We should expect some movement soon," Sandra confirmed, marking a few notes in her digital planner.

"And the local operations?" Jerry inquired, shifting his focus to more immediate concerns.

"The warehouse surveillance paid off. They started moving something big last night—could be evidence they don't want us to find. I've got a team ready to raid as soon as we have just cause," Sandra reported, her tone indicating readiness for swift action.

"Make sure they're prepared for anything. This group has proven they're not above violence," Jerry cautioned, his experience dictating a careful approach.

"Understood," Sandra nodded, her expression serious. "Switching gears for a moment, how are we handling the media? There's been increased interest since the raid last week."

"We keep it tight. Only the information we want to release goes out. No details on ongoing operations or anything that could compromise our position," Jerry stated firmly, aware of the delicate balance between transparency and operational security.

Sandra agreed, "I'll brief the communications team again. We can't afford any leaks."

"As for our next steps," Jerry continued, leaning back in his chair and crossing his arms, "once we know more from the Luxembourg lead and the warehouse, we may need to coordinate with federal agencies. This is bigger than we thought, and it might go beyond our jurisdiction."

"I'll set up preliminary contacts. It's better to have them on board early rather than scrambling to get them involved later," Sandra suggested, always thinking a step ahead.

"Exactly," Jerry said with a nod. "We're doing well, Sandra, but we can't let up. This network is extensive and well-funded. We need to stay ahead of them at every turn."

Sandra looked back at her screens, her mind already on the multitude of tasks at hand. "We will, Jerry. They've had free rein for too long. It's time to end that."

With their plans outlined and their strategy set, Jerry and Sandra prepared to continue their day, the weight of their responsibility ever-present but tempered by their commitment to see justice done. As they left the strategy room, the sun had fully risen, casting light into the darker corners of the city, much like their investigation was doing to its hidden criminal elements.

In the dimly lit surveillance room of the police station, Jerry and Sandra were joined by a select group of their top analysts and detectives, each one focused intently on the live feeds from various strategic points around the city. The morning's revelations had spurred a series of actions that were now unfolding in real-time.

"Alright, let's go through the updates. Any movements from our primary suspects?" Jerry asked, his eyes scanning the multiple screens displaying drone footage and street-level surveillance.

"We've noticed increased activity at several properties linked to our main targets. In particular, there's been a lot of coming and going from the warehouse we raided last week. It seems like they're trying to clean house," one of the detectives reported, pointing to a specific screen showing a busy industrial area.

"That aligns with our intel suggesting they might be moving the last of whatever they didn't want us to find during the initial raid," Sandra added, her voice steady but concerned. "We need to decide quickly how we want to approach this."

"Do we have enough to go in again?" Jerry questioned, turning to look at Sandra directly.

"Not yet. We need just a bit more to justify another raid. However, I've placed undercover assets in the vicinity to keep a closer eye on the situation. They're ready to act the moment we get something solid," Sandra explained, coordinating the surveillance operations with precision.

"Good. Keep the pressure. If they're cleaning house, they might slip and move something important in their haste," Jerry suggested, looking back at the live feeds. "Any word from our contacts overseas about the Luxembourg situation?"

"Yes, actually. Our liaison reported that the frozen accounts have triggered a series of financial moves that are traceable. They're pulling out all stops to secure their funds, which means they're getting nervous," another analyst chimed in, his eyes not leaving the financial tracking software on his laptop.

"That's exactly what we need. Use their panic to our advantage. Every transaction they make in response can lead us directly to other assets and maybe even 'The Accountant' we've been chasing," Jerry stated, hopeful that this could be the lead they needed to dismantle the financial backbone of the network.

Sandra nodded in agreement. "I'll ensure our financial team doubles down on that. The more they move their money, the more they expose their network."

"And the chatter? Anything from the communications intercepts?" Jerry inquired, always keen on gathering as much information as possible from all available sources.

"Actually, yes," Sandra pulled up another screen, which displayed intercepted text messages. "They're definitely aware of the pressure. There's talk of meeting up to discuss 'new management strategies,' which could mean they're planning to restructure to avoid our reach."

"That could be a crucial meeting. Do we have a time and place?" Jerry asked, his mind already planning the next steps.

"Not yet, but I suspect we'll know soon. Our source is getting close to one of the key players who might be involved in organizing it," Sandra replied, updating Jerry on the undercover operations.

"Keep me posted on that. If we can get into that meeting, it could lead us directly to the upper echelons, maybe even 'The Accountant' himself," Jerry mused, considering the possibilities.

"We will, Jerry. We're closer than ever," Sandra reassured him, her confidence bolstered by the progress they were making.

As they continued to monitor the screens, coordinate with field agents, and analyze incoming data, the room was a hive of activity. Every officer and analyst knew the critical nature of their tasks and the impact their work had on the safety of Greendale.

"Let's stay sharp, everyone. We're making progress, and it's only a matter of time before we crack this wide open," Jerry encouraged his team, standing tall amidst the buzz of operations.

Sandra nodded, her focus returning to the screens, ready to guide their team through the intricate dance of surveillance and response. As the city outside moved unknowingly about its daily business, inside the police station, a critical battle was being waged—one that would determine the fate of many.

Late afternoon shadows began to lengthen across the Greendale Police Station as Jerry and Sandra convened once more in the strategy room, surrounded by the vital tools of their trade: screens displaying maps, intercepted communications, and surveillance footage. They were joined by the financial analysts and the tech team, who had been working tirelessly to decode the data trails that led deeper into the criminal network.

Jerry, standing by the main screen, adjusted the display to show a complex web of financial transactions. "We've traced the latest series of transfers to three key accounts. These link directly back to our primary suspects, and possibly even to 'The Accountant' we've been chasing. What do we know about these accounts?"

One of the financial analysts stepped forward, holding a tablet loaded with graphs and figures. "These accounts have been quite active over the last 48 hours. We've noticed a pattern consistent with previous money laundering operations we've uncovered. There's a good chance these movements are their response to our recent actions."

"Are we able to freeze these accounts, cut off their resources?" Jerry asked, his gaze intense as he considered their options.

"We've started the process with our international partners. However, due to jurisdiction issues, it might take some time to fully block their access," Sandra added, her expression one of focused concern.

"This is crucial; we need those accounts frozen. Every minute they have access is another minute they can use those funds to regroup or disappear," Jerry stressed, his frustration evident.

"We're pushing hard on that front," Sandra reassured him, "I've got calls in with our contacts in law enforcement overseas. They understand the urgency."

As they discussed their financial strategy, the tech team had been quietly working at another station. One of the technicians called out, "Jerry, Sandra, you might want to see this."

They approached the workstation where the tech team had managed to decrypt a batch of emails that had previously been secured. The screen displayed an email chain that included detailed instructions for transferring large sums of money.

"Look at this," the lead technician pointed out, "These emails mention a meeting. It looks like they're planning to consolidate their remaining assets. They're getting ready for something big."

"Do we have a time and location for this meeting?" Jerry asked, his mind already racing through potential tactical responses.

"The details are vague, but we're close to breaking through their last layer of encryption. We should have something concrete by tonight," the technician replied, his fingers poised over the keyboard, ready to dive back into the data.

"That could be our best shot at catching them in the act, and perhaps finally identifying 'The Accountant,'" Sandra said, turning to Jerry with a look of resolve.

"Keep at it. Every piece of information brings us closer to shutting them down

----

As the evening waned into night, the dimly lit backroom of Greendale's downtown diner played host to a pivotal meeting between Jerry, Sandra, and a few trusted members of their task force. They gathered around a scarred wooden table, strewn with papers and digital devices, under the buzz of a flickering fluorescent light. The weight of their findings pressed heavily in the air, thick with the scent of stale coffee and determination.

"Alright, we've got a lot to sift through. Where do we stand?" Jerry asked, his voice a gravelly echo in the cramped space.

Sandra, looking over a laptop screen filled with digital maps and notes, responded, "Our leads from the warehouse raid have opened up several potential threads. We're particularly close to pinpointing 'The Accountant's' operations. This might be the break we've been waiting for."

One of the detectives, a young woman with sharp eyes, chimed in, "We've also managed to decrypt more communications. It looks like there's a bigger plan in play here, not just the scattered hits we thought. They're organized, planning something large."

"And our field teams?" Jerry leaned forward, his hands clasped tightly.

"They're in place. Based on the patterns we've seen, we expect some movement tonight. We're ready to intercept as soon as we get your go," Sandra explained, marking a point on the map displayed on her screen.

Jerry nodded, his gaze lingering on the map. "Good work. Now, about these communications—any more mentions of 'The Accountant'?"

"Yes, several. All cryptic, but it's clear he's central to their financial operations. There's mention of a meet-up soon. If we can tap into that, it could lead us right to him," the detective added, tapping a key to bring up the decrypted messages on a projector screen.

"The sooner, the better. We need to disrupt their cash flow to really shake them up," Jerry stated firmly, standing to stretch his legs, his mind racing through the implications.

Sandra glanced at her watch, then back at Jerry. "It's almost time. We should get ready to move out. Are we all clear on the action plan?"

Jerry gave a brief nod, his expression hardening with resolve. "Yes. Tonight, we hit them with everything we've got. It's time they learned Greendale isn't open for their business."

As the team gathered their gear and prepared to leave, the hum of activity grew. Outside, the sun had set, leaving the streets bathed in the glow of street lamps. Sandra and Jerry shared a final look, an unspoken acknowledgment of the risks and necessity of their next steps.

Stepping out into the cool night air, they moved with purpose, driven by the urgency of their mission. The town of Greendale, usually quiet at this hour, was unaware of the silent war waged in its shadows. But for Jerry, Sandra, and their team, the evening was just beginning—a critical juncture in their relentless pursuit of justice and safety.

Chapter 22
Unsettled Scores

Dawn was just breaking over Greendale, casting a pale light over the quiet streets that belied the intense activity of the night before. Jerry and Sandra had spent the early hours coordinating a series of targeted actions against the criminal network that had ensnared their city. As the first rays of sunlight filtered through the blinds of the makeshift command center, it highlighted the tired but determined faces of the team.

The operation had been meticulously planned, based on the wealth of information uncovered from the financial trails and the communications decrypted by their tech team. Now, as they gathered around the cluttered table strewn with coffee cups and high-tech equipment, the atmosphere was tense with the anticipation of the results.

Jerry stood at the head of the table, looking over the maps and notes spread out before him. He was deep in thought, piecing together the last bits of information that could lead to the apprehension of key figures within the network. His focus was occasionally interrupted by updates coming in over the radios, each one marking progress or setbacks in real-time.

"Teams are reporting in," Sandra said, breaking the silence as she listened to the crackling radio. "Alpha and Delta teams have secured their targets. No casualties reported."

Jerry nodded, his expression unreadable. "And the others?"

"Some resistance at the northern sites, but under control. Bravo team is still engaged," she replied, her voice steady despite the undercurrent of stress.

The room was filled with the soft glow of computer screens, each one displaying different aspects of the operation. Maps with GPS markers showed the movements of their teams and suspects, while others streamed video from body cams worn by officers in the field. The technology made it possible to command the complex operation from a distance, but it also laid bare the stark realities of the risks involved.

As updates continued to flow in, Jerry and Sandra worked seamlessly together, their years of experience evident in their calm, efficient communication. They were a well-oiled machine, anticipating each other's orders, adjusting tactics on the fly.

Outside, the city was waking up, oblivious to the crucial operations that had been playing out in the shadows. Commuters began their day, coffee shops started grinding beans, and morning joggers took to the parks, all under the watchful eyes of law enforcement who protected them silently.

Back in the command center, the mood was cautiously optimistic as more positive reports came in. Yet, both Jerry and Sandra knew the day was far from over. The network they were dismantling was extensive and deeply embedded within the city's underbelly. Today's victories were significant, but the war was not yet won.

As they prepared for the next phase of operations, there was a brief moment of quiet. Jerry looked out the window, watching the city come to life. He then turned back to his team, ready to keep pushing forward.

"Let's keep the pressure on. We've got them on the ropes; let's not give them a moment to regroup," he stated, his voice a resonant command that filled the room.

Sandra, checking her watch, nodded in agreement. "I'll coordinate with the units. We'll maintain surveillance on all known locations and prepare for further searches. We're not done yet."

The team mobilized quickly, energized by the morning's successes and the leadership of Jerry and Sandra. As the day unfolded, their relentless pursuit continued, each officer and detective playing a crucial role in the intricate dance of justice that sought to reclaim Greendale from the grips of organized crime. The morning light grew stronger, a symbol of the new hope that dawned with each breakthrough they achieved.

As the morning progressed, the operations room was abuzz with the constant flow of information. Jerry stood by a large table cluttered with papers and digital devices, studying the latest reports with an intensity that reflected the gravity of their undertaking. Sandra, meanwhile, was on a call, her tone firm as she coordinated efforts with other agencies involved in the operation.

Outside, the city of Greendale went about its day, the normalcy of the scene contrasting sharply with the urgency inside the police station. The sun climbed higher, casting shadows that shifted subtly across the room, marking the passage of time in a space where it seemed to stand still.

"Update on the northern sectors," Sandra announced, ending her call and turning to Jerry. "We've secured all but one of the targeted locations. The team is still working on the last site, but they've encountered some complications."

Jerry looked up from the map, his brow furrowed. "Complications? What kind of complications?"

"Structural issues within the building. It's slowing down the search. But the team is adapting. They're bringing in additional support to ensure it's done thoroughly," Sandra explained, her gaze returning to the laptop screen, where she monitored the live feeds streaming from various team body cams.

Nodding, Jerry returned his attention to the reports. Each piece of paper, each digital entry was a critical part of a larger puzzle they were desperately trying to solve. He shuffled through the documents, pulling out one that detailed financial transactions linked to suspected members of the criminal network. His fingers traced lines of numbers and names, connecting them with the faces of suspects displayed on a nearby digital board.

In another part of the room, a technician called out, "We've got something you'll want to see." Jerry and Sandra approached, watching as the tech pulled up security footage from a hidden camera they had placed near one of the suspect's frequent haunts.

On the screen, a group of individuals could be seen transferring boxes from a van into a nondescript building. "This was from last night. Looks like they were moving something important," the technician explained, enhancing the image to try and identify faces or license plate numbers.

"Keep an eye on that building. Any change in activity, I want to know immediately," Jerry directed, his voice steady but filled with urgency.

"Will do," the technician affirmed, turning back to his array of screens.

The morning wore on, with Jerry and Sandra barely taking a moment to rest. They moved from station to station within the operations room, reviewing data, making calls, and issuing orders. Their focus was unwavering, driven by a shared commitment to end the reign of the criminal network that had plagued their city.

As noon approached, the room was filled with a low hum of conversations and the clicking of keyboards. Reports continued to come in, each one adding a small, crucial piece to the evolving picture of the network's operations. Sandra paused beside Jerry, watching as he annotated a map with various notes.

"We're getting closer, Jerry. Every bit of information is another step toward shutting them down," Sandra said, her voice a mixture of fatigue and determination.

Jerry didn't look up from his work. "We are. But there's still a lot to do. Let's keep pushing."

Their dedication was a beacon for the rest of the team, who continued their tasks with renewed vigor, knowing that each action taken was a vital strike against the shadows that had loomed over Greendale for too long. As the day unfolded, the operations room remained a nexus of activity, a command center from which the battle against darkness was directed, with Jerry and Sandra leading the charge.

The afternoon was waning as Jerry and Sandra convened in a quieter corner of the operations room, away from the flurry of activity. Maps and screens around them continued to display the ongoing efforts of their teams across Greendale, but here they took a moment to assess and strategize their next moves based on the latest influx of data.

"Where do we stand with the extraction of data from the devices we confiscated last night?" Jerry began, his tone indicating he was ready to cut straight to the chase.

"We've made significant headway," Sandra replied, tapping through her tablet to bring up a report. "The tech team has managed to break through the last of the encryption. They've uncovered a series of messages that are proving to be very revealing."

"Revealing in what way?" Jerry leaned in, his interest piqued as he glanced over the digital report Sandra was holding.

"The messages outline a meeting scheduled for tomorrow night. It appears it's going to include several high-ranking members of the network. We think this might even include the elusive 'Accountant' we've been chasing," Sandra explained, her eyes not leaving the tablet as she scrolled through the detailed analysis.

"That's exactly the kind of break we needed. We should focus our resources on this meeting. It could be our chance to catch them all together," Jerry said, a strategic spark in his eye.

"I agree. I've already set up surveillance on the suspected location, and I'm arranging for additional undercover assets to be nearby," Sandra confirmed, her readiness matching Jerry's.

"Do we have enough for a warrant, or do we need more to go on?" Jerry asked, considering the legal ramifications.

"We're close. I think with a bit more surveillance tonight, we can confirm the identities of those attending. That should give us the leverage we need for a warrant," Sandra suggested, already thinking ahead to the logistics of such an operation.

"Make it happen. This could be a major turning point for us," Jerry stated firmly, his gaze fixed on a screen showing real-time movements in the area of interest.

"As for the rest of the network, let's not ease up on them either. Keep pressure where we can, and maintain surveillance on all known associates.

We can't afford to let anyone slip through the cracks now," Jerry continued, outlining a comprehensive approach.

"Already on it," Sandra replied, her tone as resolute as ever. "I'll also make sure our communication lines are secure. We can't risk any leaks about tomorrow's operation."

"Good thinking," Jerry nodded in approval. "And keep the council updated. They're anxious about the operation's progress, especially with the public safety concerns."

"I'll draft an update for the council this evening," Sandra said, noting down this additional task.

The sun began to set outside, casting long shadows across the room that seemed to echo the lengthening reach of their investigation. Jerry and Sandra remained at their post, their discussions a quiet counterpoint to the buzz of activity that continued around them.

As they wrapped up their strategic session, Jerry stood, stretching slightly. "It's been a long few days," he remarked, a rare admission of fatigue.

"It has," Sandra agreed, "but hopefully, it'll all be worth it after tomorrow."

With a mutual nod, they returned to their tasks, each aware of the critical nature of the next 24 hours. The weight of responsibility was heavy, but so was their determination to see the operation through, to restore peace and order to Greendale's streets. As the day shifted into evening, the operations room remained a beacon of light and activity in the fading light.

The evening had deepened into night, casting a veil of darkness over Greendale. Inside the police station, the operations room was still a hub of activity, though the atmosphere had shifted to a more focused, intense anticipation of the coming operation. Jerry stood by a window, looking out over the city he had sworn to protect, his mind tracing the myriad paths of the investigation that had led them here.

Sandra approached him, her footsteps soft against the hum of the computers and low conversations of the remaining staff. She handed him a cup of coffee, her expression serious. "Here, you'll need this. We've got a long night ahead."

Jerry accepted the coffee with a nod, his gaze still fixed outside. "Thank you, Sandra. Any updates from the tech team on the surveillance setup for tomorrow?"

"It's all in place. Cameras and mics at every possible angle. We won't miss a thing," Sandra assured him, checking her digital device for real-time updates. "And the undercover assets are in position. They'll blend in with the evening crowd at the venue."

"That's good to hear," Jerry said, finally turning from the window. He sipped his coffee, feeling the warmth seep into his tired bones. "We need a clean operation. It's crucial we get this right."

"We will," Sandra replied with quiet confidence. She looked up from her device, her eyes meeting Jerry's. "Everyone's prepared, and we've double-checked all contingencies. We won't get a better chance than this to take down the core of the network."

Jerry set his coffee down and walked over to the large table littered with maps and documents. He traced a route with his finger, deep in thought. After a moment, he looked up at Sandra. "Once this is over, we'll need to move fast on the follow-up. This network is extensive; taking out the leadership will cause ripples. We need to be ready to manage the fallout."

"We've already started planning for that," Sandra assured him. "I've scheduled a strategy session first thing after the operation. We'll need to reassess and realign our resources."

The clock ticked on, marking the late hour, but neither Jerry nor Sandra showed signs of leaving. They moved through the operations room, checking in with different teams, ensuring everything was set for the morning's crucial operation. Each team member responded with a nod or a thumbs-up, their faces set with determination and focus.

Back at his desk, Jerry reviewed the final details of the operation. He looked over every element, from entry and exit strategies to emergency response plans. Sandra joined him after a while, standing beside his chair, looking over his shoulder at the documents.

"We've done all we can," Jerry finally said, leaning back in his chair. "Now, it's up to the team and a bit of luck."

Sandra placed a reassuring hand on his shoulder. "They're ready, thanks to your leadership. We'll see this through, Jerry. We'll see it through to the end."

As they prepared to catch a few hours of rest before the operation, the station settled down into a watchful quiet. The night outside was still, but the energy inside the station was like the calm before a storm, poised and waiting to break at dawn. Jerry and Sandra, united in their resolve, were ready to lead their team through whatever the next hours would bring. Their commitment to justice was unwavering, a steadfast beacon in the challenging times ahead.

Chapter 23
Final Stand

The early morning hours in Greendale were quiet, the streets nearly empty as the city slept. Inside the police station, however, the tension was palpable. Jerry and Sandra, along with their core team, were making the final preparations for the pivotal operation that was set to unfold at dawn.

"Okay, let's go through this one last time," Jerry said, his voice steady and clear, cutting through the murmur of last-minute activity. He stood in front of a digital map displayed on the wall, pointing to various locations highlighted on the screen. "Sandra, confirm the positions of our undercover assets."

Sandra, her eyes on her tablet, responded without missing a beat. "All assets are in position around the venue. We have visual confirmation from two; the others are on standby. They're ready to move on your command."

"Good. And the surveillance setups?" Jerry continued, his gaze shifting to the tech team on the other side of the room.

"We've got eyes and ears on every angle. All feeds are live and recording. There's no way anything happens in that area without us knowing," one of the tech specialists assured him, adjusting the feeds displayed on multiple screens.

Jerry nodded, satisfied with the response. He turned back to Sandra, "What about local law enforcement support?"

"They're all briefed and in position. We have uniformed units blocking off nearby streets under the pretext of a routine inspection. It should keep the area clear without raising suspicion," Sandra explained, her tone indicating the precision of their planning.

"Excellent. Let's talk through the approach once more," Jerry said, shifting his focus to the tactical aspect of their operation. "Once we confirm the targets are on site, we'll give the signal to move in. I want a smooth entry; minimal force unless absolutely necessary. We can't afford any mistakes."

"Understood, Jerry. All teams are aware of the rules of engagement. We're to detain and secure, not escalate," Sandra affirmed, her expression serious as she relayed the final orders through her headset.

"And our communication lines?" Jerry asked, knowing that in operations like this, communication was as vital as action.

"Secured and double-checked. We have a direct line to all team leaders, and backups in place should anything go down," Sandra confirmed, her efficiency evident in the thoroughness of her preparations.

Jerry took a deep breath, surveying the room filled with dedicated officers and agents. "This is it, everyone. We've worked hard to get to this point. Let's bring them down and bring them to justice. Stay sharp, stay safe, and look out for each other."

Sandra stepped up beside him, her presence a solid support. "We're ready, Jerry. Let's do this."

As the clock ticked closer to the operation's go-time, the team members performed final checks on their equipment and communications devices. Each member was a blend of focus and adrenaline, prepared for the challenges ahead.

Jerry and Sandra took a moment to themselves, standing slightly apart from the hustle and activity. "No matter what happens, we've done everything we can to prepare for this. I'm proud of this team," Jerry said quietly, a rare hint of emotion in his voice.

Sandra nodded, her eyes meeting his. "I am too. Let's bring them home, Jerry."

With that, they turned their attention back to the operation, ready to lead their team into one of the most significant mornings in Greendale's recent history. The city was still dark, but as dawn approached, the light began to seep through the horizon, symbolizing the new hope that justice would soon be served.

Dawn was breaking, casting a soft glow over the city of Greendale as the operation swung into full gear. The quiet of the morning was a stark contrast to the flurry of activity inside the unmarked vehicles that lined the streets adjacent to the target location. Jerry and Sandra, stationed in the lead vehicle, monitored the situation through live feeds transmitted to their laptops.

As the light grew stronger, it revealed the outlines of the decrepit warehouse where the high-stakes meeting of the criminal network was supposed to take place. The area was cordoned off discreetly by law enforcement under the guise of a routine operation, with officers positioned strategically, blending in with the early morning workers starting their shifts.

Inside the warehouse, hidden cameras installed by the tech team provided a clear view of the interior. The screens flickered occasionally as figures began to arrive, each person's entry logged and cross-referenced instantly with the database of known suspects.

Jerry watched intently, his focus never wavering from the screens. He was looking for any sign of 'The Accountant,' the elusive figure whose capture could potentially dismantle the financial backbone of the criminal enterprise. Next to him, Sandra kept an eye on the communication channels, ensuring that every piece of information was relayed accurately and immediately to all units involved.

The operation was the culmination of months of meticulous planning and investigation. Every agent and officer knew their role, the silence in the vehicles punctuated only by the occasional crackle of the radio confirming positions and movements.

As the sky lightened, a subtle tension hung in the air, mirroring the anticipation that built up among the team. Sandra finally broke the silence in their vehicle, whispering into her headset, "All units, stand by. Targets are on site. Repeat, all targets are on site."

Jerry gave a slight nod, his hand hovering over the radio, ready to give the go-ahead to move in. His other hand was clenched tightly around his knee, the only outward sign of the pressure he felt. This moment was critical, and everything hinged on the precision and timing of what was about to unfold.

The warehouse was now fully occupied, with the last of the suspects having slipped through the large, rusted doors, which creaked slightly as they closed. On the screens, the suspects congregated, unsuspecting of the eyes watching their every move.

With a deep breath, Jerry picked up the radio. "On my mark," he said quietly, his voice steady despite the adrenaline that surged through him. He waited, watching as the suspects settled, the final pieces of their illicit puzzle coming together in front of the hidden cameras.

Then, with a single word, "Now," Jerry set the operation into motion. Like a well-oiled machine, the teams moved. Doors were breached, and officers swarmed the building with practiced efficiency and calm authority.

The suspects, caught by surprise, were quickly subdued and handcuffed. No shots were fired; the operation was clean, just as Jerry had intended. He and Sandra stepped out of their vehicle, moving towards the warehouse to oversee the final arrests.

As the suspects were led out into the burgeoning daylight, the sense of accomplishment was palpable among the team, but so was the recognition of the road still ahead. They had struck a significant blow against the network, yet the battle against crime in Greendale was far from over.

Jerry and Sandra stood side by side, watching as the suspects were secured in police vehicles. The early morning light cast long shadows on the ground, shadows that seemed to stretch far beyond the warehouse, hinting at the lingering challenges they faced. But for now, a crucial victory was theirs, and it was a moment to acknowledge the skill and bravery of their team.

After the successful operation, the atmosphere at the police station was subdued yet charged with a cautious optimism. The suspects, including several high-ranking members of the criminal network, were now in custody, their interrogation imminent. Jerry and Sandra had returned to the strategy room, which was quieter now, the maps and screens still displaying the remnants of the morning's activities.

Sandra was at her desk, reviewing the initial reports from the raid. Each document detailed the evidence collected, from financial records to encrypted digital devices that might hold the key to dismantling the remaining network structure. Jerry, meanwhile, stood by the window, watching the activity in the parking lot below where officers were securing the evidence in the forensic units.

"We did well today," Jerry finally said, breaking the silence. His voice was reflective, tinged with the fatigue of the long hours they had put in.

"We did," Sandra agreed, looking up from her papers. "But this is just the beginning. There's a lot of work ahead to ensure this sticks."

Jerry nodded, his gaze still fixed outside. "I know. The interrogations will be crucial. We need to get them talking."

Sandra stood, joining him at the window. "The team is ready. We've got our best people on it. They know how important this is."

The room fell silent again, the weight of their responsibility settling around them like a heavy cloak. They both understood the complexity of the task ahead. Breaking the criminal network was one thing; ensuring the prosecutions stuck and that the trials were successful was another.

"How are the teams holding up?" Jerry asked after a moment, turning to face Sandra, concern evident in his expression.

"They're tired but motivated. Today's success has given everyone a boost. They see the results of their hard work," Sandra responded, her voice imbued with pride for her team.

"That's good to hear. We'll need to maintain that momentum," Jerry replied, his thoughts already shifting to the next phases of their operation.

Sandra nodded, then glanced back at her desk strewn with reports and digital devices. "I'll start compiling the evidence for the prosecution. The sooner we get everything in order, the better."

Jerry took a deep breath, his mind racing with the tasks that lay ahead. "And I'll oversee the interrogation process. We need to ensure we're extracting every possible piece of information."

As the morning gave way to afternoon, the strategy room began to fill again with officers and analysts, each returning to their post-operation duties. The buzz of conversation slowly built up, a stark contrast to the earlier quiet.

Jerry and Sandra continued to coordinate the operation's aftermath, their experienced hands guiding the many moving parts. The successes of the morning were just one part of a larger battle, one that would require every ounce of their dedication and resolve.

In the corridors of the police station, the sense of purpose was palpable. Each officer, each detective carried the weight of their duty with a solemn pride, aware of the stakes involved. The city of Greendale depended on their vigilance and their ability to follow through.

As the day progressed, Jerry and Sandra remained at the heart of the operation, their leadership critical in steering their team through the complex web of crime they were determined to dismantle. The challenge was immense, but so was their commitment to seeing justice served.

Late in the afternoon, Jerry and Sandra convened an urgent meeting with the key members of their investigative team in the strategy room, the urgency of their recent successes casting a serious tone over the gathering.

"We've made significant inroads," Jerry began, his voice echoing slightly in the quiet room, "but our work isn't done. We need to capitalize on the momentum. What's the status of the interrogations?"

Sandra, looking over her notes before responding, stated, "We've had some breakthroughs. Two of the suspects are cooperating, providing details that confirm much of what we suspected about the network's operations and their reach."

"That's excellent," Jerry responded, leaning forward with interest. "Do we have anything that directly ties the remaining suspects to the operations, something concrete we can use for further charges?"

"One of the cooperators mentioned a series of transactions that we hadn't traced yet. They're going to provide account numbers and dates. It could be the evidence we need to solidify our case against the higher-ups still at large," Sandra explained, shuffling through her digital tablet to pull up relevant data.

"Good. We need to move quickly on that information. Verify it, cross-reference it with our existing data, and prepare it for the prosecutors," Jerry instructed, his tone decisive.

"I'm on it," Sandra assured him. "I'll have the financial team work through the night if necessary."

"What about the material from the warehouse raid?" Jerry shifted his focus, his strategic mind mapping out their next moves.

"We're still cataloging it, but so far, we've uncovered more encrypted devices and paperwork that could potentially outline the entire structure of their operation," replied one of the lead forensic analysts, who was also present at the meeting.

"That could be a gold mine. Prioritize decrypting those devices. Any information on how they communicate, how they move money or goods, could help us prevent future operations," Jerry pointed out, his gaze steady on the forensic analyst.

"Understood, we're treating it as high priority," the analyst responded, noting down Jerry's instructions.

"And what's our strategy moving forward?" Sandra brought the conversation back to the broader picture. "We've disrupted their operations, but to truly dismantle this network, we need a comprehensive approach."

Jerry nodded, "We continue to pressure all known associates. Surveillance remains tight. And we start looking at their international connections more closely. We know they're not operating in a vacuum."

"Exactly," Sandra agreed. "I suggest we also enhance our cooperation with international law enforcement. We need to cut off any potential escape routes or financial safe havens."

"That's an excellent point. Set up a meeting with our federal contacts. Let's ensure they're fully briefed and on board with our next steps," Jerry decided, seeing the critical need for a coordinated effort.

The meeting continued with discussions on logistics, legal strategies, and operational tactics. Each member of the team was fully engaged, offering insights and suggestions. The room was a hive of activity, reflective of the importance and intensity of their work.

As the meeting drew to a close, Jerry looked around at his team, a sense of pride swelling within him. "This is outstanding work, everyone. We're not just reacting anymore; we're staying two steps ahead. Let's keep it that way."

Sandra, gathering her materials, echoed Jerry's sentiments. "We're making a real difference. Let's keep the pressure up and close this case out strong."

With the setting sun casting long shadows into the room, the team dispersed, each member motivated by the progress and aware of the challenges that lay ahead. Jerry and Sandra lingered for a moment, reviewing their notes.

"We've got them on the run, Sandra. Let's finish this," Jerry said quietly, determination lining his features.

"We will, Jerry. We will," Sandra affirmed, equally resolute.

Together, they left the strategy room, ready to face the next phase of their operation. The night ahead would be long, but neither of them had any intention of stepping back now.

Chapter 24
Closing Cycles

As dawn crept over the horizon, casting a pale light across the city, the Greendale Police Station was already a flurry of activity. Despite the early hour, the energy was palpable, with officers and detectives moving about, their steps quick and purposeful. The operations room, usually bustling, had been transformed into a quiet hub of strategic planning, where Jerry and Sandra were deeply immersed in refining their approach to dismantling the remaining criminal network.

The pair sat at a large table strewn with maps, digital tablets, and a myriad of papers that contained the gathered intelligence from months of investigations. Every so often, Sandra would update a digital map, marking off areas where they had confirmed criminal activity, while Jerry reviewed reports from the overnight surveillance teams.

"We've tightened our grip, but they're still moving," Jerry observed, his voice low as he scanned the latest updates. "The surveillance last night picked up activity in the eastern district—looks like they're trying to regroup."

Sandra, looking over the map, added digital pins to several locations. "Yes, I saw that. I've already dispatched additional units to increase patrols and surveillance in that area. We're not giving them any room to breathe."

Jerry nodded in approval, his focus returning to a series of photographs that showed several individuals they were tracking. "Good. Keep the pressure on. Any word from the tech team on those encrypted devices?"

"They're making progress, but it's slow. The encryption is more complex than we anticipated," Sandra replied, her tone mixed with frustration and determination. "They assure me they'll have something by the end of the day."

"That could give us the edge we need to finally close this down," Jerry said, setting the photographs down and rubbing his temples. The strain of long days and short nights was beginning to show, but his resolve remained firm.

Outside, the streets of Greendale began to fill with the morning rush, the city waking up to another day, oblivious to the critical operations being orchestrated from within the police station. Inside, the contrast was stark, as the team continued their relentless pursuit of justice.

The room fell silent for a moment, both Jerry and Sandra lost in their thoughts, reviewing their next moves. The silence was eventually broken by the buzz of Sandra's phone; she glanced at the screen and then at Jerry.

"We've got a lead on one of the safe houses we've been monitoring. Looks like there's significant movement—could be they're trying to move critical evidence," Sandra reported, her voice a catalyst for renewed urgency.

"Let's not waste any time then," Jerry responded quickly, standing up. "Coordinate with SWAT and get a raid team there ASAP. I want to catch them in the act."

Sandra was already on her phone, issuing commands with a calm efficiency that had become her hallmark. As she coordinated the teams, Jerry watched the screens, which now displayed live feeds from the area around the safe house.

The stakes were high, and both knew that the coming hours could be pivotal. With each passing minute, the network they were striving to dismantle was working just as hard to survive. It was a race against time, each side maneuvering for the upper hand.

As Sandra finished her calls and looked up, her expression was one of steely resolve. "Teams are en route. We should have eyes on the target within minutes."

"Good," Jerry said, his gaze fixed on the screen. "Let's bring this to an end."

Together, they watched the live feeds, waiting for the operation to unfold, the early morning light growing brighter as the city stirred to life. The day ahead promised more challenges, but Jerry and Sandra were ready to face whatever came their way, driven by a shared commitment to their city and its safety.

The raid was in full swing as Jerry and Sandra monitored the situation from the command center. Outside, the early morning quiet of Greendale was shattered by the sudden rush of police vehicles converging on a nondescript warehouse on the outskirts of the city. Inside the command center, the air was thick with tension, each officer and technician focused intently on their screens.

"Status?" Jerry's voice cut through the low murmur of the room as he watched the live feeds from body cameras worn by the raid team.

"We're inside. No resistance so far," came the crisp reply over the radio from the team leader on-site. "Proceeding to the main storage area."

Sandra, standing beside Jerry, kept her eyes on a secondary screen showing the layout of the warehouse. "According to the blueprints, there should be a hidden section behind those panels. That's likely where they're keeping anything they don't want us to find."

Jerry nodded, processing this information. "Make sure the team checks that area thoroughly. I want everything documented before anything is moved."

"Understood," Sandra responded, relaying the instructions through her headset. "Check the panels for any hidden compartments. Document everything."

The camera feeds showed the SWAT team moving methodically through the warehouse. The beams of their flashlights cut through the dim interior, casting long shadows as they moved past rows of high shelving filled with boxes and crates.

"There, on the right," Sandra pointed out as one of the camera feeds showed a section of the wall that looked slightly different from the rest. "Focus on that area."

The team leader acknowledged her instruction, directing two officers to inspect the wall. Moments later, the feed showed one of the officers pulling away a false panel to reveal a hidden room filled with computer equipment and files.

"We've found something," the team leader's voice announced, a note of triumph mingled with the seriousness of the discovery. "Looks like a lot of documentation and some hard drives."

"Secure the area. No one touches anything until forensics gets there," Jerry instructed, his gaze fixed on the screen as he watched the officers cordon off the newly discovered room.

Sandra quickly coordinated with the forensics team, ensuring they were en route to the warehouse with all necessary equipment. "Forensics is fifteen minutes out. They're bringing everything needed for a full sweep."

As they waited for the forensics team to arrive, Jerry and Sandra reviewed the footage, noting each step taken by the raid team. The meticulous nature of the operation was crucial, not just for gathering evidence but also for ensuring the legality of the process, which would be vital when the case went to trial.

"The team's doing great," Sandra commented, a slight relief in her tone as she watched the professionalism of the raid unfold.

"They are," Jerry agreed, allowing himself a moment of pride in his team's efficiency and thoroughness. "Today's going to be a long day, but it's worth it. Every piece of evidence we gather is another step toward cleaning up this city."

As they continued to oversee the operation, the early morning began to give way to full daylight. The initial quiet of dawn now seemed like a distant memory, replaced by the reality of their significant find. Jerry and Sandra remained vigilant, ready to handle any developments that might arise from the raid, each aware of the potential impact of their discoveries on the broader fight against the city's criminal enterprises.

With the forensics team on their way, and the secure documentation of every piece of evidence, the morning's operation was shaping up to be a turning point, one that could potentially lead to the dismantling of the entire network. The command center remained a focal point of activity, a testament to the ongoing commitment of the Greendale police to uphold justice and order.

In the aftermath of the morning's successful raid, the forensics team had taken over the warehouse, meticulously cataloging and collecting evidence. Jerry and Sandra, back at the police station, were huddled with their team of detectives and analysts in the strategy room, poring over the initial findings relayed from the scene.

"Forensics has already identified several key documents that tie back to our broader investigation," Sandra updated the group, her eyes scanning the digital files on her laptop. "They've also secured hard drives that could contain the accounting records we've been after."

"That's excellent news," Jerry responded, his focus sharp. "Have we made any progress on cracking the encryption on those drives yet?"

"Our tech team is working on it as we speak. They're optimistic about breaking through given some of the new data we retrieved which may help bypass some of the security protocols," one of the tech analysts chimed in from the corner of the room.

"Keep me posted on that, every hour. The sooner we access that data, the sooner we can put together the full picture of how this network has been operating," Jerry directed, his tone conveying the urgency of the task.

"Will do, sir," the analyst replied, already typing away on his keyboard.

Sandra shifted her attention back to Jerry and the rest of the team. "What about the suspects we detained? Are we ready to move forward with their interrogations?"

"We've scheduled them to start this afternoon. Our legal team has been briefed, and they're ensuring that all procedures are followed to the letter," Jerry stated, knowing the importance of each step being legally sound.

"Good, we can't afford any mistakes. Not now when we're this close," Sandra agreed, her voice steady. "I'll oversee the interrogation process myself. We need to leverage the information we've found today to pressure them into revealing more about the network's operations."

"Exactly," Jerry nodded in agreement. "And what about the international connections we uncovered? Any word from our federal partners?"

"We have a meeting lined up tomorrow morning with them. They're bringing in their international liaison to help coordinate our efforts, especially focusing on the financial trails leading overseas," Sandra updated, organizing her notes for that upcoming discussion.

"That could be a game-changer. Keep pushing for as much cooperation as possible. We need to cut off all escape routes and financial backing," Jerry emphasized, aware of how crucial international collaboration was in modern law enforcement operations.

The rest of the team listened intently, each aware of their role in the upcoming tasks. The room was filled with a sense of collective purpose, each member prepared to follow through on their assignments with precision.

"Let's also ensure that we keep a close watch on any potential retaliation or movement from other members of the network. They'll be feeling the pressure now, but that could make them unpredictable," Jerry added, his strategic mind always considering the next steps.

"We've increased surveillance on all known associates and have alerts set up for any unusual activity. We won't let them regroup," another detective added, affirming the proactive measures already in place.

"As we move forward, remember, the information we gather in the next 24 hours is crucial. It could dictate our actions in the coming weeks," Jerry concluded, setting the tone for the critical phase they were entering.

The team nodded in understanding, each member ready to carry out their tasks with diligence and urgency. Sandra and Jerry gave each other a brief look of solidarity before preparing to leave the room and begin their respective duties.

"We're making real progress, Jerry. Let's keep the momentum going," Sandra said quietly as they walked towards the door.

"We will, Sandra. We're going to bring this network down," Jerry assured her, his resolve as firm as ever. They stepped out of the strategy room, ready to face the challenges ahead, guided by a shared commitment to seeing justice served in Greendale.

As the day progressed into late afternoon, Jerry and Sandra reconvened in the strategy room, where they were joined by key members of their team. The mood was intense as they prepared to discuss the results of the interrogations and the implications of the data extracted from the secured hard drives.

"How are the interrogations going?" Jerry began, his eyes scanning the room for updates.

Sandra responded, her voice reflecting the gravity of their findings. "They're yielding results. One of the suspects has confirmed the identity of 'The Accountant,' along with several key operational details about the network. It seems we were right about their next planned moves."

"That's excellent news," Jerry said, visibly relieved. "What about the hard drives? What have we found?"

"Our tech team has done a remarkable job," an analyst interjected from the back of the room. "We've decrypted the drives and uncovered detailed financial records, as well as communications that tie directly back to several high-profile individuals we've been tracking."

Jerry leaned forward, intrigued. "Can we use this information to extend our reach beyond the local network? Are there connections that lead us to bigger players?"

"Yes, the records link back to several international accounts, and there are implications of involvement by individuals in positions of significant power," Sandra elaborated, her tone serious as she considered the broader implications. "We need to tread carefully but assertively. The evidence is solid enough to pursue higher-level targets."

"Let's make sure our legal team is on top of this. We need everything iron-clad if we're going to take this to the next level," Jerry directed, thinking ahead to the potential legal battles.

"I've already briefed them, and they're reviewing all the material as we speak. They'll prepare the necessary warrants and liaise with international authorities," Sandra assured him, always one step ahead in coordination.

"What's our strategy for rolling this out?" Jerry asked, his strategic mind mapping out the next phases of their operation.

"We keep tightening the noose. Increase surveillance on all known associates of these high-profile targets. Prepare for a series of coordinated raids if we get the green light on those warrants," Sandra outlined the plan, her demeanor focused and commanding.

"And the public?" Jerry inquired, aware of the potential backlash and media frenzy. "How do we handle the inevitable attention this will bring?"

"We control the narrative. I suggest we prepare a press release detailing parts of the operation, emphasizing the successful dismantling of a major criminal network. We keep the higher-profile targets confidential until we're ready to make those moves," Sandra proposed, thinking through the implications of public awareness.

"That sounds like a prudent approach," Jerry agreed, nodding thoughtfully. "We need to keep the upper hand, both operationally and in the public eye."

"Exactly," Sandra said, standing to signal the end of the meeting. "Let's move forward with that. I'll coordinate with public affairs and make sure our teams are ready for the next steps."

As team members began to file out of the room, each with tasks clear and a sense of urgency renewed, Jerry stayed back, looking over the maps and data screens that still illuminated the strategy room. Sandra paused beside him, both taking a moment to reflect on the progress and the daunting tasks ahead.

"We're changing the game, Jerry. It's a big step forward," Sandra remarked, a hint of satisfaction in her voice despite the challenges.

"We are," Jerry agreed, a determined glint in his eye. "Let's keep the momentum going. We've got a lot more to do, but today, we made a difference."

With that, they left the strategy room, ready to continue their relentless pursuit of justice, knowing that each step forward was a step toward a safer Greendale. The evening shadows lengthened across the city, mirroring the deepening complexity of their mission, yet with each passing hour, their resolve only strengthened.

Chapter 25
Greendale's New Dawn

Morning light filtered through the blinds of the strategy room where Jerry and Sandra convened an urgent briefing with their team. The recent successes had given them a slight upper hand, and they were eager to maintain their momentum. Maps and digital displays encircled them, each a testament to the depth of their ongoing investigation.

"Let's get right to it," Jerry started, his voice carrying a weight of authority and expectation. "Last night's operations gave us a wealth of information. How are we integrating this into our current strategy?"

Sandra responded, her focus evident, "We're cross-referencing the new data with our existing intel. The connections are starting to form a clearer picture. There's a pattern to their financial movements that we missed before."

"Good. We need to anticipate their next steps based on this pattern. What does it suggest about their likely actions in the coming days?" Jerry probed, looking intently at the financial flow charts displayed on the screen.

"Their funds are moving quicker than usual, which suggests they might be trying to liquidate assets and possibly flee the area. We've got alerts set up on all known accounts, so we'll see it immediately if large sums begin to transfer," Sandra detailed, manipulating the data on her tablet to bring up the relevant figures.

"Have we identified any new potential safe houses or meeting points from the communications we intercepted?" Jerry asked, shifting his attention to the tactical side of their operations.

"Yes, we have two locations that were mentioned multiple times in the communications. They're under surveillance as we speak. I propose we prepare raid teams, ready to move on short notice," Sandra suggested, her tone decisive.

"That's prudent. Set up the teams but hold off on moving in until we have a clearer indication of significant activity at those locations. I want to avoid tipping them off unless we're certain," Jerry cautioned, his experience guiding his conservative approach.

"Understood," Sandra acknowledged. "I'll keep the teams on standby and continue monitoring the locations around the clock."

Jerry then turned to another crucial aspect. "What about our informants? Are they providing any additional insights that could help us tighten the noose?"

"One informant came through late last night with information about a possible escape plan involving a private airstrip on the outskirts of the city. I'm having that verified and, if it pans out, we'll need to be ready to intercept," Sandra reported, her eyes scanning a list of their undercover assets and informants.

"That could be our best chance to catch more of the high-value targets. Make it a priority to confirm that intel," Jerry directed, his mind already racing through potential scenarios.

"Will do," Sandra confirmed, typing a quick message on her device to initiate that verification.

"Lastly, let's talk about public perception. We've managed to keep most of this under wraps, but some details are starting to leak. How are we handling the media?" Jerry shifted the discussion to the equally important battle of public opinion.

"I've drafted a preliminary statement that emphasizes the success of our operations without revealing specifics about ongoing activities. It's ready to release should we need to control the narrative more tightly," Sandra replied, always prepared for the multiple fronts on which they had to fight.

"Release it. Better to shape the story than react to it. Keep it vague but positive. Reassure the public that we're making significant progress," Jerry decided, knowing the importance of maintaining community trust and support.

"Consider it done," Sandra said, her fingers swiftly navigating her device to coordinate the press release.

As the meeting concluded, the team dispersed, each member charged with specific tasks, all contributing to the intricate dance of law enforcement and intelligence work that kept the city of Greendale safe. Jerry and Sandra remained behind, briefly reviewing the decisions made, each aware of the delicate balance they needed to maintain to bring their operation to a successful close.

"We're moving the pieces into place, Sandra. Let's keep up the pressure," Jerry said, his gaze returning to the maps that seemed to hold the hidden secrets of the city's underworld.

"We will, Jerry. We're closer than ever now," Sandra affirmed, her determination echoing in her voice as they prepared to step back into the fray.

As the day progressed, the operation against the criminal network reached a critical juncture. Jerry and Sandra, entrenched in the operations room, were surrounded by multiple screens that displayed real-time data and communications from various surveillance teams spread across the city. Each piece of information that came in was a potential key to preventing the flight of high-value targets suspected of attempting to escape the tightening net of law enforcement.

The focus was particularly intense on a private airstrip on the outskirts of Greendale, where recent intelligence suggested that a significant movement was expected late in the afternoon. Sandra had coordinated with the aerial surveillance units to monitor any unusual activity, while ground teams were discreetly positioned around the perimeter, ready to move in on her command.

"Any updates on the airstrip?" Jerry asked, his voice low as he approached Sandra at her station.

"Nothing significant yet," Sandra replied, keeping her eyes on the live feed. "But our teams are in place. We won't miss anything."

Jerry nodded, his gaze fixed on a secondary screen showing a map dotted with the locations of all active units. "Keep me posted. The moment you see anything, I want to know."

Sandra acknowledged with a quick nod, her attention never wavering from the task at hand. The room hummed with the sound of whispered communications and the soft clicking of keyboards, a stark contrast to the high-stakes drama unfolding beyond its walls.

As the hours passed, the tension in the room grew. Each member of the team was acutely aware of the importance of their role in the operation's success. The wait was a test of patience and nerve, as they monitored the channels for any sign of the suspects making their move.

Outside, the city continued its usual pace, oblivious to the critical operation underway. The ordinary scenes of daily life provided a surreal backdrop to the high drama hidden in plain sight. Inside the operations room, Jerry and Sandra occasionally exchanged glances—each look a silent communication of their shared resolve and anticipation.

Finally, a call came through from an agent stationed at the airstrip. "Movement on the east side of the airstrip. A vehicle just pulled up, looks like they're unloading something."

Sandra immediately zoomed in on the feed from the drone hovering above the area. "I see it. Looks like four individuals. Can we get a closer look?"

"Adjusting altitude now," came the response from the drone operator. On the screen, the image sharpened, revealing the figures more clearly.

"Let's hold our position for now," Jerry said decisively. "We need absolute confirmation before we move in."

Sandra relayed the instruction swiftly. "All units hold. Maintain surveillance but do not engage."

Minutes dragged like hours as they watched the suspects make several trips between the vehicle and a small, nondescript airplane. It was clear that the operation was at a tipping point.

"Prepare to move on my command," Sandra whispered into her headset, her finger poised over the radio button.

The suspense in the room was palpable, with every officer and analyst holding their breath, waiting for the moment of action. Finally, as the last of the cargo was loaded into the plane, Sandra made her decision.

"Move in now, secure the airstrip," she commanded, her voice firm and authoritative.

The response was immediate. Within seconds, the screen showed the swift convergence of police units on the airstrip. The suspects, caught by surprise, were quickly apprehended with no time to react.

As the operation concluded successfully, Jerry turned to Sandra, a slight smile breaking through the tension. "Well done, Sandra. Well done, everyone."

Sandra nodded, allowing herself a moment of relief. "Thanks, Jerry. It's a good day."

The operation's success was a testament to their meticulous planning and execution. As the room began to buzz with the debriefings and follow-up plans, Jerry and Sandra started to discuss their next steps. The battle was far from over, but today's victory was crucial. They had prevented a potential escape and secured more evidence, each step bringing them closer to dismantling the network that had plagued their city for too long.

As the afternoon faded into evening, Jerry and Sandra convened a meeting in the strategy room to assess the operation's aftermath and plan their next steps. The room, lined with screens and maps, buzzed with subdued activity as various team members updated databases and compiled reports.

"Let's start with the aftermath of today's airstrip operation. What's the status of the suspects we apprehended?" Jerry began, his tone indicating the urgency of securing actionable intelligence from the day's events.

Sandra, flipping through her tablet for the latest updates, responded, "All suspects are in custody and currently being processed. Interrogation teams are set up and ready to go. We expect to start getting information soon."

"Excellent," Jerry nodded. "The evidence we collected from the site—have we begun analysis?"

"Yes, the forensic team is sorting through the materials as we speak. They've prioritized digital devices and documents that appear to be financial records," Sandra stated, her focus on ensuring no detail was overlooked.

"Good. I want a preliminary report on my desk first thing tomorrow morning. Any leads we can get on their financial operations could help us unravel more of their network," Jerry directed, thinking ahead to the broader implications of their discoveries.

"Understood," Sandra confirmed, making a note. "Also, the coordination with federal agencies has paid off. They're sending in additional support to help with the data analysis."

"That's great news," Jerry said, visibly pleased. "Now, regarding public relations—how are we handling the media? There's going to be a lot of interest after today's operation."

Sandra looked up from her tablet. "I've prepared a brief statement that gives the basics of the operation without going into specifics. It highlights the successful collaboration between agencies and reassures the public about our ongoing efforts to ensure safety."

"Perfect. Release it as soon as we're done here," Jerry agreed, always cautious about managing their narrative. "Now, let's talk about our next steps. We've made significant progress, but the network is still operational. We need to keep the pressure on."

"Agreed," Sandra said, leaning forward. "Based on today's success, I suggest we use the momentum to increase our surveillance on other potential targets. We've seen that when they feel pressured, they make mistakes."

"Absolutely," Jerry concurred. "Have we identified any new leads from the materials seized today or from the suspects' communications?"

"We have a few. There's mention of another location that might be used as a fallback for their operations. I've already dispatched surveillance teams to monitor the area," Sandra informed, demonstrating her proactive approach.

"Excellent foresight," Jerry complimented. "Keep me updated on any developments. And Sandra, make sure our teams are rotating on a reasonable schedule. I don't want anyone burning out."

"Will do, Jerry. I'll personally check on the shifts and ensure everyone gets the rest they need," Sandra promised, understanding the physical and emotional toll such intense operations could take on their team.

As the meeting drew to a close, Jerry and Sandra remained behind, reviewing the updated maps and digital feeds from their ongoing surveillance. The room slowly emptied, leaving them in a quiet contemplation of their responsibilities.

"We're doing good work, Sandra. Tough, but good," Jerry finally said, looking over the city lights beginning to twinkle outside.

"We are, Jerry. Let's keep it up. For Greendale," Sandra replied, her tone resolute.

Together, they left the strategy room, ready to face whatever challenges lay ahead. The evening settled around them, the darkness outside mirroring the deep shadows they navigated in their pursuit of justice, yet each step they took was a step toward the light of security and order for their city.

The evening stretched into night as Jerry and Sandra continued their vigil in the operations room, now quiet with the late hour. The rest of the team had gone, either to field positions or to grab some much-needed rest before the next shift began. Alone, Jerry and Sandra reviewed the latest surveillance feeds and reports that trickled in from their various sources throughout the city.

On one screen, a live feed from the newly discovered fallback location flickered quietly in the dim light. Sandra monitored it closely, watching for any sign of unusual activity. On another, digital maps displayed the movement of their teams and the known associates of the network, each icon a chess piece in the intricate game they were playing.

"Anything new from the surveillance teams?" Jerry broke the silence, his voice low, almost blending with the soft hum of computer fans.

"Not yet," Sandra replied, her eyes not leaving the screen. "It's been quiet. Too quiet. It feels like they know we're watching."

Jerry nodded, considering her words. "They might be laying low for now, trying to figure out their next move. Keep the teams on alert. Any change in pattern could give us the lead we need."

"I'll make sure of it," Sandra assured him, tapping a few commands into her tablet to send a reminder to the surveillance teams.

The room was filled with the tension of waiting—a tension they had both become accustomed to over their careers but never comfortable with. Each moment could be the precursor to a breakthrough or a setback.

"How are you holding up, Sandra?" Jerry finally asked, his concern for his colleague evident in his tone.

"I'm fine, Jerry. We've been through worse," Sandra said with a tired smile. "What about you?"

"I'm okay," Jerry said, though his weary eyes told a different story. "We're close, Sandra. I can feel it. We just need to stay focused."

"We will," Sandra responded, her conviction matching his. "We've got a good team. They're doing everything they can."

Jerry glanced at another report that had just come in, scanning the text for any crucial information. "This operation has stretched us thin, but you're right. The team is strong. They're committed."

As they talked, a soft alert sounded from one of the screens—a motion sensor from the fallback location had been triggered. Both Jerry and

Sandra turned their attention to the live feed, watching as shadows moved across the view, indicating someone was there.

"Looks like we might have something," Sandra said, zooming in on the feed. "I'll alert the response team."

"Do it," Jerry responded immediately, standing to get a closer look at the screen. "Let's see who our night owls are."

Sandra made the call, her voice calm and clear, even as her heart raced with the potential implications of this activity. Within minutes, a team was en route to the location, ready to intervene if necessary.

As they waited for updates, the weight of their responsibility lingered in the air, mingled with the hope that this night's work would bring them closer to their goal. The city outside the windows lay dark and quiet, most of its inhabitants asleep and oblivious to the drama unfolding in the shadows.

Jerry and Sandra remained at their posts, the guardians of Greendale's peace, their commitment unwavering as the night deepened around them. Each understood the stakes, and neither would rest until the job was done. The work continued, silent and relentless, as the night marched on.

Conclusion

The final threads of the conspiracy began to unravel as the early morning sun cast long shadows across the operations center. Jerry and Sandra stood side by side, a palpable sense of anticipation and fatigue mingling in the air. The latest operations had dealt a significant blow to the criminal network that had been operating under the guise of shadow and silence, penetrating deep into Greendale and beyond.

Through the large glass windows of the operations center, they could see the first stirrings of the city. People began their day, unaware of the complex and shadowy battles fought in their names. It was a morning like any other, except for those within the center, for whom the weight of the night's achievements hung heavily.

"We've done more than disrupt them; we've dismantled key parts of their operations," Jerry remarked, his voice a mix of weariness and relief. He shuffled through the reports detailing the captures, the seizures, and the vital intel gathered from their last raid.

Sandra nodded, her eyes reflecting the gravitas of their endeavor. "Yes, and we've gathered enough evidence to keep the legal wheels turning for a long time. It's a significant victory."

The room around them buzzed with activity; officers coordinating follow-up raids, analysts poring over the newly acquired data, and the constant back-and-forth of communication with other departments and agencies. It was organized chaos—a symphony of law enforcement and justice being meted out in real time.

Jerry turned to look at Sandra, a small, tired smile playing at the corners of his mouth. "You know, this all started with a series of small, seemingly unrelated incidents. It's almost hard to believe we've come this far."

"It's a testament to your persistence, Jerry. We wouldn't be here without your dogged determination," Sandra replied, placing a hand on his shoulder in a rare gesture of camaraderie and support.

Their attention was drawn to a large screen displaying the map of Greendale and the surrounding areas, dotted with markers and lines that traced the spiderweb of the criminal network they had uncovered. Each line, each marker represented a story, a lead followed, a danger faced.

"The city owes you a debt, Jerry. This peace we're feeling this morning, it's thanks to you and your team," Sandra said, her voice earnest.

Jerry shook his head slightly. "It's thanks to us, Sandra. All of us. And we'll need to keep at it. The peace is... fragile, as long as people like Marco are out there."

As they spoke, a young officer approached, a folder in hand. "Captains, we've just received confirmation. Several more arrests have been made this morning based on the information from last night's raid. It looks like we've caught a couple of big fish."

"That's excellent news," Sandra responded, taking the folder and flipping it open. "Let's keep the momentum going."

Jerry watched as Sandra briefed the officer, her leadership as steady as ever. As they dispersed to continue their work, Jerry's gaze lingered on the map, his mind already racing ahead to the next challenges they would face.

Outside, the city of Greendale stirred under the rising sun, its streets safe for now, its enemies retreating into the shadows from which they came, but the light of justice, hard-earned through the night's endeavors, held steady, promising a fight for every inch of shadow that remained.